SHE KNEW THEIR LIGHTHEARTED BANTER WAS OVER AND DONE

Perhaps the die had been cast when Lindsay had invited him to dinner. Deep inside she wanted the innocence of the day to end and the promise of the evening to begin. Perhaps her eyes now told him this.

As they stood in her kitchen drinking wine, Lindsay understood that to make the fantasy of that first night possible again they had needed a day grounded in reality. Was that why Blake had wanted her to be with him, to commune in the unpretentious, natural surroundings of the woods? In order to experience his magic again, she first had to experience him in his candid simplicity, in his boots walking among the trees.

Now the result was unfolding. Their relationship had elevated to a new, even more exciting plane. The spark he had struck was smoldering once again. The difference was that this time, she would know the man in her arms.

ABOUT THE AUTHOR

It was natural that Janice Kaiser's first romantic heroine be a lawyer. This vivacious mother of two has a Ph.D. in English and now practices law in the San Francisco peninsula area. A longtime fan of romances, Janice is also an avid world traveler who intends to use a lot of fabulous settings in future romances.

Janice Kaiser

HARMONY

Harlequin **Books**

TORONTO • NEW YORK • LONDON
AMSTERDAM • PARIS • SYDNEY • HAMBURG
STOCKHOLM • ATHENS • TOKYO • MILAN

Published November 1985

First printing September 1985

ISBN 0-373-70187-X

To Edith Small
and the memory of Loraine Kidwell Smith

CHAPTER ONE

BLAKE PRESCOTT GLANCED UP at the man sitting across the desk then down again at the glossy photo lying in the file folder. "Not bad looking, is she?" he said as much to himself as to the man.

The other nodded but said nothing.

Prescott examined the photograph. She was pretty, all right, but it wasn't the vapid, superficial beauty of a homecoming queen or a photogenic model in a department store catalog. This woman had something more, intelligence for one thing. He could see it in her eyes; there was a depth to them. Something was going on in that pretty head. He looked up again. "Doesn't look all that dangerous, does she?"

"Dangerous?"

An ironic smirk moved across Prescott's mouth. "I doubted it myself at first. But my lawyer tells me I've got trouble."

"Used to be a pretty girl couldn't be dangerous unless she had something on you—personal I mean."

"Well, times have changed. I've never laid eyes on Lindsay Bishop and she's got a goddamn knife at my throat." Prescott examined the face in the photograph again. The mouth in particular he liked. It was wide, with the lower lip full, sensuous. He liked a woman with a sensuous mouth. Her dark hair came to her shoulders. She looked too young to pose such a threat—she couldn't be older than in her late twenties. "How recent is this, Jerry?"

"Within the past year or so."

"Where'd you get it?"

"We have our methods, Mr. Prescott."

"Well this is a portrait, not a candid shot. You must have a source."

"As a matter of fact we do. That particular photo is a file shot from one of the local papers. I've got a friend there."

A smile crossed Prescott's handsome face. "I bet you do." He was holding the photo up now, studying it as though the answer he sought was hidden somewhere in it. Strangely enough, however, he was as fascinated with the woman as with the problem she posed. "What's her body like?"

The other man grinned. "Good, Mr. Prescott, good. She's a nice piece, if I do say so."

"Hmmm..."

"Sorry I don't have a full-length shot in there. Didn't occur to me."

"For the money I pay you, Jerry, there ought to be a full layout of nude pictures."

The man chuckled. "I'm afraid that would cost a lot more—a whole lot more—but it could be arranged."

"You know, Randall, sometimes you amaze me." He tossed the photo back into the folder. "I'm a businessman, not a pervert."

Jerry Randall didn't respond.

"What else have you got on Lindsay Bishop?"

"There's a data sheet in there."

Prescott leafed through the file until he came to a neatly typed sheet of personal data. He read through the information quickly. *Born St. Louis, Missouri, thirty years of age....* "Oh, she's thirty. I'd have guessed less."...*hair black, eyes blue, fair complexioned, no distinguishing marks or characteristics, height five feet, two inches...* "She's tiny."

"Yeah. She's a little thing. Really cute."

Prescott frowned and continued reading. *One hundred and five pounds...resides Palo Alto, California... graduate of Stephens College, B.F.A....Stanford Law School...law office in Palo Alto, California... home telephone number...* He looked up at Jerry Randall. "You must be getting old, Jerry, you didn't get her shoe size."

The man laughed. "You're wrong there, Mr. Prescott. She wears a six double A shoe. I assumed you wouldn't care about that sort of thing."

"Never assume anything."

Randall shrugged. "She wears a size five dress, but I'd have to guess on her bra size, probably thirty-four B..."

"Okay, okay, you made your point," Prescott said with some disgust. "You should have stayed in the divorce business, Jerry."

"I still would be if they hadn't changed the law on me. Anybody can get a divorce for any reason nowadays."

"There must be enough jealous husbands around to keep your prurient interests satisfied."

Randall grinned and shrugged again.

Prescott toyed absentmindedly with the photograph, then flipped through the several more pages in the file before sighing in exasperation. He leaned back in his chair, clasped his hands behind his head and looked at Randall vacantly.

"What do you think, Mr. Prescott?"

He shook his head. "I don't know what to think. I don't know what to do."

Randall looked perplexed. "What exactly were you hoping to find out about Miss Bishop?"

Prescott laughed. "I don't know that either, Jerry." He rose to his feet and stretched his large, well-proportioned frame, running his fingers through his thick auburn hair. "That's the hell of it. I just couldn't sit around waiting. You know me. I've got to know what I'm up against, who the enemy is." He pointed at Randall. "That's the first principle of war—know the enemy."

"Well, I hope it was worth it to you, Mr. Prescott. This wasn't cheap."

"Yeah, I know. I suppose it's worth it if it makes me feel better, though. It's the same as when I have you check someone out before a business negotiation. I don't like surprises. That's what it boils down to, I don't like surprises."

"Sounds like she has you worried."

"My attorney says she's good. Best there is at what she does. He knew her at Stanford. Says he hasn't seen her in years, but she's well respected in the legal community." Prescott dropped back into his chair and looked at Randall. "I don't suppose you found any dirt on her...."

"No, she's clean."

"That's what I expected." He sighed again and looked at the pretty face in the photograph. "How about a boyfriend?"

Randall looked perplexed. "What difference..."

"None," Prescott cut in, anticipating the question. "I was just curious."

"Oh. Well, so far as I know she doesn't have much of a social life. She works a hell of a lot, though. That's for sure."

"Yeah, busy readying lambs for slaughter." Then he slapped the desk top with his hand to underscore the thought that had settled in his mind. "Jerry, I'm going to talk to her."

The private investigator raised his eyebrows in surprise.

"Somehow I've got to manage a casual encounter with her. I can't just go waltzing into her office."

"If you don't mind a crowd you can see her at the Flint Center in Cupertino Wednesday night. She's giving a speech."

"A speech?"

"Yes, I believe there's a flyer somewhere there in the file."

Prescott found the flyer and broke into a broad grin, his emerald eyes gleaming.

"If there's anything else you'd like for me to check into, Mr. Prescott, just give a whistle."

But Blake Prescott was looking at the photograph again, his mind working. Damn if she didn't have a sexy mouth. That lip intrigued him. The hair. The face. She didn't look sinister in the least. He tried to imagine what the flesh-and-blood woman would be like, realizing it was more the woman than the lawyer that had captured his imagination. The male in him sensed a challenge, and the anxiety he had felt began fading even as his curiosity grew.

"SEX HAS NOTHING to do with it." Laughter rippled throughout the auditorium as the young woman standing behind the lectern answered the questioner. Her dark glossy hair swung freely as she iterated, "Really, why should sex in a relationship affect the principle of law?"

From the back of the auditorium Blake Prescott could see a smile cross Lindsay Bishop's pretty face as she looked at the student. Jerry Randall was right, she was "a nice piece"; the picture didn't do her justice.

The girl in the audience shrugged. "Well, there isn't much of a marriage without sex."

The predominantly female audience again laughed and all eyes shifted back to the podium.

"You may be right about that," Lindsay rejoined, "but is sex an *essential* element of marriage? You see, the famous case of *Marvin v. Marvin*, involving the actor, concerned an unmarried couple living together—what we lawyers call a meretricious relationship. The question I'm asking is this: when the couple breaks up and the woman claims the same rights as if they had been married, as in the *Marvin* case, what does the woman have to prove? Should she have to prove they had sex? Should the man get off if he can prove that their relationship was platonic?"

Prescott saw a mischievous little quirk on her face.

"I almost hate to say this," the speaker continued, "but sex can be either good or bad—in court as well as bed."

There was raucous laughter throughout the hall and sporadic applause. Even Blake Prescott found himself smiling in amusement.

Watching the woman who seemed totally in her element, he was reminded how a creature could at the same time be alluring and yet deadly. The image of Lindsay Bishop standing before a jury tearing some poor bastard limb from limb came to his mind. Yet, that sensuous mouth that was too far away to be seen clearly also preoccupied him. He knew he couldn't take her lightly because she represented danger, but he couldn't rid himself of the growing fascination with her either.

From where he sat he could see her fingering the thin bow of her white tailored blouse. Her face reflected a businesslike self-assurance, yet she was strikingly beautiful in her navy suit and matching pumps. Prescott wondered what she would be like offstage, whether there might be a soft, feminine vulnerability beneath that artful veneer. He mused on how difficult it would be to find and touch the woman in her.

Lindsay looked around the audience. "Are there any more questions?"

After a brief silence, a deep baritone boomed from the back of the room. "I have a question, Miss Bishop."

She raised her hand to shield her eyes against the bright lights, searching for the source of the unexpected male voice. A sea of heads turned back to one corner and she located the man who rose to his feet. He was a tall, attractive man in a business suit and even at a distance she saw the wry expression on his face. That fleeting impression told her there was some kind of challenge in the offing.

"You said sex has nothing to do with it," the resonant voice continued. "What about gender?"

Was it the visual image of the man's imposing good looks or the remarkable timbre of his voice that distracted her? She had missed the point. "Gender?"

"What I mean to ask," he replied, "is if your legal theory applies only to women or would you represent a man in one of these cases?"

"You mean an action based on the *Marvin* case? Where the plaintiff is a man?"

"Yes."

Lindsay studied him for an instant, trying to divine what might be behind his question. She wondered what he was up to. Obviously well into his thirties, maybe forty, the man was much older than the rest of the audience. He stood out like a sore thumb. Maybe he was a man in need of legal counsel. "Sure," she replied at last.

"Why not? If the facts support it a man could, in my opinion, sue successfully. I suppose, for example, a wealthy woman could take a man as a lover and offer to share her property in exchange for his contribution to the relationship."

There was tittering around the audience.

"Is there anything *you'd* like to tell us?" she asked whimsically.

There was laughter.

"I didn't know a guy had to make a public confession to get legal representation," he replied.

Lindsay liked the way he deflected her barb. She doubted his seriousness, though. "Normally I don't hold client conferences in public," she rejoined, "but your story sounds so interesting I..."

"I believe," he interrupted, "any prurient implication was in your supposition, not my question."

"Touche," she said conceding the point. "Perhaps I was flip. I apologize. But, if you have a legal matter you'd like to discuss, maybe we'd best talk after the lecture."

She watched him smile and sit down as some of the young women hissed their disappointment. Lindsay sympathized with their frustration. The brief glimpse of the man fascinated her as well.

Blake Prescott watched her as she turned to take another question, but he had tuned out the dialogue, being too charmed by the verve and vivaciousness of the woman on stage. She had turned to the other side of the hall now, her hand resting on her hip. She leaned against the lectern in a relaxed manner. Prescott had become engrossed in his observation. He was admiring the fine shape of her calf and ankle. Her suit jacket masked her torso, but he could see that she was trim and well shaped.

He couldn't help appreciating her feminine grace; she moved and gestured with assurance. She was funny too, but that made her seem disarming, a danger Prescott knew he'd have to guard against.

Just as Lindsay finished with her questioner a great crash of thunder shook the building and Prescott was as surprised by it as everyone else. The paper had forecast thundershowers that evening, but it still was a little shocking to hear thunder in California. It was rare along the coast, with years sometimes passing between such storms.

"I hope that was a concurring opinion from a higher authority," Lindsay said over the hushed silence in the room.

Everyone laughed and the hall buzzed, but another clap of thunder silenced them.

"Almost like being home in the Midwest," she added. "Anyone besides me forget to bring their umbrella?" People chuckled and began stirring. "If there aren't any more questions, perhaps we'd better go before we all get rained on. Thank you for coming this evening and for being such a great audience."

The room filled with applause and Prescott watched her gracious acceptance of the crowd's approval. He smiled to himself. Her invitation to speak with her after the lecture had eliminated the problem of finding a way to approach her. That would be the easy part now. With a little luck he could manage to delay her long enough for the audience to clear out. Then he could speak with her alone.

By now most of the audience was filing out so Prescott grabbed his trench coat, rose to his feet and made his way to the aisle. But he soon saw there was going to be a sizable mob of admirers clustering around the young attorney. It looked like she would be tied up for some time.

Turning from the scene at the front of the auditorium, he walked back up the aisle to the foyer. He decided to wait a while until the crowd thinned before approaching her.

It was raining hard outside. Darkness had fallen and the students were girding themselves against the rain before dashing toward the parking lot. He watched the spectacle for a while and thought about the woman inside the hall. He realized that what attracted him was her appeal, not the challenge she represented. She had completely captured his imagination. He knew that what he wanted was not just a brief conversation, he wanted to spend time with her, to find out what she was like—perhaps take her someplace for a drink or a bite to eat.

She didn't seem like a woman easily charmed into going off someplace with a strange man. It could be done, but Prescott wanted better odds than what he saw. He contemplated various ruses and strategies when an idea popped into his mind.

He poked his head back in the doorway and saw that the group at the foot of the stage was still large. He estimated she would be tied up for at least another ten minutes or so. Prescott searched his mind for the description of Lindsay Bishop's car. Not having Jerry Randall's file, he couldn't be sure of the description but he recalled it was a BMW, but what else? Her license plate was personalized, though he didn't remember what it was.

Prescott stepped to the outer doors and peered into the darkness. The parking lot was vast. She probably would have parked near the auditoruim, and the cars should have thinned out by now. Though there were lights scattered around the lot he couldn't see well from the building. Deciding to go out and have a look, he slipped on his trench coat and went outside.

The rain had let up, but was still falling as Prescott wandered out into the parking lot. There were not many vehicles but he saw nothing that might be hers. He spotted a BMW but it was an older car and had standard plates. It wouldn't be Lindsay's. Walking further into the lot he finally found a late model BMW, with plates reading "MS JD".

Knowing that "J.D." stood for "juris doctor," the degree given to attorneys, he decided the car had to be hers.

He looked around. Fortunately there were no lamp posts nearby. It was relatively dark in the vicinity and another car was parked next to the BMW on the driver's side, blocking the view of people who might approach from the direction of the auditorium. After glancing around him again, Prescott stepped quickly between the cars and squatted down just as a bolt of lightning seared the sky, followed an instant later by a rumble of thunder.

Finding the air valve on the left front tire of the car, he unscrewed the cap and took his car keys from his pocket. Using the narrowest key on the ring he pressed in on the pin until air came gushing out. After holding the key against the valve pin for several minutes he had succeeded in completely flattening the tire.

Standing up cautiously, Prescott looked around and, seeing no one nearby, stepped around to the other side of the car and deflated the front tire on the passenger side. Having finished, he walked quickly back toward the auditorium in a light rain accompanied by flashes of lightning and rolling thunder. Entering the building, he saw by his watch that ten minutes had elapsed since he left. Several young women were exiting the inner doors as

Prescott approached. Looking inside the hall, he saw that only a handful of people remained clustered around the young lawyer.

Before walking down the aisle to join Lindsay Bishop's coterie of admirers, Prescott removed his trench coat and wiped the moisture from his face and hair with his handkerchief. He smiled to himself, seeing the lively expression on her face as she spoke to the students. Blake Prescott felt much better knowing he had changed the odds enough to virtually ensure his success. Before the evening was through, he knew he'd have the upper hand.

CHAPTER TWO

LINDSAY BISHOP WAS BEGINNING to tire of the questions. Her feet hurt from standing for nearly two hours and she wanted to leave. The young woman in front of her was going on at length and Lindsay was about to cut her off when she saw him walking up behind the small group of students.

The first thing she noticed was the complacent expression on his handsome face. He looked at her in a way that almost said, "See? I'm here. I decided to take you up on your invitation." He smiled at her rather rakishly, even defiantly, as though his manner in itself should command respect. After a moment Lindsay realized that she had been staring into his emerald eyes unabashedly when several of the students turned around to see what she was looking at.

Her lapse in self-control left her momentarily flustered and Lindsay blushed. She quickly managed to regain her poise and tried to pick up the thread of the student's monologue, but she could concentrate with only half a mind. Whenever she stole a glance at the mysterious man at the back of the group, she found his eyes riveted to her, almost as though he was daring her to look at him again. Wondering if he was brazen enough to think this would unnerve her, Lindsay finally refused to even glance at him. She would not give him the satisfaction!

"Look, let me sum up my views this way," Lindsay said, at last interrupting the girl. "There are advantages as well as disadvantages in being a woman—even in the field of law." She could almost feel the man's presence, but she was determined not to look at those green eyes. "But, you know as well as I do," she continued, "what counts in the end is how hard you're willing to work."

The girl started to respond, but Lindsay cut her off. "I'm sorry, I know you have more questions, but I do have to go." She smiled at them sympathetically, patting her principal questioner on the arm. "It happens to me all the time in court where judges rule the roost."

The small covey of students started out the hall and Lindsay gathered her notes, put them in her briefcase and took her raincoat out from under the lectern. She knew he was still there so she directed her gaze at him.

He was alone at the foot of the stage watching her. His auburn hair glistened under the bright lights. Those brilliant green eyes were flashing but friendly. He was placid, mute. He just seemed to be waiting for her to say something.

After a moment Lindsay started feeling a little awkward. "So it's not palimony you're after. No wealthy widows that you feel owe you a living?"

He grinned. "No."

She studied him. "What's your legal problem then?"

"No problem actually. Just curiosity. I'm here out of curiosity."

Lindsay went to the corner of the stage, descended the stairs and made her way back toward him. Level with him now on the auditorium floor, she realized just how large he was. Well over six feet tall, and looking rather lean in an Italian-cut suit, though his shoulders were broad. The greens and browns in his tie nicely matched the dark brown gabardine of his suit. He was rather imposing, really, and Lindsay felt a little trepidation knowing she was alone with him in this vast hall.

"You see," he explained, "I'm interested in the kind of law you practice. You and Millicent Woodward have made quite a name for yourselves with all the big palimony awards you've been getting for these women."

"Thanks for the compliment, Mr..."

He hesitated and she saw a strange look pass over his face before he smiled. "Price," he said extending his hand. "Bill Price."

Lindsay felt her hand swallowed in the large warmth of his. "Nice to meet you." Conscious of his touch she pulled her hand away feeling a little uncomfortable with his magnetism.

He was looking at her as though she were a bird in a cage and he a big tom cat. In spite of herself she felt flustered again.

"You look uncomfortable," he said in a low, mocking tone.

Lindsay's eyes flashed. *Because of you?* she thought scornfully. But the words she uttered were more tempered. "I suppose I'm a little confused. You implied earlier you were in need of legal representation, now your motive seems to be curiosity." She felt the need to lash back at the charm with which he was assaulting her. "What *is* your motive, Mr. Price?"

He laughed. "Do I need one?"

"No, I suppose it's perfectly normal for a man to come out on a stormy night to listen to a lecture on women's rights in meretricious relationships."

He shrugged.

Lindsay found his coyness disconcerting, yet she was acutely aware if his attractiveness. The combination seemed unfair and she resented him for it. "Mr. Price, you're being terribly mysterious. Is it a secret or are you going to tell me what you're up to?"

"No secret. The subject matter interests me and I find you very stimulating—a stimulating speaker."

Lindsay could tell now he was definitely not sincere. He wasn't concerned with her law practice, his interest seemed personal. She knew she had to be careful. "Mr. Price, I'm flattered, but..."

"Please, call me...er...Bill."

"Okay Bill. Who are you?" She examined the face, which reflected amusement. He was enjoying his game. "You're no attorney, that much I'm reasonably sure of—they usually aren't this imaginative."

His laugh was disarming, though she sensed danger. "You are perceptive, Lindsay, and you're right, I'm no attorney."

"You're not a teacher either—too well dressed."

He nodded.

"But you are here by design, not accident, that much I'm sure of."

"Right again."

His caginess was beginning to annoy her, and he must have sensed it.

"The truth is there's a reason for my evasiveness. And I'm afraid the truth is a little embarrassing."

"Oh?"

"You see, I was supposed to meet someone here at your lecture—a lady friend—but she stood me up."

A devilish grin crossed Lindsay's face. "Maybe she just wanted to put the fear of palimony into you!"

He laughed. "No, we didn't have that kind of relationship, Lindsay."

She studied him with uncertainty, her intuition sounding an alarm, but some part of her refused to heed the warning. He seemed every bit the spider and she the fly, but Lindsay couldn't bring herself to take flight. "Bill, I don't believe you," she challenged.

Just then a door slammed at the rear of the auditorium and the janitor called out to them, "Will you be long? I need to put out the lights."

"No, we're leaving right now," Lindsay called out.

There was a smile on Bill Price's face as he took her arm, sending an unexpected tremor through her. They were walking up the center aisle toward the doors when a clap of thunder echoed through the deserted hall. Lindsay glanced warily at the towering man beside her, realizing she was literally in his hands. It was a strange sensation for a woman accustomed to being total mistress of her destiny.

"Quite a storm," he said as though he sensed some benign comment was called for.

As they entered the foyer she saw the rain outside falling in sheets. "Just look at that," she groaned.

Bill Price had released her arm, perhaps content in the knowledge the rain had trapped her there with him. "I'd offer to share my umbrella," he said ironically, "but unfortunately I didn't bring it with me."

"That makes two of us."

They stood looking out the glass doors at the downpour.

"Do you suppose it will let up?" she asked.

"I hope so."

Lindsay's eyes lingered on him before trailing away. What was it about him that left her doubting his every word? She looked at her watch. It was nearly nine o'clock. It was late and she was tired. The obvious thing to do was to make her farewells and be gone, rain or no rain, but something was holding her there. She felt the need to resolve it before she could go.

"What sort of work do you do, Mr. Price?"

The look in his eye left her doubting his response before he had uttered it. "I'm an inventor."

"Oh. What do you invent?"

"High-tech, electronic things." He smiled at her provocatively.

Lindsay was shocked to feel a sudden irrational urge to slap the man. She didn't want to hurt him, just send him a message. On reflection, she realized it was her own frustration that caused her to want to lash out. Why? He hadn't said or done anything improper, but he was affecting her as surely as if he had. Nonetheless Lindsay decided that she'd been manipulated...and it was an unfamiliar, uncomfortable feeling.

Looking at him again she saw that he had been watching her. She felt exposed and turned abruptly away, toward the pelting rain on the windows. Why couldn't she just walk away?

"No sign of it letting up, is there?" His tone was as bland as it had been earlier. He seemed to sense when to give her space and ease up.

Lindsay sighed with exasperation. "Well, I think it's become a monsoon and much as I hate to get wet and ruin a perfectly good pair of shoes, I think I'll make a run for it."

She was a bit surprised when he showed no dismay at the announcement. Instead he extended his hand, which she took automatically.

"Lindsay, I enjoyed your lecture this evening," he said, covering their right hands with his left. "And it was nice talking with you."

Her heart fluttered, both in nervousness and from the energy transmitted by his touch. She looked up at the jade disks of his eyes and his smiling mouth. Two distinct and conflicting emotions consumed her, one positive, one negative. She didn't know whether to flee or stay. What was happening to her? This man was a total stranger. "Nice to have met you," she mumbled when he finally released her hand.

Lightning lit the sky, thunder followed almost immediately.

"I think I'll give it another five minutes or so," he said. The words were innocent enough but his tone was almost jocular. He seemed totally bemused with their parting. Why did it distress her? Or, was it annoyance she felt at his reaction?

Lindsay took her raincoat from her arm and started to slip it on when Bill Price reached over and helped her. His hands rested for the briefest moment on her shoulders before he stepped back. The gesture hinted at affection and the resulting surge of emotion propelled her toward the door. She gave him only a sideward glance and a perfunctory salute before stepping out.

"Good luck," she heard him call as she charged into the blowing rain.

Lindsay descended the steps and ran across the wet pavement toward the parking lot. She had not gone a hundred feet before her open-toed pumps and her feet were soaked. Half an inch of water covered the pavement everywhere, making the parking lot an enormous puddle. Her hair was plastered to her head and as she ran she could feel the water running down her face and neck.

Squinting into the rain and darkness, she had run halfway to her car, when suddenly her foot sank into a hidden pothole, pitching her forward and sending her sprawling onto the pavement.

Lindsay lay for a moment in the water, stunned. She tried to sort out the barage of sensation going through her body, searching for the pain she instinctively knew would come. Awkwardly she raised herself to a sitting position when the pain hit her, first in her hand and wrist, then in her right calf, which was twisted under her.

His voice reached her first through the pain and numbness. Then she looked around as Bill Price came running up, a distraught and anxious expression on his face.

He dropped down beside her. "Are you all right?"

"I think so," she groaned.

His arm was around her shoulder, supporting her tightly, and his face was over hers, just inches away. Lindsay looked at him, feeling the throbbing ache in her entire right side, but her attention was focused on his face. She saw how the water on his cheek glistened in the light of a nearby lamppost, saw the vapors from their breathing billow and mingle between them in the cold wet air. In spite of the pain hovering about her consciousness, more than anything else she was aware of the absurdity of the situation.

"Are you sure you're all right, Lindsay?"

The green eyes were there next to her face, but they were no longer dangerous. She nodded.

"Can you stand?"

His arm slid around her back and under her arm. It tightened as he lifted her. The legs under her straightened but he held her so securely that her weight was barely on her feet. The trench coat he wore was open and she was enfolded by it, held closely against his body.

"Are your legs okay?" he asked as he eased her weight down upon her feet.

"My leg hurts, but it's okay."

He wrapped his coat farther around her, sheltering her from the downpour. Through the pain and the rain Lindsay's primary sensation was of the warmth of him. She shivered, and the man pulled her more closely against him, protectively. When she lifted her eyes again his head was bowed close to her face, so close the warmth of his breath touched her cheek. She saw his parted lips and the white of his teeth in the semi-light. Then the corners of his lips curled slightly and she looked into his eyes. He was observing her mouth, smiling. The concern had faded from his face. The look he gave her now betrayed a more intimate emotion. She sensed desire and shuddered, even as her own physical awareness of him heightened.

"We've got to get you out of this rain. Can you walk?"

Lindsay looked down at her feet, realizing she had broken the heel of one shoe in the fall. "I think so." She took a tentative step. "Yes, I'm okay."

"Here, wait," he said, then reached down and picked up her purse and briefcase from the pavement.

"What a disaster," she mumbled as he put his coat around her again.

"Where's your car?"

"Just over there."

When they arrived at the BMW she took her purse and began fumbling through it for her keys.

"Uh oh," he said, "I'm afraid this is not your day, Lindsay."

Seeing him look at the car she spun around and saw that the front tire was completely flat. "Oh, damn."

"Well, you get inside. I'll see what I can do."

She felt like a sponge as she sat on the seat, squishing water all over the upholstery. There wasn't a square inch of her that was dry and there was nothing she could do about it. Bill Price had walked around the car and was back tapping on her window. She lowered it.

"Don't have two spares, do you?"

"No, why?"

"Your other front tire is flat too."

"Oh, no! Two flat tires? How can I have *two* flat tires?" Water was dripping from his chin and nose. He shrugged. She searched his eyes, feeling totally miserable. "Damn! Must've been kids. What'll I do now?" she wailed.

"We'll have to get someone to come out."

"I can call the auto club. Could I trouble you for a lift to a phone?"

"Sure, let me go get my car." He gave her a reassuring smile then turned and disappeared into the darkness.

For a time Lindsay sat dazed, her body rigid, her eyes frozen on the stream of water flowing down the windshield, distorting the outside world, leaving her feeling isolated and helpless. A flash of lightning illuminated the sky to the west. In a few seconds, she was not only wet and aching, but also terribly cold. She began shivering.

Just as her misery was getting to the point of being unbearable, she saw the lights of Bill Price's car. She couldn't remember ever feeling so grateful to a man in all her life. In a moment he was tapping on her window and she had to struggle against the violent shaking of her body to open the door.

One look at her and he took her quickly by the arm. "Come on, young lady, we've got to warm you up." He helped her out of the seat and around to the passenger side of his car, a sleek Porsche Carrera. Grabbing a blanket from the back, he opened it on the seat and helped her in, wrapping the blanket around her trembling body. He closed the door, ran around to the driver's side and jumped in. The engine was running and the heat was on, but Bill pushed the fan on full blast, sending hot air swirling around Lindsay.

She moaned through her chattering teeth.

"It'll be like a sauna in here in a minute," he said reassuringly. "Let's see, I'd better lock your car. Where are your keys?"

"In my purse on the front seat," she said, her teeth rattling.

He got out of the car and in a minute was back again with Lindsay's purse and briefcase in hand. He put them in back and climbed in. "All locked up."

"Bill, I can't thank you enough. I feel terrible putting you through this."

He turned to her with a benevolent expression on his face. "I'm sorry you fell. How are you feeling now? Getting warmer?"

Lindsay pulled the blanket tightly around her neck and nodded. She was still shivering, but the bone-chilling cold had abated.

He put the car in gear and drove out of the parking lot to the boulevard. Several blocks up the street they came to a gas station and he pulled in. Lindsay sat shivering as Bill Price got out and went to talk to the attendant. A moment later he was back.

"Looks bad, Lindsay. Both their trucks are out, and it could be forty-five minutes or an hour before they could get to us."

She looked at him in desperation. "What shall we do? Try another station?"

"We could, but it's a bad storm and I'm afraid we'll get the same story everywhere." He watched her shivering for a moment, his face sympathetic. "Look, you're in no shape to sit around gas stations. I think we ought to tend to you before we worry about your car." He paused. "I live nearby in Saratoga. Why don't I take you to my place to get warm and dry before we take care of the car."

His words set off an alarm bell in Lindsay's head. "Thank you, you're very kind Bill, but no. I'll just wait for a tow truck."

"Lindsay, be practical. If you don't take care of yourself you'll probably come down with pneumonia."

"Really, no. I couldn't impose, you've done more than enough already."

He studied her. "That's not what concerns you, and you know it. You're thinking I'm a strange man, you don't know me."

She returned his look. "Well, you must admit..."

Bill lifted his hand and a quirky smile brushed the corner of his handsome mouth. "Here," he said opening the glove compartment and removing an aerosol can. "Mace. Use this if there's a problem."

Lindsay took the can and looked at it. "This isn't Mace, it's insect repellant!"

Bill grinned. "I know, but it was the only thing I could think of to reassure you. Trust me, Lindsay, I'm better for you than pneumonia."

Lindsay trembled, feeling so miserable it was difficult to think. Her teeth chattered uncontrollably and she knew she was on the verge of surrender. "No criminal record, Bill?" she managed.

"Not even crimes of the heart."

"How do I get myself into these situations?"

He started the engine.

"My mother would kill me," she mumbled.

As they drove west toward the exclusive town of Saratoga nestled in the hills, Bill chatted away amiably. Lindsay hardly heard a word, longing to be free of her intense discomfort. After about ten minutes they wound their way through a posh residential neighborhood in the hills, and Lindsay found herself mesmerized by the rhythmic sweep of the windshield wipers and Bill's soothing voice. Before she knew it they pulled into a great circular drive, drove past the front door of a large rambling Spanish-style home, and turned into the garage at the far end of the house. He pushed the button on the dash and the door closed slowly behind them.

"After a shot of brandy and some warm dry clothes, you'll be good as new," he said, grinning.

Lindsay let herself be led into the house, knowing she was totally at the man's mercy. He took her through the kitchen to a bathroom. "Get out of those wet clothes. I'll get you something to put on."

He left and Lindsay looked at the soaked and trembling woman in the mirror. She was too upset to think, too uncomfortable even to care how she looked. All she wanted was to be warm and dry. With difficulty she slipped off her suit jacket, which was soaked through. Her silk blouse wasn't quite as wet, but it was bad enough that it was plastered against her skin so that her bra showed plainly through the film of fabric.

Lindsay had slipped off her shoes and was wiping her face with a hand towel when Bill Price returned. He tossed a large white terry cloth bathrobe on the vanity. "This will do until I can find something else." Reaching into the shower he turned on the hot water. In an instant steam began billowing out of the stall. "Get those clothes off and get into the shower.'' His eyes passed briefly over the front of her wet blouse and he left the room, pulling the door closed behind him.

Lindsay went to the door, pushed the button lock on the handle and with trembling hands began undoing her blouse. As she stepped out of her skirt and peeled off her blouse, she realized that she didn't have the vaguest idea where she was. Not a soul in the world knew she was there—except of course for Bill Price—but it was *his* bathroom and *his* house. Looking at the inviting warmth of the shower, she hoped everything would be all right.

Lindsay removed her bra and began pulling down her panty hose when she saw the gash at the back of her calf. The blood had coagulated in the thin mesh of the nylon and the wound hurt when she pulled away the hose from her skin. There was an abrasion on the side of her thigh and hip, but it wasn't bad, though she was sure there'd soon be a nasty bruise.

There was a sharp clap of thunder outside. Lindsay quickly stepped into the shower, her taut muscles and clammy skin craving the soothing hot water. She hunched under the flow of it, her head and shoulders taking the direct force of the jet, the rest of her gradually relaxing under the warm sheets of water.

The sensation of warm pleasure, in contrast to the insidious cold she had endured, made Lindsay unwilling to leave the shower. She stood there, her eyes closed, her mouth slightly open, her hands entwined and holding the nape of her neck. Her entire being was aware only of the hot steaming liquid.

After a long time the deep chill was finally expunged and her natural vitality started returning to her. She stepped from the shower feeling warm, relaxed and restored. As she dried herself with a bath sheet, she dis-

covered with dismay that the wound on her right leg was
bleeding freely now. She took some tissue and pressed it
against the scrape to stem the flow of blood. Then she
looked in the medicine cabinet and the drawers of the
vanity for bandages. Not finding any, Lindsay left pieces
of the tissue on the wound and turned to finish rubbing
her skin and hair dry with the towel.

She looked through the drawers until she found a
comb. After working through the tangles in her hair, she
wrapped it up in a hand towel. Slipping on the heavy terry
cloth bathrobe, she pulled it snugly around her and tied
it securely about her waist. After hanging out her wet
clothing on the towel racks and over the tub, Lindsay was
tidying the bathroom when there was a knock at the door.

"Yes?" she said, pulling the lapels of the bathrobe together at the neck.

"How are you feeling?" came the familiar baritone
voice through the door.

"Much better, Bill."

"Good, I've got some cognac for you. Are you
decent?"

Lindsay looked into the mirror and felt completely
unprepared to greet him. Her nudity under this strange
man's bathrobe left her feeling vulnerable. Considering
she hadn't laid eyes on him until a scant hour or so earlier, she realized she had conferred a great deal of trust on
him with very little basis for it. Earlier she had been in a
sad plight and had accepted his assistance almost out of
necessity, but now the man outside the door seemed like
the greater threat, not her injury, not the elements. With
the door locked between them she felt secure. Once she
stepped from the bath her fate was in his hands.

She found herself staring at the doorknob, but was
unable to open it. Was she being silly? The man had be-

haved perfectly well and with no small sacrifice on his part. But now, in his house, she would be completely at his mercy. They would be alone—the point could hardly be lost on him—yet she couldn't stay where she was.

"Lindsay? Are you all right?"

Thunder crashed outside in the night sky then rolled away from the house into the western hills. Lindsay set her jaw and opened the door.

CHAPTER THREE

LINDSAY'S FACE REFLECTED UNCERTAINTY when the door finally opened and Blake Prescott smiled to reassure her. But the smile broadened at the surprising beauty of the vision before him.

The turban atop her head gave her an exotic yet vulnerable look. It was completely at odds with the sophisticated, businesslike attorney at the lecture or even the injured and distressed woman in the parking lot. Her suggested nudity beneath the oversized bathrobe underlined a femininity that normally a man only encountered in more sexually intimate circumstances. But although the image she presented was different from what he had previously seen, there was still the sensuous mouth with its lower lip that looked even more inviting than it had before. She glanced at the brandy snifter in his hand before he had the presence of mind to extend it to her.

"This ought to warm your insides."

She smiled tentatively and brought the glass immediately to her lips, sipping the fiery liquid.

Prescott let his eyes meander down the front of the bathrobe, which she still clutched at the neck. "Better?"

"Yes, it's nice. Thank you."

She gave his clothing only the briefest glance.

He had changed into a bulky fisherman's sweater, an old pair of jeans and tennis shoes. He looked her up and down again, this time making no attempt to disguise the candid appraisal of her. "Any permanent damage?"

Lindsay looked down at her leg and turned her calf toward him. "This cut and some bruises. That's all."

"Looks like you can use some patching."

"Maybe if you have a bandage..."

"Sure. You enjoy the brandy. I'll get my first-aid kit." He was gone only a minute, and by the time he had returned Lindsay had removed the towel from her head and was combing through her wet hair. Their eyes met in the mirror as he stepped up behind her. He found himself transfixed. She immediately turned her attention back to her own image as she finished the last stroke, enabling him to observe her. His eyes rested on her lower lip until she turned squarely to him.

"Sit there on the edge of the tub," he said. She had an uncertain look on her face and he hastened to reassure her. "I'm certain all that first-aid training I got in the service was to prepare me for this moment."

Lindsay smiled hesitantly and sat on the tub. He kneeled down at her feet and opened the box he had carried with him. As he rummaged through it, he became aware of the woman's legs and couldn't help glancing at the shapely ankles and small, narrow feet just inches from him.

Looking at them he saw that her toenails had been pedicured in a soft shade of coral. On her big toe, he noticed in surprise, was a delicate butterfly, so finely painted that at first sight it looked like a photograph.

Lindsay was aware of his candid examination of her, and her feet pressed more closely together and slid a few inches back against the tub. Prescott looked up at her with a grin on his face. "Did you know there was a bug on your toe?"

She chuckled. "Yes, and it wasn't cheap getting it there either."

Prescott shrugged. "Women do the damnedest things."

"You don't like my butterfly?"

"It's pretty, but what good does it do hidden under your shoes? Who'd see it...?"

Now it was Lindsay who grinned. "I don't always have my shoes on."

Prescott looked up at her. "Do you have a friend with a butterfly fetish?"

With a bemused expression, she answered, "No, I do it for me."

Lindsay saw a twinkle in his eye as he turned away and continued ferreting through his box, finally pulling out a rather sinister little bottle that she had associated with pain since childhood.

"Merthiolate!" he announced triumphantly.

"You needn't look so pleased!"

"But Lindsay, I just love killing germs."

Without comment, he turned to his task of doctoring while Lindsay bit her lip in fear.

Bill pulled away the bits of tissue in preparation for the swabbing.

"Will you do it quickly?" she asked anxiously, feeling the pain justified the cowardice she let show.

The glass applicator was poised in his hand when Lindsay winced and jerked her leg back reflexively, though the dreaded medicine was still three inches from the wound.

"I don't have a bullet for you to bite on," he teased, "so..." Without hesitating the man grasped Lindsay firmly by the ankle with his free hand and virtually nailed her foot to the floor with surprising strength.

For an instant Lindsay didn't know whether she should fear the forceful masculine grip or the impending pain of the antiseptic. She closed her eyes and started trembling until she felt the touch of the applicator on her wound. It felt cool at first, then began to burn, but far less severely than she had expected.

Bill continued to swab the cut, all the while holding her ankle tightly in his large hand. After a while she looked away from her leg, becoming aware of the absurdity of what was happening to her. This handsome man, whose shoulders seemed so broad to her in the sweater, was kneeling at her feet, holding her by the foot and painting her leg with a little glass rod.

From her vantage point above him on the tub she couldn't see his face, just the top of his head and the rich auburn of his hair that she had first noticed in the lecture hall. The longer they remained in this attitude of unconscious intimacy, the more Lindsay became conscious of his raw masculinity.

The fingers that were clamped about her ankle gradually seemed more instruments of dominance. Lindsay, of necessity, had exposed her leg to the man without really thinking of her nakedness under the garment and the realization suddenly evoked sexual awareness in her. Her skin seemed to tingle as much from his touch as the medication, and she saw him once more as a physical being. Lindsay found her knees pressing together in response to the disturbing signal from her body, and she wondered if only she was aware.

Bill looked up as if to inquire about her condition. "Are you all right, Lindsay?"

She blinked at the incongruity between the words and her thoughts, even as fear and titilation cavorted in her body. "Yes," she replied vacantly.

"Are you sure?"

The aberrancy of her tone had struck even Lindsay.

"Yes, Bill. I'm fine," she said recovering.

The corners of his mouth twitched, as if he knew very well she *wasn't* fine, but he quickly masked his amusement. "Good. You're a good soldier, the worst is over." Setting the captive ankle free at last, he turned to his kit, taking some gauze patches from the box. Tearing one bandage from its protective wrapping he looked closely at Lindsay's injured leg, running his fingertips lightly around the periphery of the wound. "I'll have you fixed up in no time." The self-satisfied little laugh he gave seemed to Lindsay more responsive to some inner thought than the words he uttered.

He managed, despite slightly clumsy fingers, to position the bandage on the wound and begin taping it. Holding her calf he couldn't help but be aware of her body. She was so petite, but her figure was quite feminine, even voluptuous given the small scale of her stature. The clean scent of her, fresh out of the shower, filled his nostrils as he worked and he found himself trying to repress his sexual awareness of her.

Prescott knew that his interest in Lindsay Bishop had drifted hopelessly beyond the point of curiosity. He was no longer taking his measure of an adversary, he was testing the depth of his desire for a woman. The danger she had represented before seemed to fade as her allure increased and he began regretting the corner he had painted himself into. It was on an impulse that he had told her his name was Bill Price and he thought in a whimsical moment that he would end up paying a dear "price" for his deception. Prescott realized that if he were ever to be more than an ambulance driver to this woman he'd have to tell her the truth, but now was not the time. Not with her sitting half-naked in his bathroom.

Working on her leg, he admonished himself to be careful. What he had intended as a conversation over a drink or a cup of coffee had become a bizarre encounter on his own turf. Ironically, the house was empty that night, enabling him to bring her there. What at first had seemed like good fortune had become a problem for him.

But even as Prescott felt regret, he enjoyed the pleasure of Lindsay Bishop's company. In spite of himself her very presence seemed to arouse him. The bathrobe was parted to a point just above her knee where she held it with her hand. If she had been his woman he'd have brushed the protective hand aside and reached under the hem of the robe to caress the milky flesh of her thigh. Yet he knew he couldn't blame Lindsay for the frustration he felt. It was his doing that brought her here, not her own.

Applying the final pieces of tape, Prescott weighed the possibility of some sort of overture, to test the possibility of any interest she might have in him. But, the situation was much too delicate at the moment. He could blow it.

"There you go. Good as new!" he said looking up.

She had been leaning forward watching the operation with interest and her face was now very near his. He could have kissed her without much trouble and when she didn't pull away he nearly took the sensuous mouth that he had found so enticing.

Sensing the man's strong vibrations, Lindsay was suddenly touched by fear. She leaned back, away from him, unconsciously tucking her dangling wet hair behind one ear. Bill Price had not taken his eyes off of her when he unexpectedly reached up and touched the ends of her hair on the other side of her face. Then, to her surprise, he pushed her damp tresses behind her other ear, just as she had, letting his hand skitter along the edge of her cheek as it retreated. This contact and the distant, hungry look in his eyes sent a tremor through her.

There was alarm on her face when he gave her a soothing smile. "Your hair's still wet. I'll get you a dryer so you won't get a chill." He stood up with the first-aid kit in his hand and shook the stiffness out of his legs. "Don't go away. I'll be right back."

When he had gone Lindsay's mind rushed to question what had just taken place. He had very nearly kissed her, she was sure of that. What would she have done? She didn't know the man but in her mind she saw herself submitting to him as readily as she saw herself taking flight. Relief and disappointment were the surprising competitors among her thoughts.

Lindsay was examining herself in the mirror when she heard his footstep in the hall. She turned to the door not knowing what to expect.

He put only one foot inside the door, handing her the hair dryer then picking up her almost-empty brandy snifter from the counter. "I'll be in the living room, at the end of the hall, Lindsay. Come on down when you're through." And he was gone.

She had nearly finished drying her hair when there was more thunder, so loud it was easily heard over the sound of the dryer. The lights flickered and the motor of the appliance labored before recovering. The rain had become so heavy that Lindsay was able to hear it pounding on the roof through the ceiling. She was running the comb through her hair under the stream of hot air when the lights flickered again and went out, plunging the bathroom into total darkness. Likewise, the hair dryer died in her hand.

Lindsay, frightened, fumbled for the doorknob in the dark and opened the bathroom door. ''Bill?'' she called out into the hall.

''I'm in the living room, Lindsay. Can you see your way?''

She peered up the hallway in the darkness and saw light flickering faintly. ''Is there a light?''

''We lost our power and I'm trying to find some candles,'' he replied. ''I've got a fire going. Can you see your way or shall I come and get you?''

She had started feeling her way along the walls. ''No, I'll make it.'' By the time she reached the end of the hallway her eyes had adjusted to the dark and she was able to see the living room clearly by the light of the fire. Bill was lighting several candles on a table by a window that was being pelted by the rain. The dark shadows on his face were erased intermittently by flashes of lightning outside.

''Yeah, it's quite a storm,'' he said casually. ''Don't remember anything like this before in California.''

Lindsay had come up behind the couch facing the fireplace. ''Me neither.''

''Your cognac is there on the hearth. Sit by the fire and warm yourself.''

She saw two snifters on the hearth, which was elevated a foot or so above the floor. It afforded a cozy place to sit by the fire, which burned brightly. Lindsay made her way toward the crackling flames.

''The full one's yours,'' Bill said and blew out the match in his hand.

She picked up the glass as he walked over to where she sat. The deep shadows gave him an altogether different look, more chiseled and nefarious, but the timbre of his voice was familiar and the white of his teeth indicated a smile.

"Did you get your hair dry?" he asked as he sat beside her.

"Just about." She peered at him over her glass and sipped at the brandy, meeting emerald green eyes. Instantly their mutual awareness flared and, after a tense, frozen moment, he lifted his hand to her face. But he didn't touch it, taking instead the ends of her hair between his fingers as he had before. "It feels dry," he said softly.

The expression on his face was benevolent, perhaps even tender. Lindsay felt her throat tighten as he toyed with her hair a bit longer before releasing it. His eyes were moving back and forth between hers. Then they dropped to her lips and without hesitation he leaned toward her.

So entranced was she, that her lips were covered by his before she fully realized that this stranger had kissed her. Their heads slowly angled around the exquisite point of contact. Lindsay was entrapped in the sweetness of the embrace, her heart beating in an uncontrollable flight and her body responding to the man on its own—without her permission.

His arm slipped around her shoulders as he moved close against her. His mouth took her more eagerly. His tongue sank into her sweet moistness. His teeth gingerly claimed the fullness of her lip.

He had taken her so unexpectedly that Lindsay found herself caught up in his passion before the full implications of his act were clear. She knew she should stop him, but her body refused to cooperate. Even as the conflict raged inside her, she accepted his affections, and returned them with her own.

When his hand went to the gap in her bathrobe and slipped inside to take her breast, Lindsay knew she had to do something. But her resolve was deflected by the sensuality of his mouth now playing with her lower lip. Her will was suppressed by the gentle caress of the hand that cupped her breast and by the thumb that ran over the hardening nub of her nipple.

Bill's hand moved down her torso to the curve of her waist, and Lindsay, still locked in his embrace, felt the robe being pulled open by his arm. Only a gentle push of his hand was needed to loosen the tie and expose her entirely to him. As his tongue explored her mouth, his hand swept across her stomach and Lindsay felt the fabric giving way. Excitement and fear buffeted her and her eyes opened to see which one deserved her trust. The man's hands had nearly captured her, but the sight of the strange face against hers was disconcerting, and her will finally asserted itself. She pulled back from him.

His face registered surprise and she was steeling herself for further resistance. Their eyes were joined in an incongruous confrontation when the lights in the room flickered then came to life, flooding the room.

There was momentary embarrassment before they began eyeing each other with uncertainty. Then Bill reached over and took the ends of the tie to her robe, crossed them and cinched the garment at her waist. Then he leaned toward her, kissed her delicately on the lower lip, and smiled. "Don't worry, Lindsay," he whispered in an ironic tone, "You're safe."

She held the robe tightly across her chest, searching his eyes, resenting him for the torment she felt, imploring him to make the moment right. He kissed her again lightly by way of concession.

"Now that you've been mended and cared for, perhaps we'd best see to your car," he said in a low matter-of-fact voice.

He was punishing her for calling a halt to their love-making. Lindsay didn't like it, but she knew she'd have to take responsibility for her own actions. "What can I wear?" she asked, looking down at herself.

"The best I could find is one of my jogging suits." He walked to a green suede chair to fetch the suit, stopping on the way to blow out the candles.

The fire at Lindsay's back was quite warm and she stood up as he returned with the clothing in his hand. He seemed to tower over her like a giant; she hadn't been so aware of his height until now. She felt shy as he looked at her and she decided he was remembering their intimacy. Ironically, she wished he would kiss her again.

Instead he handed her the jogging suit. "Let me get you a bag for your wet clothes. You can change in the bath if you like."

Several minutes later Lindsay was looking at the comical creature in the bathroom mirror. The pants were pulled up to her ribs yet the crotch hung halfway to her knees. The elastic at the ankles kept the legs bloused up, making her look roly-poly. The jacket top hung well over her hips to the middle of her thighs and the shoulders drooped halfway to her elbows.

She found Bill in the kitchen rinsing out the glasses. He couldn't help grinning at the image she presented. Then he noticed her little bare feet on the linoleum. "That won't do. Hang on." And he left the room.

Lindsay looked around her and was struck by the tidiness of the kitchen. Either Bill Price was terribly neat for a man or there was the hand of a woman in evidence. A maid perhaps? The bath she had used must be some sort of guest bath, as it showed no signs of regular use. She stepped toward the counter and her eye was caught by a colorful object beside a canister. It was a plastic cup with Disney characters painted on it. She picked it up as Bill came walking back into the room. He saw the cup in her hand.

"Kind of funky, huh?" he said with a chuckle.

"Yes," she said wryly. "Some sort of mid-life crisis?"

He laughed. "Beneath this conventional-looking exterior is a true eccentric."

Lindsay laughed too. Bill winked and handed her a pair of sweat socks that seemed nearly as long as her legs. She took them and went to the table where she sat down and pulled them onto her slender feet.

She wondered about the child's cup. Perhaps, she thought, he was a divorced father who saw his child on weekends. In any case, he didn't seem to want to talk about it.

He was watching her from his vantage point at the sink. "Are thirteens a little big for you?"

"Considering the heel comes to the middle of my calf, they're not bad. At least all this baggy stuff is easy on my cuts and bruises."

"How are you doing, by the way?" He had walked around to the table and was looking at her with a bemused expression.

"Do men ever have to go through this kind of embarrassment?"

"I don't know about other guys, but I think I'd go nude before trying to squeeze into a pair of panty hose."

She laughed in spite of herself. "Sometimes I wonder if the people who organize the world are all tall."

"Well, let me add to your paranoia with some bad news. The auto club is pretty busy because of the storm. I called a couple of gas stations and they're tied up too."

Lindsay's sinking feeling was all over her face for Blake Prescott to see.

"But don't despair. I've got a solution. I'll drive you home now. If you'll give me your car keys I'll have my garage pick up your car first thing in the morning, fix the tires and deliver the car to your house."

"Would they?"

"It's all arranged."

She felt relieved and grateful. "Again, Bill, thank you."

"The least I can do. Well, m'lady, may I show you home?"

The storm had pretty well dissipated by the time they left. Only a light rain was falling, and the puddles remaining in low spots were the sole indication a storm had passed through.

"What time is it anyway?" Lindsay asked a few minutes later as they sped along the freeway.

"Just past eleven."

"So late? Hope I haven't kept you up with my disastrous evening."

"Wouldn't have missed it for the world."

Something told her he was genuinely pleased. Of course, the evening *had* clearly been a change of pace from a routine night with the television set, but Lindsay sensed some extra measure of satisfaction in this man.

Glancing at her companion, she realized that he had a quality that piqued her interest. Something that seemed gentle and dangerous at the same time. She knew also he was disingenuous, but she couldn't tell why or exactly how. Something about him was staged, but at the same time she could find nothing nefarious about him.

Perhaps the most disturbing aspect of the night had been the conflict within her that he had provoked. He seemed both too much and too little at the same time. When he had kissed her and touched her she was alarmed, although excited. At the moment she had the curious feeling of being cheated, as though he had denied her an experience to which she was entitled.

She directed Bill to her town house located in a pleasant neighborhood in Palo Alto. He had been rather quiet for most of the ride, seemingly as content in his thoughts as she had been in hers.

After indicating the final turn, Lindsay began gathering her purse, briefcase and the bag of clothes.

"I'm awfully sorry about all the misfortune that's befallen you tonight, Lindsay."

"You're hardly responsible. To the contrary, if it weren't for you I'd have been in a sorry state." She pointed to her house. "That's mine."

"Well, incongruous as it sounds, I enjoyed it. You're a fun lawyer." He pulled over.

"I *guess* that's a compliment."

"Oh yes, indeed." He had stopped the car. "Hold on. Wait there, I'll help you." Bill got out and walked around the car. It had stopped raining, but when he opened the door for her Lindsay could see the ground was still quite wet.

She looked up at him feeling rather helpless again, her arms overflowing with baggage.

"Can you handle all that?"

"Yes, if I can just get out."

Before she knew it he had reached down and in one easy motion had lifted her and all her things. He stepped back from the car and kicked the door closed with his foot. Lindsay looked at him in surprise, feeling like a small waif snatched away by some congenial ogre.

"Can't have you getting your feet wet, can we?"

"Really, Bill…" But her murmured protest was stifled by his disarming laugh.

As he carried her to the door, she became acutely aware of his indulgent air. His statement was so pointed, so proprietary, that she felt even more compromised than she had by the earlier intimacy, though his manner remained wholly proper, even solicitous.

Never could Lindsay remember feeling so small and vulnerable. His strong arms held her so certainly that she found herself automatically—and completely—surrendering to the gesture. When he had climbed with her to the top of the steps he stopped and turned his emerald eyes on her, embracing her with them. There was no mistaking the message.

The corner of his mouth bent upward a bit as if the frightened expression on her face was amusing. He let the moment dangle like a cat might with a captured mouse. She waited.

His face was just inches from hers, giving him the opportunity to savor her, to enjoy her as he had earlier. Precisely at the instant in time when her own feelings had evolved to desire, he lowered his mouth to hers and kissed her carefully, gently, on the lips, caressing her like a bee would a blossom, until his lips trailed away, leaving her free.

The man placed her carefully on the threshold, waiting in silence for her to open the door with her key, then seeing her safely inside, he quietly left.

CHAPTER FOUR

BLAKE PRESCOTT stared out the window as his fingertips unconsciously drummed the highly polished wood of
the desk. His mind cavorted through memories of the
previous evening, pausing to recall brief scenes of Lindsay Bishop in the lecture hall, in the rain, sitting in his car.
But mostly he saw those wide eyes signaling surrender
just before she submitted to his kiss.

The image of her in his mind was at once delicious and
tormenting. His feelings were not the result he had
wanted and he berated himself for the dalliance, even as
he enjoyed it. Prescott knew himself well enough to know
he'd do his damnedest to have it both ways. That had always been his style.

He was stubborn. Doing what he wanted usually got
him the things he desired, but he was shrewd, too, and
that meant knowing when to pull back, when to punt.
Lindsay Bishop had caused him to vacillate—behavior
uncharacteristic of him—and it troubled him that she
should. It was almost as though the little victory she had
permitted him by the fire was really his Waterloo. Common sense and good judgment told him to pull back and
wait. Instead he picked up the telephone and dialed the
number listed in the file lying open on his desk.

He continued staring out the window as the phone
rang, waiting for her to answer. "Well, good morning.
Thought I'd call and see if you survived the night."

"Bill?"

"Yes, it's me. How are you feeling?"

"I'm feeling great, thank you."

"Judging by your tone they must have gotten your car to you."

"Yes. As a matter of fact the man just left a few minutes ago. The car's parked out in front, good as new. He said the tires were fine. The air had been let out of them, that's all."

"You were right then. It probably was a prank."

"By the way, I wish you hadn't paid the garage. It was awfully nice of you, but unnecessary. Rescuing me last night was more than enough."

"No, it was nothing. Actually, the reason I called is I'd like to get together with you again. I'd like to take you to dinner tonight."

There was a brief pause. "Well, I accept in principle. I want to see you again to thank you properly and to return your clothes, but I insist that you be my guest."

"May I suggest a compromise?"

"Dutch treat?"

"No, I'm sufficiently traditional that I prefer to pay, but I will agree to negotiate the arrangement for future dinners with an open mind."

"Okay, I'm sufficiently liberated that I'll accept that. When and where shall I pick you up?"

Prescott couldn't help but smile at the woman's spunk. He was glad, though, she wasn't there to have the satisfaction of seeing the expression on his face. "I'll be at the Supreme Court in Palo Alto at seven. You can pick me up there."

"The Supreme Court? You mean the municipal court?"

"No, Lindsay, it's a *racquetball* club just off Embarcadero Road, not a court of law!"

She laughed. "Sorry, I have a tendency to see things through lawyers' eyes."

"An unfortunate tendency, but I'll learn to live with it."

Lindsay ignored the comment. "I'll see you tonight at seven then." And she hung up feeling rather pleased.

From the moment the door had closed after his kiss the night before, Lindsay's mind had been a crucible of emotion. In one bold gesture he had traversed the gap that had opened between them after the advances he had made by the fire. His touch had completely electrified her and she had come close to giving herself to him completely.

For an hour after he had gone she had been obsessed with the way he had so quickly and easily aroused her. She became obsessed with that dangling moment in which she was suspended in his arms, helpless, waiting to be kissed. Never had vulnerability been so sweet and never had promise been so gently fulfilled. She had tempted danger and she had won. What began as disaster ended in a remarkable experience. Still, Bill Price was a mystery to her. The excitement engendered by that notion only served to spur her on and Lindsay knew she had to be careful, particularly until she got to know him better.

Her hand still rested on the telephone beside the bed, as though by touching it she was able to sustain the satisfaction of the call. Looking down at the instrument her mind suddenly churned and her face reflected the perplexity that had just come upon her. Bill Price had called her, but how could he? Her number was unlisted and she hadn't given it to him.

She quickly considered the possibilities. Had he called the office first? No, it was only a few minutes past eight, there'd have been no one there yet. Would he have found it somewhere? In her purse? On her checkbook? But why would he be so sneaky? No, there must be another explanation, probably an innocent one. Still, it was baffling. She would ask him about it at dinner.

BRIGHTLY COLORED LEAVES drifted from the maple trees on University Avenue as Lindsay made her way along the sidewalk. The ground was still wet from the storm the previous night, but the sun had come up to warm the crisp October air. There was promise of a beautiful day.

She turned from the walk and climbed the steps of an old Spanish house now converted to professional offices. The soreness in her right leg was an unpleasant reminder of her fall, but there was no evidence available to the outside world save a small adhesive strip that had replaced the large bandage administered by Bill Price. Even that was hardly noticeable below the hem of the pencil slim skirt of her pale gray wool suit.

Lindsay's straight black hair glistened in the sunlight, a perfect foil to her ivory skin and the shell-pink blouse with a mandarin collar she had selected to go with the suit. When she entered the double doors emblazoned with the words Woodward & Bishop, Attorneys-at-Law in gold relief letters, her face radiated the happiness in her heart.

"Well, good morning, Lindsay," the receptionist said cheerfully. "You're looking chipper."

"Thank you, Karen. It *is* a nice morning, isn't it?" She stopped at the girl's desk and took the message slips that were handed to her.

"What did you think of all the thunder and lightning last night?" Karen asked.

"Quite a show, wasn't it?" Lindsay looked up from the pink message slip she'd been reading.

"I've never seen anything like it in my life!"

"You're a true Californian," Lindsay said and glanced back down at the message in her hand. Her mind slowly moved from the storm to Bill Price then to his call that morning. "By the way, Karen, was anyone in the office early this morning?"

"No. I was the first one in and I got here at eight-fifteen, as usual. Why?"

"I had a call this morning from an acquaintance and I don't remember giving him my unlisted number. It only occurred to me after the call. Then I thought he might have gotten it from someone here."

"Not that I know of, unless the answering service gave it to him. Want me to check?"

"No, it's no big deal."

"I can call them. It's no trouble."

"Well, if you have a minute, call, but I'm not really concerned." Lindsay smiled at the girl again, then walked on through the suite toward her office. "Good morning, Jean," she said arriving at the desk of her legal assistant.

"Morning, Lindsay. How'd the speech go?" The woman, a veteran paralegal in her early fifties, had—as Lindsay remembered hearing innumerable times—been working in the legal field since Lindsay was in grammar school.

"It was marvelous!" Lindsay enthused.

Jean looked at the younger woman over the tops of her bifocals. "Standing ovation?"

Lindsay chuckled. "I mean it was a great experience. But, now that you mention it, some of my demagoguery did bring them to their feet."

"Doesn't surprise me. With some of those college kids all you have to do is whisper 'ERA' or 'No Nukes' and they're in a tizzy."

"Jean, all you need is a little consciousness raising," Lindsay teased.

The older woman gave her an admonishing look. "You know how I feel about *that*."

Lindsay smiled and nodded. The topic was a familiar one between them.

"Guess I shouldn't be surprised, though. The girls got just as excited in my day, only then it was over Frank Sinatra."

Lindsay laughed approvingly. "Have anything for me this morning? Anything from Millicent?"

"She called to say she had an appointment out of the office and that she'd be in about ten."

"Okay. Anything in the mail?"

"We got the interrogatories in from Martin Blum on the *Moretti* case."

"Oh, wonderful! I've been looking forward to seeing those."

Jean handed Lindsay a large thick manila envelope. "Have fun," she said dryly.

Lindsay went into her office, sat in the high-backed swivel chair at her desk and was scanning her calendar when the intercom buzzed. She picked up the receiver. "Yes?"

"Lindsay, it's Karen. Answering service had no calls at all on our account this morning."

"All right, Karen. Thanks for checking." She hung up, disappointed the mystery hadn't been solved. Forcing her thoughts from Bill Price, she turned to the envelope Jean had given her a few minutes earlier. Inside it was one version of the story of two lives now dissolved into a bitter feud over rights to money. It was, she thought, a classical example of what she had talked about in her lecture the previous day.

Terry Moretti, her client, had lived with a wealthy man for ten years. She had a child by him, a son named Rusty who was now nine years old. The man had admitted paternity and given the child his name. Terry, a professional singer, had lived with this man all these years without benefit of marriage, and now that things had gone bad, he was tossing her out. The case was a perfect example of a woman used.

The intercom on Lindsay's desk shattered her musings as though they were crystal. She blinked and picked up the receiver. "Yes?"

"Lindsay, Martin Blum on line three."

She pushed a button on the phone. "Lindsay Bishop."

"Hi, doll. Need a favor."

She hadn't laid eyes on Martin Blum in years but they had talked a number of times on the phone and had corresponded extensively on the *Moretti* case. "What is it, Martin?"

"My client's attorney has a real big problem shaping up over that deposition you have a week from tomorrow..."

"Your client's attorney? You mean you?"

"Hey baby, you're sharp as a tack for so early in the morning."

"Martin if you're going to act like an ass, I wish you'd save it for when we're in court. It would serve me better then."

He laughed. "I've got a conflict."

"Then let's reschedule."

"What are you doing tomorrow?"

"Tomorrow!"

"I know it's short notice, but I'm going to be socked in with an *important* case for three weeks or so starting Monday. Big, big trial."

Martin's subtle put-down was not lost on Lindsay, but she chose to ignore it, just as she had with his jibes during their rivalry in their law school years. She turned the page of her calendar, sighing in exasperation. "Well, I'm going to be in the office tomorrow, but there's the matter of the court reporter and…"

"I've already arranged that. They were reluctant to send someone until I suggested they extort some money out of me for the extra service."

Lindsay laughed. "Well, what about preparation time? I only got your answer to my interrogatories this morning."

"What's the problem? You've got all day and night. Besides, you know there's nothing in there."

"I wish you'd grow up, Martin. When will you stop expecting the world to operate at your convenience?"

"Then you'll do it, doll?"

She groaned. "I suppose so."

"Great. I'll ask my client if it's okay."

"Martin! You haven't asked him yet?"

"I had to know if you could first. Besides, I don't think there's a problem. We were scheduled to spend the morning together anyway for a predep. We'll just have to skip the rehearsal and do the real thing."

Lindsay shook her head in disgust. "What time?"

"Same as we scheduled, only a week earlier."

"Well, I'll expect you unless I hear differently then."

He ended the conversation with a telephonic kiss. She hung up, wishing Marin Blum didn't always insist on pushing even the most routine conversation beyond the bounds of propriety. She knew it was all calculated to unnerve her, but she resented being forced to keep him in line.

Lindsay speculated on the possible ulterior motives Martin might have. The purpose of the deposition was to enable her to question the defendant before trial and thus save time and expense later. It also focused the issues of the case and often led to settlements before trial. Since Martin didn't have much to do but sit and listen to her question his client, he could have asked an associate to stand in for him. Why was it important that Martin be there himself? As plaintiff's counsel *she* would have all the work. On the other hand, she had heard the defendant was a difficult man. Martin's reasons probably had more to do with client relations than litigation strategy.

Taking Martin's answers to her interrogatories from the envelope, Lindsay scanned through some of the pages at random to get a feel for the tack he had taken in answering the written questions she had submitted. Most of what he wrote would be couched in careful terms, giving no more information than absolutely required under the law, but she hoped there might be a damning admission hidden in there, something she could use to nail the defendant to the wall at the deposition the next day.

Lindsay turned around and found the Moretti file on the rack on the credenza behind her. She eyed the thick folder full of pleadings, correspondence and dozens of pages of her notes. Seeing the mass of material she would have to master by the time of the deposition the following morning, Lindsay began regretting she had been so quick to accommodate Martin Blum.

On top of everything else her leg was starting to ache and stiffen up and Lindsay wished she could climb into a nice hot bath. Sitting at her desk all day was not a prospect that she looked forward to, especially since she would be a lot more comfortable at home where she could prepare for the deposition much more efficiently and without interruption. Millicent would be arriving soon and the office would be covered. She decided to gather up her things and head for home.

The pleasant ambience of Lindsay's town house with its interior of blue and apricot tones afforded a welcome refuge. She could truly relax amidst her plants and the smattering of antiques she had collected over the years.

She spent most of the day on her bed with documents and files spread all around her, going back through Terry Moretti's life step by step, matching facts with issues, identifying the principal lines of questioning she would follow the next day. At noon she broke for a bowl of soup and in the middle of the afternoon she had the hot bath her body craved. By six she had pretty well completed her preparation for the deposition and her mind was crying out for relief from the tedium. Lindsay let herself think about the upcoming evening and Bill Price.

As she dressed again her mind churned with speculation about the way it would be. She decided that tonight it would be different. She would not let him seduce her as she had the night before. Dignity and propriety were called for. Instead of romance she would focus on getting to know him. If that weren't acceptable to him, she'd know she should forget all about Mr. Bill Price.

It had been years since Lindsay had been emotionally involved with a man, though she had had relationships, flirtations. In truth, her career had stolen her life the past few years and men had been a growing disappointment to her. At times she worried that her cynicism was serving her badly, that she was ensuring a bland and barren romantic life by her unwillingness to devote some energy to it.

But Lindsay had always subscribed to the theory that you couldn't find love, it would find you. Perhaps it was that fatalism that had caused her to take such an interest in Bill Price and the bizarre little episode of the night before.

Stepping back into her gray suit, Lindsay decided the smartest course was to relax and try to have a good time. Fate, inner wisdom, or the mystery of human emotion would take care of the rest. Experience had taught her not to count on anything, and she wouldn't.

CHAPTER FIVE

BLAKE PRESCOTT, sweating heavily, left his partner to take on another opponent, then climbed the steps to the second floor and walked past a glassed-in room. Inside, several dozen people dressed in designer leotards and sweat suits struggled through their routines on exercise machines.

Glancing in as he passed by, Prescott wondered about their motivation, suspecting that vanity and socializing were behind their zeal. He couldn't see it himself. He didn't have the patience or the desire to preen. Racquetball, on the other hand, made sense. It was exercise that compelled you by the competitive urge; the demands placed on the body were tied to the immediate, tangible goal of victory. It suited him much better.

As he entered the noisy and crowded men's locker room, he looked up at the clock. Six thirty-five. He would have to hurry if he wanted to be outside waiting when she arrived. Walking along the banks of lockers he squeezed by a crowd of men and shifted the balls and racquet in his hands so that he could fish the key to this padlock out of the pocket of his trunks.

"Hi, Blake," a youngish man said as Prescott approached.

"How's it going, Don?" he replied, stopping in front of his locker. The other man had a towel around his neck and was obviously headed for the shower.

"Haven't seen you for a while. How's your game?"

Prescott dropped on a stool and looked up with fatigue. "Neglected. That'd be the best way to describe it."

"Playing in the tournament next week?"

"No, I'm lucky to get in an hour a week for a casual game."

"You work too hard, Blake. You'll give entrepreneurs a bad name," the man said turning away. "Give me a call sometime and we'll play."

"Sure," Prescott called after him.

He finished undressing, stuffed his things into the locker carefully so as not to get his business suit wrinkled or wet, took his towel and headed for the shower.

After soaping himself down and rinsing off under one of the dozen or so nozzles in the room, he stepped into the outer area, which contained a Jacuzzi and doors leading to a steam room and sauna. Glancing at the clock on the wall, he elected to soak himself in the hot tub for a few minutes to relax his tired muscles.

Several minutes later he was back at his locker, running a little behind schedule because of his self-indulgence. He moved rather quickly as he dressed, not wanting Lindsay to get in the building where he was known by too many people. After drying his hair he put on his tie and suit jacket, checking himself in the mirror. He looked at his watch. It was seven o'clock.

Prescott hit the lobby a minute later, half-running. His equipment bag was in one hand, his towel was in the other. As he approached the desk he looked out the front door and saw Lindsay coming up the walk. "Hey, Norm, here's my towel. Give me my keys. I'm in a hurry."

The girl Norm was waiting on looked at Prescott in disgust.

"Sorry." He shrugged and took his keys in exchange for the towel. He turned to the door.

"Hey, Blake," the clerk called, "fifty cents!"

"Put it on my account," he called back.

"There ain't any accounts," Norm shouted after him, but Prescott was stepping out the door just as Lindsay reached for the handle.

"Hi, counselor!"

"Well, good evening, Bill," she said to the tall man with auburn hair.

They stood for a moment on the sidewalk, motionless, mute with the delight of being together again. Lindsay noticed the ruddy glow of Bill Price's skin. His green eyes seemed full of fire and he exuded the physical verve of an athlete, a man full of life.

Although he was once again impeccably dressed and groomed, Lindsay detected the subtle signs that he had been in the shower not long before. There was a hint of dampness to his hair and his cologne was fresh, not yet having mellowed and blended with the masculine musk of his body. The thought had never occurred to her before but somehow a man—or at least this man—seemed most primal just after donning clothing when the body hadn't yet become habituated to the fabric. Only moments ago that body had been free, full of the exhilaration of sport and immersed in the sensuality of water.

As he smiled down at her, Lindsay had a real sense of his size. He must be at least six three, over a foot taller than she, but with a graceful, well-proportioned body. He stood erect and proud in a way that told Lindsay he liked his height—and hers.

Bill took Lindsay by the arm and they headed back down the walk. "You're looking beautiful this evening," he said smiling down at her.

Lindsay unconsciously touched the string of pearls she had added to her outfit that evening. "Thank you." Their eyes met briefly and she surprised herself with the shyness she felt.

The sight of him, large and protective at her side, immediately brought to mind the previous evening. She felt again his warm hand on her breast as she sat naked, save for his bathrobe, by the fire. She remembered her mounting excitement as he carried her in his arms, sensing her desire before kissing her at the door.

Last night her emotions and her thoughts of him had been a confusing jumble. Fear, gratitude, attraction had competed, but tonight it was different. For her, he need play no role but himself.

They had gone a few steps along the sidewalk, Bill still holding her arm, when he directed her to the black sports car parked at the curb. He reached down with his key in hand to unlock the door.

"Hey!" she protested, "I was driving *you*, remember?"

"Maybe next time," he replied and firmly guided her into the Porsche. "I know where we're going. It'll be easier." He tossed his equipment into the back then closed the door behind her.

"So how was your day, Bill?" she asked as he climbed into the car.

"Hectic. As a matter of fact I spent most of it in Los Angeles."

"Is that what inventors do, fly off somewhere at the drop of a hat?"

"This was a meeting, not a pleasure trip. How about you? Put anybody in jail today?"

"Hardly. Spent most of the day at home, preparing for a deposition."

"You barristers actually have to practice being nasty, don't you?" He laughed.

It was cheeky, but Lindsay liked it anyway—sometimes he said the most unexpected things. She found herself admiring him without feeling totally comfortable. "Where are we going for dinner?"

"That's a secret. I hope you're not too hungry, though. It'll take a while to get there."

"No, I'm fine. No hints where we're headed?"

"It's bigger than a bread box."

She gave him a sideways glance. "Thanks."

They drove through Palo Alto into the countryside and headed west toward Woodside. In the darkness it seemed they were traversing some remote country road, but Lindsay knew they were passing through an area scattered with large estates and expensive homes. When they had passed through the town of Woodside she turned to him in puzzlement. "Are there restaurants out here?"

"Yes indeed."

Soon they were winding their way up the side of the mountain ridge that separated San Francisco Bay from the Pacific. The car twisted and turned up the narrow deserted road, its headlights penetrating the heavy darkness of the forest. Bill lowered his window a crack so that the damp earthy smell of the redwoods filled the car. Lindsay grew a bit uncomfortable alone with him in such an isolated spot, but reassured herself with the thought that if the man were up to no good, he'd have done something the previous night. Still, his taciturn air left her feeling a little uneasy.

She gripped the door handle as the car first roared into the sharp curves in the road then lurched ahead when Bill accelerated.

They finally gained the top of the mountain and turned north along Skyline Drive, where the comparatively straight road freed them to race at high speed down the undulating ribbon of asphalt.

After a while Bill slowed down. Ahead on the right side of the road Lindsay saw lights through the pines. When they drew nearer, a building became visible as well as a number of cars scattered around it.

"Here we are," he announced as he guided the Porsche off the highway. When he had stopped between two trees in the grove of sugar pine that doubled as a parking lot, they got out and walked toward the building.

"What's the name of this place?"

"The Bella Vista," he said taking Lindsay's arm.

She was glad for the support because of the darkness and uneven ground. As they walked she glanced up at the moist vapors drifting through the trees. "Look at the fog!"

"Yes, it can appear rather suddenly up here. Let's hope we haven't already lost the view."

The outside of the building was rather inauspicious. Lindsay almost expected to see a neon Coca Cola sign with the word Eat over the front door. However, the ambience inside was significantly different. They walked first through a knotty pine bar to the wide but rather shallow dining room wrapped in glass.

The room itself was darkened, lit primarily by the candles on scattered tables. Soon the maître d' arrived and led them to a corner window table with a white linen cloth and a single rose in a bud vase. The woody-rustic feel of the building was in stark contrast to the formality of the dinner service. Outside, nearby trees at the periphery of the vista were revealed by floodlights, forming a backdrop for the drifting vapors. The swirling fog made the room seem even warmer and more intimate.

The waiter promptly appeared and they soon got through the business of ordering, permitting them to relax and savor the ambience of the setting. They were both quiet for a few moments. Lindsay was distracted, looking first at the room then out the window beside them. When she finally turned to him, she was surprised to find a rather wistful look on his face. But knowing she saw it, he recovered, immediately assuming a mask of self-assurance and aplomb. Lindsay decided he was preoccupied and wondered why.

Blake Prescott saw the inquisitive innocence in her eyes and felt a certain resentment, but it was inner-directed resentment, impatience with the circumstances and the feelings within him that were getting out of hand. He gave her his best enigmatic smile, a ploy that would keep her at bay, but it did nothing to solve the real problem. He cursed the timing of the thing. Why *this* woman? And why *now*?

Prescott knew that if he had any sense at all he would make the evening as polite and pleasant as he could, tell her the truth, justifying himself by flattering her, and be on his way as surely and quickly as possible. But he was enough of a realist to know it wouldn't happen that way. It wasn't his style to sacrifice what he wanted until he was forced into it. No, the truth would be told later, at a time when he would be in control.

She had been talking about the view and the fog, but now her eyes were on him again, evaluating, wondering. He had to be careful.

"You look as though you might still be in Los Angeles," she said softly.

"I'm sorry. It *has* been a rough day, but frankly I wasn't in Los Angeles just now."

"Where then? Or is it indiscreet of me to ask?"

"Not indiscreet. I was speculating about you, actually."

His directness hit her unexpectedly. "Oh? What conclusions?"

"None really. More questions than conclusions, I'd say."

"That's not surprising, Bill. We hardly know each other. I know, for example, that you're an inventor who lives in Saratoga. You drive a black sports car and occasionally rescue damsels in distress, but I don't know much more." She was toying with the rose, turning it slowly in the vase with her long slender fingers.

Prescott realized this would be an obvious time to come clean and be done with it. He let the idea run through his mind a moment before dismissing it. No, he wasn't prepared for a roll of the dice. Her delicate, fragile beauty was enhanced by the candlelight and she was having the effect on him that he had both hoped for and dreaded. She was drawing him into some sort of spell; he wanted her so much.

He watched her spinning the flower for a time, her lashes laying on the ivory smoothness of her cheeks until she looked up. The violet eyes engaging his were innocent, intelligent, inquisitive, uncertain. This petite, lovely lawyer—the same that had looked at him from the glossy photograph in the file—was real, a woman with feelings, questions and perhaps desire. Prescott saw in her face something of himself, a connection that superseded the uncertainty she doubtless felt about him. It was Bill Price she was trying to know and understand, not him.

Prescott felt the sting of his own deception. "What is it you'd like to know?" he asked reluctantly.

"Just about you, your life."

"Well, I'm thirty-eight. I've got a degree in electrical engineering from MIT and an MBA from Harvard. I've been in the high-tech game for ten years." He stopped and shrugged.

Lindsay frowned. "What about *you*?"

"Besides racquetball I play a little tennis. My spectator sport is ice hockey. I like antiques and old movies, especially Hitchcock."

"How am I supposed to judge your character and personality from that?"

"Okay. I was an Eagle Scout at fourteen and I've never been in jail, though they've threatened to take away my driver's license. I used to have a bad temper—now it's only...questionable."

Lindsay remembered the child's cup she had seen in his kitchen. "Do you like children?"

"Yes."

She saw he had decided to pass on the opportunity she had given him to talk about children, if he had any. Lindsay contemplated asking him but something told her it wouldn't be politic to be too blunt. "Tell me about your family."

"My father is a retired history professor from Princeton and my mother was a music teacher. They live down in San Diego now."

"Is that all?"

A droll expression crossed his face. "It's a small family."

Lindsay rolled her eyes. "What's your favorite color, Bill?" she asked with obvious sarcasm.

"The color of your eyes." He was grinning at her now.

"I can't tell if you're trying to be predictable or unpredictable."

"Oh, definitely predictable."

"I guess that's your idea of being cooperative."

"Am I too difficult?"

"Yes."

"Well, Lindsay, if I make it too easy for you, you might lose interest. You see men have to be a little mysterious, don't they?"

"Do they?"

"Yes."

She could see he was having great fun with her and it was flattering, but she was loath to give him the satisfaction. "Hearing you describe yourself, Bill, is like reading your résumé—lots of facts, not much sense of the person," she teased.

"I *do* like your eyes. That's the most important thing I said. The rest of it doesn't count for much in the end."

He meant what he said and would have liked to add that the truth about who he was shouldn't matter either. Not compared to feelings. They were all-important. Still, he understood her reaction to impersonal facts. He remembered *his* frustration with Jerry Randall's file and all the detail about Lindsay that told him nothing—at least not what he had wanted to know. What it succeeded in doing was to make him curious. Now he was becoming obsessed with the woman, not the lawyer. She was so enticing, yet she had the potential to destroy much of what he'd done in his life.

The waiter arrived with their wine and Prescott escaped into the distraction of the moment.

In a while their food came and they ate in a mood of shared contentment. The wine, the candlelight, the man all conspired to entice Lindsay to forget her sensible side.

They were sipping the last of the cabernet, their dishes having been cleared from the table. Lindsay was feeling a little tipsy, uninhibited, when his smile stole her attention.

"What are you smiling at?" she asked, amused.

"I was thinking that you know so much about me, but you've told me so little about yourself."

"Fair enough. What do you want to know?"

His response was totally unexpected. "Have you ever been in love?"

She searched for the motive behind the question, but his face betrayed no hidden intent beyond mere polite curiosity. "That question's not as easy to answer as you might think."

"Is that the lawyer speaking, or the woman?"

"It's the woman."

"Why is the question tough to answer?"

"Because there was a time when I would have told you I was in love, but now, from a perspective of years, it looks different to me."

"You had a crush on a teacher?"

"I almost married my high school sweetheart."

"Really?"

"I came this close," she said holding her fingers a fraction of an inch apart. "Of course I wouldn't have gone on to college. Probably would've had a few children...." The thought was not altogether displeasing. But Lindsay mentally shook herself and raised her chin a little. "Can you imagine—" she laughed "—what I'd be like today?"

"A house in the suburbs and dishpan hands?"

"Probably, and I'm sure I'd be frustrated. I have no idea what Peter is doing today, but my life would be totally different. *I'd* be totally different."

"And since then?"

"The usual flirtations. The usual experiences and relationships, but nothing I'd call serious, not love certainly."

There was a gentle smile on his face.

"How about you, Bill?"

"I've been married to my career. No close calls as far as marriage is concerned."

"Is there a woman in your life?"

"You mean someone I care for? No."

She studied him. He remained at ease, almost serene. "I'm a lawyer, but I'm also a woman. My intuition tells me there's something I should ask, something I should discover."

She saw his expression grow pensive, but in Blake Prescott her words had a more profound effect. This woman understood him—she seemed to look right inside of him like no one else ever had. The notion excited him, but there was also guilt. He would have much preferred at this moment to be confessing the truth. "I think that's maybe the past talking to you, Lindsay. Our experiences and fears affect the way we read the moment." Bill fell silent but Lindsay saw the monologue continuing within him.

"Are you sure you're an inventor? You seem more like a philosopher to me."

He grinned at her. "I'm not used to a woman like you. You're a rather unique experience for me."

"How so?"

"It's rather difficult to explain, but most women I have known have fit comfortably in the compartment of my life reserved for them. You don't fit very well."

His words had a strange effect on Lindsay. He'd given her a glimpse inside she hadn't expected. It was, she was sure, the kind of admission people reserved for those they were intimate with. His tone of voice, his eyes, betrayed him. A flutter of excitement rippled through her as though he'd just kissed her again.

"Perhaps it's the way we met."

He shook off the suggestion, smiling. "No. It's something different. I'll admit it creates a fascination I'm not entirely used to."

Lindsay felt her cheeks redden and her eyes finally dropped, eluding his frank gaze. She searched for something to say, but his admission had so unnerved her that she was at a loss. Unconsciously her fingers went to the rose. She watched it spinning in the vase, so that she wouldn't have to look at him.

Bill permitted Lindsay her silence, turning instead to the waiter and calling for the bill. When he had paid they made their way out. Lindsay glanced at the fire blazing in the large stone fireplace in the bar before they stepped into the foggy autumn air.

He took her hand, squeezing it firmly in his large, warm palm. More than courtesy, she knew it was affection. She sensed they had crossed the line where tenderness needed no justification. Holding his hand, Lindsay thought, seemed the most natural thing in the world and yet just yesterday she didn't even know the man. She felt in awe of the mystery of it.

They got into Bill Price's car in silence, but the tension of uncertainty was gone. Now expectation fueled her. She looked at the man only a little shyly. "Thank you for the lovely dinner."

Lindsay thought for a moment he would lean over and kiss her, but he didn't, letting the opportunity slip by, content in the knowledge she was willing.

CHAPTER SIX

HE SAT ON one of the two soft-blue velvet love seats that faced each other in front of the traditional fireplace. A faded-blue oriental carpet with a design in apricot and beige covered much of the hardwood floor. An antique regulator clock ticked in the hallway. Blake Prescott liked the simple elegance of the room. It had charm but also warmth, not unlike Lindsay herself.

"Put on some music if you like, Bill," she called from the top of the stairs, "tapes and records are in the cabinet right below the stereo."

He glanced across the room at the wall opposite him lined with books and stereo equipment. Putting his glass of sherry down on the coffee table he went over to the stereo and picked up the cassettes lying on top of it. It was a recording of madrigal music by Jannequin and Monteverdi. Prescott didn't know much about medieval music, but he was curious about Lindsay's taste. He turned on the machine and inserted the cassette.

He waited, then heard the haunting sound of a male tenor voice soon interwoven with other voices, particularly a female soprano singing in counterpoint to the male lead. There was no instrumental background, only the subtle symphony of human voices, an ethereal fabric of sound. Prescott pictured an ancient monastery or Gothic cathedral, but not Lindsay Bishop. Still, he listened, searching for the element in it that might reveal to him something of her.

"Not a good choice," she said softly from across the room. "Much too reflective."

He turned and watched her saunter toward him; her body graceful and assured, her face delicately beautiful. There was just a hint of reproach in her smile. Prescott stepped aside as Lindsay ejected the tape, put it back on top of the stereo, then bent down and looked inside the cabinet.

"Would you prefer Handel's Water Music or some Vivaldi harpsichord?" she asked.

She had removed her suit jacket, looking much softer now and more feminine in the shell-pink blouse. Prescott looked down on her glistening hair and slender shoulders under the soft silk garment, aware of his strong desire to touch her. Her upturned face silently restated the question.

"You choose, Lindsay."

She stood up, her body just inches from his as her fingers quickly and expertly removed the cassette from its container and inserted it into the slot in the stereo. She adjusted a knob, waited until the melodic music filled the room, then made another adjustment of the equipment, all the while a scant foot from him. She seemed to sense how close he was to her just before looking up into his eyes. "Better?"

Prescott felt his heart rocking in his chest as the floral scent of her touched his nostrils. His mouth stretched a little wider and his hand rose almost in reflex, taking her by the arm so that she would not escape. His thumb stroked her through the silk in an unconscious motion that revealed a more portentous objective.

She dropped her eyes, unwilling to risk the response he was demanding of her, but she made no attempt to withdraw. Her fingers nervously went to the pearls around her neck and hesitated there before she touched the button of his shirt.

Slowly finding her courage, she turned her face upward only to find him much closer. Amusement faded from his lips even as they parted in anticipation of her. "You're irresistible," he whispered, but the words were so softly spoken that the caress of his breath on her skin told her more than the sound. She was frozen for the eternal moment before his mouth began moving toward her, preparing to take of her sweetness and possess her.

When at last his soft lips touched hers, all the world collapsed into that exquisite point of contact. All desire, latent and apparent, coalesced into one remarkable shared sensation.

Lindsay let herself be taken up by him, more eager for his kiss than she had herself realized. The growing exuberance of his lips and tongue began spilling over into her, igniting fires long dormant. His intimate contact now summoned her womanly awareness and she became aroused, inflamed with desire, as she had the night before.

"Lindsay, I want you," he murmured into her ear. "Ever since I saw you standing on that stage, I've wanted you."

And I want you, she thought, but the words couldn't be uttered, not yet. This was too quick. Her own passion was flaring out of control and she fought it, but only halfheartedly, unable to deny the insistent mouth on her lips. "Bill, I didn't want this to happen..."

"But it's right, Lindsay," he said silencing her objection and biting at the fullness of her lip. His hands roamed anxiously over her shoulders and back, frustrated with the clothing that kept him from her. He hadn't intended this, it was a foolish surrender to his desire, but even as he knew it was dangerous, he knew he had no choice.

For an instant he released her mouth, pulling back to take measure of her, seeking some sign and then telling her again with his eyes that he wanted her. She trembled slightly, her violet eyes a blend of desire and trepidation, but there was no hiding that she wanted him too.

"I don't even know you," she whispered more in wonder than objection. "This isn't me, Bill." But there was no denying her own imperative craving, any more than she could deny him. Yet she couldn't bring herself to submit either.

Sensing her vacillation made him ache for her all the more. The longing deep in his belly became more urgent and he tried without success to quench it by taking her mouth. But the nectars he found there only heightened his excitement and drove him to still more urgent supplication. "I must have you now."

Lindsay's will lurched at his words, first toward submission, then toward resistance. He was so large, so overwhelming, that she felt helpless, but more than his size it was the pleasure of his touch that weakened her. She had become caught up in his excitement to the point of being lost in it. She wanted him now as much as she had ever wanted any man. But she was afraid.

Prescott studied the little dovelike creature in his arms, sensing her fear, knowing his own passion could overwhelm her if he weren't careful. "I won't hurt you," he said tenderly.

"I know." But she couldn't look at his eyes. Instead she laid her head against his chest, slipped her arms around his waist and clung to him.

They stood that way for a long while until Lindsay finally felt she had regained herself. Bill had let her off the hook and she was grateful. She smiled up at him and he kissed the end of her nose.

"Can I get you some more sherry?" she asked.

"All right."

She pulled away from him and he watched her walk across the room toward the kitchen, admiring her legs, the rounded curve of her hips and waist. The ample femininity of her, in spite of her small stature, aroused him, hardening his determination. Prescott realized now how important it had become to him that he have her.

He had drifted back to his place on the love seat when Lindsay returned with the decanter of sherry and her glass. She refilled his, then hers and sat down across from him. He watched her pick up her glass and slide back on the couch, engaging his eyes as she did.

In the background the horns sang their regal song and he knew why he liked the music—it suited her. It was stately, refined and beautiful at the same time. Examining her closely, he decided Lindsay's beauty was warm, inviting. This was the alluring beauty that attracted, mesmerized, incapacitated a man. Black silky hair framed the ivory skin of her face and hyacinth eyes waited, questioning him, pronouncing some unspoken feminine prerogative. She accepted his masculinity with cautious grace, leaving him aching for her, wanting her.

Lindsay crossed her legs, deliciously aware of the man's rather candid observation of her. Her skin tingled from his caresses and even now she felt his mouth against her, almost as though she were still in his arms. The space separating them as they sat facing each other became cruel, a torture neither of them desired, but one which circumstances had dictated.

"Do you feel safe over there?" he asked as though he'd been listening to her thoughts.

"No, not safe. In control."

"Is that important?"

"Very."

"Why?"

"You'd understand if you were a woman."

"I'm not a woman, so tell me."

She started to demur, then wondered if it was a feeling she could explain and share. "I wouldn't know how to explain it."

"It's not fear?"

"No, it's one of two choices a woman has. Submission or control."

"There's no middle ground?"

"Not at certain stages."

"Is that where we are now, Lindsay?"

She couldn't help blushing. Talking about it in the abstract was one thing, but having him personalize it was another matter entirely. "How do you like the Water Music?" she asked, hoping the sound of the hunting horns, trumpets, oboes and bassoons in the background might serve as an ally.

"I like it," he said simply.

He had let her off the hook again, and she sank back more comfortably, watching him over the rim of her glass as she sipped the sherry. Bill Price himself seemed to ease back and let the moment drift, a sort of self-assured serenity on his face.

The inspiring music claimed her thoughts and Lindsay found herself picturing Bill as King George I listening to the composition the first time it had been played for him on the Thames. But after a moment she decided Bill was much more like a young Henry VIII with his auburn hair, large stature and self-indulgent demeanor.

"You look like you're hundreds of miles away," he chided.

"Thousands actually."

"Oh?"

"Yes, I was picturing you as Henry VIII."

"Henry VIII? Me?" He laughed. "Do I look like somebody who runs around shouting 'Off with her head'?"

"No, but you look like someone who's master of his destiny."

"Is that bad?"

"And probably insists on having his way with women," she added without acknowledging his question.

"Now *that* doesn't sound bad at all. But if I *were* Henry VIII," he added diabolically, "I'd make you come and sit beside me."

"But you aren't Henry VIII."

"I might make you do it anyway."

"This is the twentieth century, Bill."

"Perhaps you're right," he said as he rose to his feet, sliding around the table and dropping down beside her.

Bill's arm came around her and she felt surrounded by him, the warmth of his body against her arm penetrating the silk of her blouse and electrifying her skin. She felt his breath against her hair and on her cheek. And as the aura of him threatened to envelop her completely, she spun the glass nervously in her fingers.

Bill, smiling, enclosed both her hand and the glass in his, ending the fidgeting, freezing her as she had been frozen in his arms the night before. He took the glass from her hand and leaned toward her, letting his breath caress her cheek as his lips hovered near her face.

Lindsay gave him a sideways glance, knowing this time she was helpless in the face of his desire. "Actually, you're worse than Henry VIII."

His low laugh gently mocked her and she turned toward him defiantly, her pansy-colored eyes emboldened, ready to challenge him. Perhaps it was the response he wanted because after pausing just long enough to touch her cheek with his fingertips, the man dropped his mouth to hers, taking the fullness of her lips with his, deftly, sensuously.

The sweet aroma of their mouths intermingled, their tongues meeting, exploring, his teeth caressing the softness of her lip. Lindsay reached up with her hand to touch his face and send her fingers burrowing into the hair at the back of his head.

His hand found the small of her back and he pulled her head against him, half lifting her from the love seat into the curve of his body. Lindsay felt his body against her breast and the eager excitement of him as she let herself respond, surrendering to his mounting passion.

Finally, their lips parted, the heavy breathing of their excitement still urgent, imperative. The man's jade eyes took in the results of the last few moments, his mouth twisted slightly in amusement, waiting just inches from her lips to take her again.

"Henry would envy me," he whispered.

"I wouldn't have wanted him," she replied. "This is much better."

Bill kissed her lower lip and leaned back against the arm of the love seat, pulling her with him so that their bodies were extended and flush together. Her breasts now rested on his chest, his thigh pressed between her legs and he caressed the curve of her buttocks with his hand.

As he grew more excited his hand found Lindsay's breast, first grasping the full swell of it, then more lightly caressing her nipple through the silk and lace of her bra. His thumb traced the bud in a slow swirling motion that brought it to taut erection. It pulsed under his touch, hungering to be caressed unencumbered by her clothing.

Prescott smothered her soft moan with his anxious mouth, plainly aroused by her excitement, eager for greater intimacy, barely able to control the desire ablaze in his loins. His hand went to the band of her skirt, toying with it impatiently then sliding up the front of her blouse to the collar and the first button, which he unfastened with anxious fingers. He took her mouth with his as he quickly released several more buttons, permitting his hand to slip through the opening in the fabric to her skin. Still kissing her, he unfastened the remaining buttons down to her skirt, enabling him to enter her blouse freely and take her breasts and run his fingertips under the lacy fringe of her bra.

Pulling away from her swollen lips, Prescott peered down at the treasures he'd uncovered, unable to resist kissing the alabaster softness swelling from her bra. As he pressed his face against her, Lindsay took his head, crushing it to her pounding heart.

"Let's go upstairs," she whispered into his ear, and he lifted his head and kissed Lindsay's cheeks and eyes before he rose, pulling her to her feet.

She searched his face as they stood together, seeking reassurance that she had done the right thing, when in the next room the phone rang, shattering the erotic focus of the moment.

Lindsay stiffened and Prescott silently cursed the criminal intrusion. She did not move for an instant, looking instead at him, her eyes blinking but unable to ignore the offending sound.

"Forget it," he murmured and kissed her cheek.

She hesitated, then winced with annoyance. "No, I'd better get it." Turning from him she stepped quickly into the kitchen to answer the phone.

Prescott tried to master his irritation. Picking up his sherry he wandered over toward the fireplace and listened to Lindsay's voice in the next room.

"Hello.... Martin! What are you doing calling me at this time of night?"

As Prescott heard the name *Martin* he drew a cautious breath. The muscles at his jaw tightened and he listened closely the woman's voice.

"I was out to dinner. I only got in a while ago.... No, I'm still available. What happened...? What's the matter? Doesn't he return phone calls...? I see. Well, can you reach him in the morning...? Okay. Do what you can.... Martin, by the way where did you get my number? It's unlisted."

Unlisted, Prescott thought. He had called it himself, the number Jerry Randall had placed in the file. He wondered if Lindsay had questioned where he had gotten it as well. Suddenly, reality was pressing in on what had been a wonderful evening.

"Well, I hope you'll be able to get your client organized," she was saying in the next room. "Talk to you in the morning."

He listened to the end of the call and waited uncomfortably until Lindsay came back into the room.

"Can you imagine," she said walking toward him, "a business call at this time of the night?" He seemed to her rather subdued, even sad. "I'm awfully sorry about the call."

He grinned unconvincingly and touched her neck with his fingertips. "Not your fault."

Lindsay had refastened all but the top few buttons of her blouse, and Bill gently touched her skin at the vee of the opening. His manner seemed more nostalgic than affectionate. She grasped his fingers and kissed them.

"Was your caller an attorney?"

"Yes, we're having scheduling problems, but I half suspect he's playing games with me."

"Why is that?"

"Some litigators engage in psychological warfare—anything to affect the outcome."

"Apparently it's not working?"

Lindsay smiled, squeezing Bill's fingers. "This fellow's underestimated me. I'm optimistic."

"From what I heard you seemed to handle him pretty well."

Lindsay was pleased at Bill's compliment and let her satisfaction show. He put his arms around her and they embraced quietly.

"You know," she said pulling back, "that call reminded me of something I was going to ask you this evening, but forgot."

"What's that?"

"Where did you get my telephone number? It's unlisted and I thought about it after you called me this morning. I hadn't given it to you."

"Probably the same place your friend that called just now got it."

"He called Millicent Woodward at home and she gave it to him."

"Well no, I didn't get it from her..."

Again the phone rang in the kitchen. Lindsay groaned and rolled her eyes. "What now?"

Prescott sighed in relief as she left the room. It was a close call and he had been lucky, but there were no guarantees his luck would hold. He saw that having his cake and eating it too would be impossible. He had probably been fortunate to carry this off as far as he had. Prescott now realized that the right thing to do was to get out as gracefully as possible. She didn't deserve this.

Lindsay's voice came from the kitchen. "Hello, Millicent.... Yes, he just called. No, that's okay.... It was an emergency of sorts. Don't worry about it.... I'm sorry you were disturbed this evening. Okay, see you tomorrow. Good night."

A moment later Lindsay was back. "I'm terribly sorry, Bill. This usually doesn't happen." The music that had been in the background came to its climactic finale and Lindsay looked over at the stereo. "What would you like to hear now, Bill? I've got jazz and soft rock too, if you don't like classical."

He took her hands. "No, I enjoyed the Handel. I like your music almost as much as I like you. But I've been thinking, it's getting late. I imagine you have a full day tomorrow. I know I do."

Lindsay felt a surge of disappointment. She looked at him, sensing something was wrong, but was at a loss to know what it might be. The telephone calls seemed totally to have spoiled the mood for him. She hoped he wasn't upset with her for answering them, but couldn't imagine why he should be.

Still holding her hand, Bill led her toward the entry hall. Lindsay got his suit coat from the closet and he quickly put it on while she picked up the jogging suit.

"Thank you for letting me borrow the clothes," she said looking up at him.

His expression was affectionate. "No thanks necessary. I enjoyed every minute, Lindsay, even the rain. I wish I didn't have to go, but I do."

She nodded and smiled lamely.

Prescott looked into her face and felt his heart wrench. He hated the circumstances he found himself in and for the first time felt guilt. She was disappointed and hurt, that was apparent, but he could no more stay now than he could have left earlier. He had to get away, clear his mind, then later he would have a talk with her. Things couldn't go on like this. He touched Lindsay's cheek. "Why don't we have lunch together the first of the week?"

"Okay."

"When's a good time for you?"

"Call me at the office tomorrow and I'll check my calendar."

Prescott looked into her eyes trying to elicit the joy they had shared before the phone calls, but he saw that it was useless. Taking her by the shoulders he waited until she looked up at him, then kissed her softly on the lips. "Good night," he whispered.

Lindsay watched him disappear into the night, his goodbye kiss bittersweet on her lips, his promise unfulfilled. She felt confused and cheated. One minute it had been wonderful, the next...nothing. He had walked out leaving her with a terrible, sinking feeling. Something deep inside her—her intuition—told her that she would never see Bill Price again. Lindsay shut the door and listened to the sound echoing through the empty house. For the first time in years she was afraid of being alone.

CHAPTER SEVEN

AT NINE-FIFTEEN the next morning Lindsay Bishop walked in the door of her offices. On seeing her, Karen started waving excitedly even while talking into her headset. "Woodward & Bishop, good morning." She listened for a moment. "One moment please." She pushed a button on her console and looked up at the young attorney. "Bill Price has been trying to get ahold of you. He said it was terribly urgent."

Lindsay looked down at the message slips the girl handed her, wondering what was happening. Karen had circled "urgent" and added exclamation marks. The first slip at eight-fifteen read "Must talk with you this morning, urgent." She looked at her watch with concern and headed back toward her office.

"Morning Jean," she said to her legal assistant.

"Good morning, Lindsay. You've had a call this morning. A man named Bill Price."

"I know, Karen gave me the message."

"Yes, well I talked with him at some length. Told him you were in Law and Motion court and he was very upset because he couldn't reach you at home or here. He demanded—yes, that's the word I'd use—he demanded that I call you at the courthouse. I told him it was impossible. He hung up very angry."

"Don't worry about it, Jean. I'll go call him now." She went to her phone and dialed the number on the slip. She looked at her watch. It was twenty-one after nine. The phone continued ringing, but there was no answer. Lindsay hung up wondering what could be so pressing.

She looked at her appointment calendar. The morning, beginning at ten, was blocked out for the deposition and she had a conference with a new client at four-thirty. Nothing else was scheduled. Fortunately the deposition would be held in her office, saving travel time, but Lindsay wanted at least twenty minutes to review her notes.

She called Karen on the intercom and told her to hold all calls.

"What if Bill Price calls?" the girl asked.

"Well, put him through if he calls before my deposition begins." She hung up and stepped out to speak to Jean.

"Did you reach Mr. Price?" Jean queried.

"No, I guess I missed him." She shrugged. "Maybe he'll call back. If I'm in the deposition when he does, would you try to find out what's wrong?"

"I asked when he called, but he said it was personal."

Lindsay shook her head in perplexity. "Where's Millicent this morning?"

"She's in the city at Sutcliffe & Orrick. She should be in about noon."

"Okay, fine. I've got the deposition for the Moretti case at ten. The defendant should be in with Martin Blum soon."

"Yes, everything's set up in the conference room."

Lindsay saw the proud smile on the woman's face. Jean loved being a step ahead of the game. "I wouldn't expect less of you," the younger woman said appreciatively and turned back into her office. Lindsay pulled the Moretti file out of her briefcase, and dropped it on her desk. She sat down, ready to begin her review when Bill

Price popped back in her head. Her watch told her it was nine-thirty, still plenty of time before the deposition was to begin. Picking up Karen's message slip, she reached for the phone and again dialed Bill's number. Still no answer.

Lindsay opened the file and had looked down through the first series of questions she had prepared when there was a knock at the door. Jean stuck her head in the office.

"Sorry to disturb you, Lindsay, but Terry Moretti is out here. She says it's very important that she speak with you."

Lindsay looked at her watch and grimaced. "I don't have much time, Jean, but bring her back."

In a minute Jean returned with a tall young woman with honey-blond hair in tow. Lindsay stood up and walked around her desk to greet her client who was twenty-eight, but looked older. Terry's eyes were heavily made up, and although she was very pretty, traces of her show-business life-style could be seen in her manner. She wore a fur jacket over a brown satin dress.

"Hello, Terry," Lindsay said smiling and extending her hand.

The other smiled nervously and shook Lindsay's hand, then dropped immediately into a chair in front of the desk.

"You know, I'll be deposing the defendant in a few minutes, Terry, so I don't have much time."

"Yes I know, Miss Bishop. That's why I'm here. You see I've been thinking about this whole thing..."

"Yes."

"Well, I think I want to settle out of court."

Lindsay looked at the woman with surprise. "But Terry, why? Your case has merit. After the deposition our case should be even stronger and your chance of a favorable settlement even better.''

"I know all that, but I know him, too. Look, just ask him if he'll give me $100,000, will you?''

"Terry, you know we could get far more than that if we go to trial.''

"Yeah, but I don't want to risk it. I want to settle. Now.''

Lindsay hadn't expected this turn of events, and the change of attitude troubled her. She knew most plaintiffs were willing to settle to get the legal matters over with as quickly as possible, but when they genuinely felt aggrieved they were willing to fight. Terry had a strong case—or at least it *appeared* strong—so why the sudden case of cold feet? Or, could it be that she had embellished the truth? Lindsay inwardly grimaced at the thought of a client deceiving her. No, Terry was honest, and the case was a strong one. Nevertheless, she knew her job was to get the result her client wanted. She studied the young woman but was unable to fathom the problem.

"Very well, I'll discuss it with Mr. Blum when he arrives and ask if the defendant is willing to settle. They're due any minute. Would you like to wait?''

Terry nodded.

Lindsay went to the door. "Jean,'' she called to her assistant, "would you take Terry into the library? Have Karen get her some magazines. She's going to wait.''

Terry stood up and smiled weakly at Lindsay. "Thanks, Miss Bishop. Just get me the money, please.''

Lindsay patted the young woman's arm and retreated to her desk.

In a moment Jean was back at her door. "Trouble?'' the older woman asked.

Lindsay relayed the gist of her conversation with Terry. "What do you make of it?"

"Want the truth?"

"Yes."

"I think she's a little gold digger and the moment of truth has arrived. I think she's losing her nerve."

"You think she's lied?"

"Who knows? I think she knew what she was getting into with this guy. She was 'kept' and she knew it. He wasn't worth anything ten years ago, now he's rich and she wants to get what she can. For my money she got a free ride for ten years."

"Jean, that's narrow-minded. You wouldn't say that if they were married. She'd be entitled to her share, regardless."

Jean shook her head. "You know how I feel, Lindsay, marriage means something."

"Well, I guess I'd better be thankful I've only got Martin Blum to contend with, not you!"

"Speaking of Mr. Blum, his office called several minutes ago to say they'd be a little late. Apparently their client was late arriving at their offices."

"Just as well. I could use a few minutes. When they arrive would you send Martin back? I want to speak with him privately about the settlement."

"Sure. The court reporter is here. I'll put her in the reception room."

Lindsay sat contemplating the latest turn of events. She already felt uncomfortable with Terry's change of heart. And Jean's comments didn't help. She glanced down at the file and began formulating in her mind good, lawyerly reasons why Martin Blum's client should give her client $100,000.

As she thought she became philosophical—where did the truth belong in all of this? Lindsay wondered if everything she had said at the lecture two days before wasn't simply rationalization.

Her reverie was broken by a brief knock at the door. "Yes?"

A slightly balding thin man with glasses stuck his head in the door. "Good morning, counselor. Got a minute?"

Although there was less hair, and a gold watch and expensive suit had been added, Lindsay immediately recognized her old nemesis from her law-school days, Martin Blum. She rose to greet him. "Martin, good to see you. You look terrific!"

The man strode across the room with the same self-assured demeanor that had so characterized him in law school. "You're not doing so bad yourself," he said taking Lindsay's hand. "Your name in gold letters on the door!" He looked around. "Nice place you've got here. Sort of homey."

Lindsay ignored Martin's put-down—she had learned how in their years together as editors of the law review at Stanford.

"Yeah. They finally gave me my oval office." He laughed, appreciating his own wit. She smiled.

"Time has been good to you, Lindsay. You still look young enough to be a brand-new associate."

"Yes, that's one of my daily dilemmas—whether to look old and intimidating or young and alluring."

"And for me you picked alluring."

"Yes, well, intimidation seemed so superfluous."

Martin playfully tapped Lindsay on the jaw with his fist. "Haven't lost the old spunk, have you baby?"

Lindsay gestured at the chair in front of her desk. "Shall we talk about our case?"

Martin Blum sat down where Terry Moretti had been sitting just ten minutes before, his lighthearted manner now replaced with the severe demeanor of a lawyer in negotiation. Lindsay knew his razor-sharp mind was now on full alert.

"Let me be rather direct, Martin. Our case is strong, I don't have to tell you that. The child, the cohabitation—it will be a tough one for you to break."

"Don't be so sure. Things aren't always as they appear, you know. My client..."

"Yes, I know," she interrupted. "Your client wants to get off scot-free after mine has devoted ten years of her life to him."

Martin's expression was sarcastic. "You're making this sound more like a cause than a law suit."

Lindsay thought of her own self-deprecating comment to Jean about her demagoguery. "Yes, well you know as well as I, Martin, these things are decided on moral issues and social policy. This is not a tax case."

"Okay, so I've got the widows and orphans obstacle. What do you want, surrender?"

"No, my client's willing to make a quick cash settlement to save both sides time, expense and grief. She'll take $100,000 cash on the barrel head." Lindsay looked directly at Martin. "You know as well as I do that's ridiculously low. I told her she'd be generous at twice that much."

Martin Blum shrugged his shoulders. "What can I say? I'll pass on your offer to my client. With him it's been a matter of principle all along. He says he won't give her a nickle."

"Well, I advise you to discuss it with him. He didn't seem to have any principles when he got a teenager pregnant and had her come live with him, and it seems to me that it is a little late now.''

"You know, Lindsay, you'd make a wonderful politician.''

"If that was meant as sarcasm, I'll just pass it off as your inexperience in divorce court.'' Lindsay's expression softened. "Just present the offer. It's a good deal for you.''

"On paper perhaps. But this guy's not easy. He didn't get where he is by being soft. Besides, he plays his cards close to his vest.''

"Maybe your problem is client control, Martin.''

"For once I'll give you a point, Lindsay. I'm a hired gun in this one. What I'm saying, I suppose, is that with this one *you've* got your hands full.''

"We can go to trial.''

"It wouldn't surprise me.''

Lindsay was frustrated. She wasn't quite sure whether to attribute it to the circumstances or Martin Blum's skill. "Well then, why don't we go depose the defendant? It may be just as well if you discuss settlement with him after the deposition.''

"No. I'll talk to him. But there is one thing first. He wants a word with you himself.''

"With me?''

"Yes, he asked me...no, he *told* me to arrange a brief meeting before the deposition.''

Lindsay studied Martin's face, trying to fathom what she was hearing. "Martin, you know I can't do that. You're his attorney. Didn't you explain...''

"He said he wanted to speak with you. He assured me it had nothing to do with the case, and no, he didn't want me there.'' Lindsay sensed something ill afoot but decided Martin was being straight with her. "Okay, but if he starts talking about the case, or raises any improper issue, I'm walking out!''

Lindsay Bishop strode through the office toward the conference room. She was anxious to get the man's game over with and get on with the deposition.

Turning the knob she quietly pushed open the door and walked into the small room.

Standing at the far end of the room was a tall man with auburn hair. As she entered he turned and looked squarely at her with his flashing green eyes. It was Bill Price.

''Bill!'' Lindsay exclaimed, startled at the unexpected apparition. ''What are you doing here?''

''I had to speak with you, Lindsay.''

''But...I thought...'' Her mind froze for an instant, then began racing. She tried to grasp why this man, the man who had so suddenly and exquisitely entered her life, was standing in this room.

''I tried urgently to reach you this morning.''

''But...why...where is...?'' her voice trailed off as the awful truth was beginning to sink in.

''Close the door, please.''

Mechanically, unthinking, she closed the door behind her, her mouth still open with the utter shock of what she was seeing—of what her mind was beginning to comprehend.

The man walked around the corner of the conference table and toward her. ''I wanted to talk with you before the deposition, but I didn't find out it had been moved up until this morning,'' he said in a firm, even tone.

''You,'' she said, her voice quivering with emotion, ''you are...''

''Blake Prescott,'' he said harshly, wanting the pronouncement completed. He had stopped several feet from her, the muscles of his jaw hard, his lips pressed in a tight line.

Lindsay was still in shock, trying to understand the implication of the incredible reality she was witnessing. She stepped back from him as though she could somehow remove herself from the shock—and the anger—that started welling within her. "You lied to me!" she whispered, her eyes wide in amazement.

"Yes, God dammit, I lied to you! But I didn't want you to find out like this. I intended to tell you differently. Next week. Before the deposition."

"You lied to me!" she shrieked.

"Listen to me!" he shouted grabbing her forcefully by the arm, his fingers biting into her flesh.

"You lied to me, you…you…rotten bastard!"

He flushed, his teeth clenched. "For God's sake, Lindsay, listen to what I have to say."

She shrank away from him, her own eyes reflecting the loathing welling within her. "If you think you're going to get away with this, Mr. Price…"

"Prescott," he interjected in a low, hard voice.

"Prescott," she repeated derisively. "You're sadly mistaken. I'll rake you over the coals. You'll be sorry you ever tried such a dirty, cheap trick with me!" She started to turn to the door but he grabbed her arm again, hurting her enough that she hit his offending arm with her fist, but he ignored the blow.

"You're not leaving until I've had my say."

"Let go of me, you bastard!"

"I'll let go of you when I'm through and not before."

She saw the determination in his eyes, the unreasoned anger and she surrendered, frightened of his violence.

Seeing her relenting Prescott pulled a chair out from under the conference table and firmly eased her into it.

He stood above her glaring down, his look as hard and hostile as her own. Then his expression softened. "I didn't intend it. It just happened, Lindsay. What started out as curiosity ended in..."

"Deception?" she shrieked derisively.

"I didn't mean to deceive you."

"Oh, I'm sure not. What was that 'Bill Price' business? A slip of the tongue?"

Blake sighed with exasperation. "For God's sake, you'd think I raped you."

"Well, it was moral rape," she shot back.

"That wasn't my intent."

Lindsay scoffed. "What *was* your intent, Mr. *Prescott*?"

"I wanted to find out what you were like. I wondered whether the truth in this case would matter to you."

She laughed bitterly. "The truth! That's a laugh."

He glared back fiercely but he saw there was no use in going on.

Lindsay stood up and cut deep into him with her eyes. "Mr. Prescott, you'll get a lesson in truth from me, be sure of that. You'll rue the day you tried this. That I'll guarantee you!" With that she turned and walked out the door, slamming it behind her.

Heads turned as Lindsay marched back to her office. Once inside she closed the door and collapsed against it, her arms pinned behind her. She tried to master the raging beat of her heart as tears of anger and hurt welled in her eyes.

When the tears finally overflowed she went to her desk, opened a drawer and took a tissue, dabbing her cheeks then blowing her nose. She sat down at her desk and tried to collect her thoughts. For the first time since her childhood Lindsay felt the urge to run from a problem. She would like nothing better now than to run from the office, get in her car and go, as far and as fast as she could.

As she thought about Blake Prescott in the guise of Bill Price she reddened. Her feelings were of utter humiliation, not just as a professional, but as a woman. Dirty tricks in legal battle were one thing—she was equipped to deal with that—but the man's unscrupulous act told her how truly vulnerable she was. He had played with her emotions and used her, and she, the gullible innocent, had permitted it. What a fool she had been!

Lindsay went to her desk and sat down feeling strangely detached and insulated from the others. It was as if she were in some great cocoon of silence, separated from them. She knew they would all be waiting for her to make a move—Terry Moretti in the library, the court reporter in the reception area, Martin Blum and Blake Prescott out there somewhere, talking—but she couldn't move.

Lindsay knew she had to get control and master the confusion reigning in her mind. She tried to rationalize what had befallen her but the personal humiliation kept crowding out the other implications. Blake Prescott had rudely forced her into a compromising situation, that much was clear. There were also elements of a conflict of interest. After all, she, attorney for the plaintiff, had very nearly ended up in bed with the defendant, albeit unwittingly. Lindsay cringed at the thought. If this became generally known—if even Martin Blum knew—she could be ruined, or at least the laughing stock of the legal community.

She wondered whether Blake Prescott had the decency to be discreet, whether the incident might be ignored, but realized that there was no way she could ethically keep this a secret. Her duty to Terry Moretti was full disclosure.

Lindsay bit her lip in anger as she thought about Blake Prescott and Martin Blum somewhere out there with their heads together, talking about her. She wondered about Martin. No, she doubted he'd have been a party to it. He wasn't that stupid. More likely Blake had conjured up the scheme himself. But, what was his motive?

Perhaps he wanted to discredit her, perhaps even subvert her. By seducing her he would have put her in a compromising situation. Leverage! That's what he was after. She would have been forced to either cooperate or quit the case. There was probably no end to what the man might do.

Contempt was welling within her when there was a knock at the door. The thought that it might be Blake Prescott sent a wave of dread through her. "Yes?" she called out.

Martin Blum entered the room. "Lindsay, what the hell's going on? Prescott won't tell me a thing except that he wants his deposition. The way he's acting, you'd think it was for *his* benefit."

Lindsay knew she needed to buy some time to sort things out. "Look Martin, perhaps I should have told you this, but I've got my client, Terry Moretti, here in the office. She's waiting to find out whether you'll accept the settlement. I'm going to need some time with her. Perhaps, under the circumstances, we'd better postpone the deposition. Why don't you take Mr. Prescott away somewhere and discuss the settlement offer with him?"

"Okay, I'll see what I can do." He started out then hesitated, looking at Lindsay's reddened eyes. "What happened in there anyway?"

"I told you I'd walk out if he got out of line. Let's just say he did. You were right, Martin, he's not easy to deal with."

Martin Blum smiled. "Glad it's not just me." He left the room.

Lindsay thought for a moment then picked up the phone. She pushed the intercom button. "Listen Jean, will you try to get Millicent on the line for me...? Yes, have them interrupt her if at all possible. Tell them it's urgent. Thanks."

Lindsay got up and paced the room, thinking. After a minute or so there was another knock at her door. She opened it only to be greeted by a doleful Martin Blum.

"I suggested we leave and he's refused," Martin said shaking his head. "He said he wants the deposition now. I told him you were within your rights to cancel as long as you paid for our time and expense, but he's refusing to leave. I also told him you'd made a settlement offer, but he won't hear it. Says he wouldn't *accept* money to settle."

"Okay, Martin. Give me ten minutes. I have to talk to my client."

When Martin turned to leave Jean was right behind him. "I've got Millicent on line three."

"Thanks, Jean." Lindsay closed her door and went to the phone.

"Hello, Millicent?"

"Yes, Lindsay. What's happened? Jean said it was urgent."

"I'm afraid it is, Millicent. Sorry to interrupt, but I'm in a pickle. I don't know what to do. I need your advice."

"What is it?"

"I'm supposed to be deposing the defendant in the *Moretti* case this morning, but the thing's blown up in my face."

"I'm listening."

"I'll be blunt. There's no way to be delicate. Last night I had dinner with a man named Bill Price. One thing led to another and I almost ended up in bed with him."

"Well, yes. I know that's done these days."

"Millicent, when I met Blake Prescott, the defendant, this morning, he turned out to be the same man. Bill Price was really Blake Prescott using an assumed name. I don't know what his motive was. His attorney, Martin Blum, doesn't know a thing about it. I'm convinced of that."

There was silence on the other end.

"Millicent?"

"Yes, I'm here, dear. I'm thinking…"

"I don't know what to do now. I've got the plaintiff in the library. She came in this morning asking me to offer to settle. The defendant is in the conference room refusing even to talk about settlement. He's insisting on having the deposition. He won't leave!"

"Lindsay, often as I've been around the barn, this is a first for me. You're breaking new ground."

Lindsay couldn't help but smile through the pain.

"Ethically I've got to tell Terry and maybe remove myself from the case."

"I agree. If necessary I can step in, unless she'd prefer finding other counsel. We must give her the option. How will she react to your…er…encounter with her…the defendant?"

"I don't know. There doesn't seem to be much love lost. I think the issue is money."

"Yes, I suppose that's the modern formulation. When I started my practice the women were always ready to go after the men with meat cleavers. But times do change."

"Well, *I* could use a meat cleaver on him." She sighed in exasperation. "What do you think I should do?"

"First, talk to Miss Moretti. Since she's there you may as well. I think I'd also have a word with Mr. Blum."

Lindsay cringed. "Do I have to?"

"Well, perhaps there's no prejudice to their side—unless, of course, they were to claim you seduced *him*..."

"Millicent, I didn't even know who he was! He made the overture!"

"Do as you see fit then. Our duty is to *our* client."

"Yes, I'll talk to her. How do I get Prescott out of here."

"Well, perhaps you needn't. I'll be finished here in another quarter hour. It's nearly eleven o'clock now. I could be there by, say, noon. If the gentleman wants to be deposed today he can wait and I'll depose him this afternoon. What I had planned can wait. I'll need an hour with the file."

"Fine, but I think he's being adamant because he wants to see me again."

"Well then, if Miss Moretti has no objection, why don't you go ahead and start the deposition? Use the time till lunch. Perhaps your pride could stand a little revenge. No need to be gentle with the man, is there?"

A smile crossed Lindsay's face. "No, Millicent, you're right. His ego needs to be deflated. I'd like nothing better than to rake him over the coals!"

CHAPTER EIGHT

"As far as I'm concerned you can marry the guy, as long as you get me what I have coming."

Lindsay winced inwardly at Terry Moretti's words. "There's no danger of me ever seeing the man after this is over, but then the way I feel about Mr. Prescott is not really at issue. As I explained, Terry, I have an obligation to disclose to you what happened."

"Yes, I understand that." Terry sat in the chair across the desk from Lindsay, her legs crossed, her expression bored. She flipped her hair unconsciously with her hand. "If Blake's trick really upset you like you say, I suppose you'd do even better by me, not worse."

"Naturally I'd do my best regardless, but it may be better if I withdraw from the case."

"Even if I don't care about your thing with Blake?"

"Yes, it's important that there be no possibility of conflict of interest. However, the choice is yours."

"Okay, so I can have either you or Mrs. Woodward?"

"If you wish, Terry. You're of course free to find other counsel. That option's always open. We would release you from our agreement."

The blond woman looked at Lindsay, flipping her hair again in a rather nervous manner. "No, I don't want to start over with someone else. You've done fine here. I'll stick with you and Mrs. Woodward. Either of you is fine with me."

"Do you have any objection if I begin the deposition?"

"No." Terry smiled. "Give him hell for both of us."

LINDSAY BISHOP entered the conference room, a file folder and legal pad in hand. She smiled at a middle-aged woman, the court reporter, seated at her machine to one side of the room. She glanced at the two men, Blake Prescott and Martin Blum who had risen when she entered.

"Please sit down, gentlemen. No need to stand on ceremony." She looked at each of the other three people in the room. "My apologies to you all for the delay." Placing the file and pad on the table opposite where the men sat, Lindsay turned to the woman. "Are you ready, Alice?"

"Yes, Ms Bishop."

Looking at Martin she asked, "Is your client ready to be deposed, Mr. Blum?"

"He is."

"Very well. Alice, will you please begin by administering the oath to the deponent?"

The woman cleared her throat. "Mr. Prescott, do you swear to tell the truth, the whole truth, and nothing but the truth, so help you God?"

When Lindsay glanced up at Blake Prescott she found his eyes focused squarely on her. "I do," he said with a level tone. His face was severe, almost defiant.

Returning his glare with a hard look of her own, Lindsay remembered his words earlier when they had been alone in the room. The absurdity of it struck her even as she looked at his loathsome face. With one breath he'd admitted his duplicity, with the next he'd denied evil intentions!

Blake refused to relent; his eyes bore into her. He had no conscience. She finally turned away. "Do you agree to the usual stipulations, Mr. Blum?"

"Yes."

Lindsay picked up her notepad. "Mr. Prescott, you are the defendant in the matter of *Moretti v. Prescott*?"

"Yes."

"Do you understand that you are under oath?"

"Yes."

"And that anything you say today may be used against you in a court of law?"

"Yes." His eyes were penetrating, his expression somber. He gave nothing away.

"Good. Do you understand that you should not guess in answering questions?"

"Yes."

"And that you must inform me if you don't understand a question?"

"Yes. I understand."

Lindsay stood across from the man, one hand on her hip, the other holding her notepad. She looked at him again and found a hard, almost demonic face waiting for her. Without permitting her eyes to retreat she drew a breath and launched her assault. "Do you know the plaintiff, Terry Moretti?"

"Yes."

"How long have you known her?"

"Oh, I guess about ten or eleven years."

"Do you know a Rusty Prescott, age nine?"

"Yes."

"Is Rusty Prescott the child of Terry Moretti, the plaintiff?"

"Yes."

"Mr. Prescott, are you the father of Rusty Prescott?"

For the first time the stony visage softened. Lindsay saw a flicker of indecisiveness before he replied. "My name is on the birth certificate."

"At the time of the child's birth were you named as the father by Terry Moretti?"

"I admitted paternity and consented to having my name placed on the birth certificate, Lindsay."

Her eyes flashed at his use of her first name. Her glare left him unrepentant though. He was not easily chastened. She could see he was a man who didn't give a damn about anything. Lindsay suspected that even the deposition meant nothing to him, except perhaps as an opportunity to use his arrogance to humiliate, to hurt. Her jaw tightened and her eyes narrowed with hatred. "Mr. *Prescott*," she said with derisive intonation, "Does the boy reside with you?"

"Yes."

"How long has he lived with you?"

"Since his birth."

"Continuously?"

"Yes, continuously." Blake's tone was definite, his eyes never quitting Lindsay's face.

Lindsay slowly paced along her side of the table. "Returning to the matter of paternity, Mr. Prescott, did you at any point object to Terry Moretti's suggesting that you be named as the father of Rusty Prescott?"

"No. As a matter of fact I insisted on it."

Alice interjected. "Excuse me, Mr. Prescott, did you say 'insisted'?"

"Yes, insisted."

"Then I take it," Lindsay resumed, "that you do not at this time deny paternity?"

"No."

"Did you at any time prior to the birth of the child cohabit with the plaintiff, Terry Moretti?"

"No."

"Never?"

"If you mean did I live with her the answer is no." Blake's tone was firm but not hostile.

"What about since the birth of the child, Mr. Prescott? Have you cohabited with the plaintiff since the birth of the child?"

"She's spent the night when visiting the boy. I always made it as easy for him as I could. I didn't want him to have to leave to see his mother." Blake looked at his questioner earnestly. "But that isn't cohabitation is it, Lindsay?"

She smirked at this use of her name and immediately proceeded with her questioning. "Did she live in the house, Mr. Prescott?"

"No more than one lives in a hotel in some city they frequently visit."

"Did she sleep in the house?"

Martin interrupted. "I think the question's been answered, Lindsay."

"All right. Did Miss Moretti have a room in the house, Mr. Prescott?"

"There was a bedroom she usually used."

"Was it for her exclusive use?"

"I have a large house. The bedroom was set aside for her visits."

"Did *you* use the bedroom?"

Blake showed signs of exasperation. "I didn't sleep with her, Lindsay. Why don't you ask me that? I didn't sleep with her—ever!"

"Never?" Lindsay's voice contained a note of sarcasm.

"No—never. Not in the house. Not after..."

"Not after the critical first time?"

Blake looked at Lindsay in silence.

"Well?"

Martin Blum interjected sharply. "The deponent has admitted paternity and he has answered your questions, Ms Bishop. Paternity is not the issue here. With all due respect, the defendant has fully met his obligations to the child. That's not in issue."

"I appreciate the fact that you are satisfied the defendant has met his obligations to the child, Mr. Blum. However, I represent the child's mother. This suit was brought because of the defendant's failure to meet his obligation to *her*." Lindsay had gradually raised her voice and now paused, permitting her temper to cool. When she resumed, her voice was calm. "My purpose is to establish the character of the relationship between the plaintiff and the defendant. I found his denial of having sexual relations with the plaintiff to be strangely inconsistent, if you know what I mean."

"That's funny," Blake said in a firm voice, "I was under the impression sex had nothing to do with this kind of case."

Lindsay reddened at his obvious reference to her statement at the lecture two days earlier. "You're right except insofar as it becomes a part of the complex web making up the relationship."

"We're not here to debate the law," Martin said impatiently, "we're here to discover the facts."

Lindsay nodded. "Mr. Prescott, when did Terry Moretti last sleep in the house?"

"I don't know exactly, but it must have been three or four months ago. Not since I was served with the complaint. She still visits the boy, I've agreed to that."

"So by your admission Terry Moretti has slept in the house regularly since the birth of her son and until a couple of months ago—the better part of nine years."

"When she visited the boy I permitted her to stay, for *his* benefit."

"You didn't answer the question."

"Yes, for nine years."

"To your knowledge did the plaintiff maintain another residence?"

"No."

"So your house was her principal place of domicile?"

"She was gone most of the time. She's a singer. She travels all over the country."

"But she didn't maintain another home elsewhere?"

"I don't know."

"Mr. Prescott, did she use your home as her legal residence? Did she receive her mail there? Did she file her tax returns and vote using your address as hers?"

"I'm not sure."

"You never saw any mail addressed to her at the house?"

"Yes, perhaps, sometimes."

"I see." Lindsay paced back and forth like a predator sensing a kill. "Mr. Prescott, have you ever been married?"

"No."

"Then you remained single during the nine years Terry Moretti resided with you?"

"Yes, of course."

"Were you engaged to be married to anyone during that period of time?"

"No."

"Did any other woman reside in the house during the nine year period in question?"

"How do you define reside?"

Martin chuckled.

"Did you cohabit with any women apart from the plaintiff?"

"Why don't you just ask me about my sex life?"

"If it's relevant, I will."

"Don't get me wrong. I don't mind the question, I just don't like beating around the bush."

Martin spoke up. "Blake, there's no need to do anything but respond to Ms Bishop's questions."

"No, that's okay, Martin. I don't mind telling her about my sex life."

"Thank you, Mr. Prescott. I appreciate your cooperation." The sarcasm in Lindsay's voice was subtle, but unmistakable. "Since the birth of your child, Rusty Prescott, have you had sexual relations with other women?"

"Yes."

"I phrased the question in the plural—'women,' more than one." When Lindsay realized her question was leading Blake Prescott dangerously close to herself she suddenly felt trepidation. Would he possibly have the nerve, the gall, to refer to their own encounter right here, on record?

"Yes, I understood the question. The answer is yes. More than one."

"Many?" Listening to her own tone of voice, Lindsay wondered if she betrayed any personal interest in the answer. Was it wounded pride at the thought of almost being the latest in a long line? She looked at Blake Prescott as dispassionately as she was able.

"How many is 'many,' Lindsay?"

Lindsay reddened, angry with herself for having pursued this line of questioning. She turned and paced again so as not to have to look at the man. "Were there more than...say fifty?"

"No."

"But more than a few...two or three?" Lindsay stole a glance at Blake. He seemed to be enjoying her discomfort more than being bothered by any of his own. This was *not* what she had intended.

"Yes. More than two or three."

"Really, Lindsay," Martin Blum intoned, "are you going to ask him to rate them?"

It was a cheap shot and Lindsay gave Martin a withering look. "If *you* would like to question the deponent in that regard, Mr. Blum, I have no objection. Otherwise, if you don't mind, I'll continue."

Martin leaned back. "No objection, counselor."

"These women with whom you've had sexual relations, Mr. Prescott, did any of them reside with you? Did you live with them?"

"Not in the sense that any of them actually moved in. Two or three days in a row was the most anyone stayed."

"I take it this occurred while the plaintiff, Terry Moretti, was absent from the home?"

Blake thought. "When you consider that Terry wasn't around that much and women didn't stay over all that often..."

"Just answer the question."

"I'm not all that sure. Actually I do have a recollection of Terry coming to visit when a lady friend was there."

"Were these 'lady friends' sort of...er...rotating in and out of the place or did you see one at a time?"

"Are you asking if I was promiscuous, Lindsay?"

"That is a value judgment, Mr. Prescott. What I'm trying to ascertain is whether you had any type of relationship that was inconsistent with your relationship with the plaintiff.''

"Let me just tell you about my love life and save you the trouble.''

"Blake, this isn't necessary," Martin said touching his client's arm.

"It's okay, Martin, trust me." Blake looked at Lindsay who had pulled out a chair and sat down opposite him. "Over the past ten years I've dated a number of women. Several I went out with for an extended period—say six or eight months. There wasn't anyone I was serious about." He looked at her, his emerald eyes flashing. "The fact of the matter is I was in love with my work, my career. I don't know whether there wasn't room for a special woman in my life, or whether I'd never found one that I was willing to make room for.''

"Then there's never been anyone you've cared for?''

"No, when I was in college there was a girl I cared for...loved, I suppose. We were 'engaged to be engaged' I think was the term, but when I left for graduate school the relationship changed, my priorities changed.''

"And there's been no one since?''

Prescott saw a flicker of softness at the edge of Lindsay's tough veneer. For the past half hour, he had seen her at her lawyerly best, aggressive, probing, attacking where he was vulnerable. But in spite of her hostility toward him, he sensed she had a personal interest in him, or curiosity that her antipathy couldn't subdue. It might prove to be the wedge he needed, but Prescott could see there was no point in pressing his case now. He would wait for another opportunity, a time when she could be forced to listen to him—in private.

"No, Lindsay, there's been no one since.''

"It's safe to say then that Terry Moretti has been a greater factor in your life than any other woman in the past nine or ten years?"

"No, dammit. She's meant nothing to me at all!"

Martin raised a restraining hand, but Lindsay's eyes had already lashed back at him. She glared contemptuously. "It's clear, Mr. Prescott, that your regard for her is nil now that it's time to divide the fruits of your life together."

"What life together?" he replied angrily. "Does the fact that I've been father to her son mean we have a life together?"

"Blake!" Martin interjected, "just answer her questions."

"But this is nonsense. She visits the boy. No court is going to hang me because I let her visit him." Prescott's bile had risen now. "And I'll be damned if her mail or tax returns coming to my house will change that!"

The expression on Lindsay's face had grown smug, further enraging him. "You're so blinded by my bank account you couldn't see the truth if it hit you in the face," he exclaimed, pointing an angry finger at her. "Champion of used women, my ass! Justice starts with the victim's financial statement and it ends there as far as you're concerned and *you* can't tell me otherwise."

Lindsay flushed and threw her legal pad on the table. "Martin, I won't take any more of this!"

Martin Blum stood up as Blake and Lindsay seethed like two raging bulls. "Why don't we take a break? We all could use it," he added.

Lindsay knew she had lost control, but she didn't care. The gall of the man was almost more than she could bear. It wasn't enough that he should humiliate her personally with a dirty, cheap trick, he had to rail at her and impugn her professional integrity on top of it.

Forcing herself to turn to Martin, she gradually regained a semblance of control. She took a deep breath and started gathering her things. "I've arranged for Millicent Woodward to depose your client this afternoon, Mr. Blum," she said in a low tone. "Would it be convenient to resume the deposition at one-thirty?"

Martin looked at Blake.

"Yes, fine with me," Blake replied. "I just want an opportunity to tell my story."

Without so much as a glance in his direction, Lindsay walked out of the room.

CHAPTER NINE

THE WOMAN WAS TALL, stately, patrician. Her gray hair was pulled back from her face in soft finger waves and fastened in a bun at the back of her head. The navy-blue wool business suit she wore was of a classical and conservative cut, her white silk blouse rather understated. There was a plain gold band on her ring finger. She wore no other jewelry.

Millicent Woodward raised her chin slightly as she drew a long breath. The tips of her fingers were resting on the desk in front of her. She stood motionless for a long moment. "Actually," she said at last, "I was pleasantly surprised at the man. I found him rather charming." A hint of a smile crossed her face and her eyes twinkled. "I'm not surprised you found him charming as well."

Lindsay Bishop reddened and looked down, not wishing to face the woman who had been her mentor, her teacher, her idol.

"And frankly," Millicent continued, "I don't quite know what to make of him."

Rising to her feet, Lindsay began pacing back and forth. Like Millicent, she reflected.

"I would say," the older woman rejoined, "that he is either extremely clever, or adamant about his moral position." She glanced at Lindsay. "I believe I would rather deal with the former."

"Yes, I would too, Millicent, but my intuition tells me he's adamant. I believe he's sincere."

The older woman looked at her and seemed to be thinking what Lindsay pictured in her own mind at that instant—the image of herself in Blake Prescott's arms. "I would feel badly for you if you didn't think him sincere, Lindsay."

She knew Millicent didn't intend it as patronizing, but Lindsay was aware that she seemed a naive fool to her partner. "I feel dreadful," she said finally. "I feel as though I've let you down, let myself down." She turned to pace again. "This has been humiliating."

"Nonsense. Mistakes don't matter—they never do. It's what you do about them. That's what matters."

Lindsay stopped and turned to Millicent. The woman's wisdom was all too evident. There was no need to express the gratitude she felt. "Perhaps it's self-serving to say so now, but I really do believe he's sincere."

There was affection on the older woman's face. "You have a wonderful quality of creative insight. You'd make an outstanding judge."

Lindsay laughed. "Funny you should say that, this morning Martin Blum said I should be a politician."

"They're the same thing, dear. The only difference is the robes."

The two women laughed.

Millicent sat down in her high-backed desk chair and Lindsay seated herself opposite her.

"Our task now," the firm's senior partner said, "is to make the best possible case for Miss Moretti. Others—perhaps those with greater intuitive insight—shall render the judgment. I, for my part, will ensure that every shred of evidence favorable to the plaintiff is before the court. I have no doubt whatsoever that Mr. Blum shall do the same for the defendant, be the gentleman innocent or a snake in the grass.''

Lindsay nodded her head approvingly.

''As for you, my dear, don't be too hard on yourself over the little indiscretion with Mr. Prescott. There's not an attorney, or human being alive, who hasn't done something they've bitterly regretted. The important thing is what you learn from the experience.''

''Like never to trust a man?''

''Hardly. That would make for a very lonely world. Maybe the problem is just the opposite. Perhaps you've neglected your social life too much, Lindsay. Hard work is important, but there must be balance in one's life.'' She walked around the desk and put a sympathetic hand on her young colleague's shoulder. ''This has been a miserable day for you. Why don't you go home and have a nice long soak in the tub?''

Lindsay couldn't speak, but the appreciation and admiration on her face was evident.

''Listen,'' Millicent said in her best chipper voice, ''if you're free this evening, why don't you come over and have dinner with Kenneth and me? We've had three consecutive quiet evenings at home. Your presence would be a welcome break from the monotony.''

Lindsay chuckled.

''Perhaps I can persuade Kenneth to open one of those special bottles of sherry he's so fond of. Shall I call Kathleen and have her set an extra place?''

''I'd enjoy it, Millicent. It's been months since I've seen Kenneth.''

''Good,'' the other said, rising to her feet. ''Shall we say half past seven?''

THE LATE AFTERNOON SUN was low in the sky as Lindsay Bishop left the old Spanish office building. A light breeze sent leaves tumbling along the sidewalk in front of her and the smell of autumn lay heavy in the air. Lindsay took a deep breath, savoring the air and the memories of other fall days that came cascading through her mind.

Her car was around the corner on a side street waiting to take her the short distance to her town house. As she walked, Lindsay felt relief at escaping the office, but also a certain sense of emptiness, knowing that the heart of her life these past years was back there in that building, in her law practice. To escape it was not escape, it was abandonment. She had made the mistake of having nothing else in her life, nothing to go home to.

She was suddenly sad, and nostalgic—the nostalgia of a child as she stepped along the sidewalk avoiding the cracks, remembering a hundred other fall days, a hundred other memories blended into one.

Glancing up from her idle reverie toward the place where her car sat waiting, Lindsay was shocked at the sight of a familiar face. It was Blake Prescott.

He was leaning against the car, his arms folded across his chest. Lindsay stopped, perhaps ten yards from the point where he waited and glared at the man who in just the space of a few minutes that morning had been transformed from an exciting new force in her life to an enemy.

"What do *you* want?" she said hatefully.

His voice was unexpectedly soft. "I have to speak with you, Lindsay." He stood up straight, waiting as she traversed half the distance between them.

"I have nothing to say to you."

"But I have something to say to you."

Lindsay looked at the face that had been so dear to her, so full of promise, but all she could think of was his deception. The handsome image had become synonymous with duplicity. Though she wished it weren't so, the eyes, the mouth, the familiar line of his jaw were as loathsome as they were attractive. "Then you'll have to say it in court." She walked around to the other side of the car and unlocked the door with her key. Before she was able to open the door and get in, Blake had gone around and held it closed with his hand.

"You have to listen to what I have to say. It concerns us, not this suit."

"Us? Mr. *Prescott*, there is no *us* to be concerned about."

Blake grimaced with irritation. "Lindsay, be reasonable. I made a mistake of judgment. That doesn't make me a monster. I'm the same person I was before. I'm the same man who held you in his arms and kissed you."

Lindsay turned away. "Please. You've done enough to me in one day. I don't need this."

"Look, my judgment was terrible, I've admitted that I was wrong. But what difference does my name make? Prescott, Price, Blake, Bill, how does it matter in the end? It's how I feel about you that counts."

She looked up into the emerald eyes that were almost pleading. Absurd as his statement was he seemed to mean it. He really seemed to think the false name was all that bothered her. Lindsay shook her head in disbelief. "Don't you understand, Blake? You're the defendant in a law suit and I'm the plaintiff's counsel. You tried to seduce me under false pretense. You tried to seduce me!" her voice flared again in anger.

"I wasn't seducing a lawyer," he shot back. "I was expressing my feelings for a woman, for you, Lindsay, not the damned plaintiff's counsel!"

"You knew who I was, Blake, so this poor innocent defendant business doesn't cut the mustard with me!"

"I'm not the *defendant*," he roared. "I'm a man."

"You're a man who's defendant in a case in which I'm plaintiff's counsel. Nothing can change that. I'm a professional and I have my responsibilities and nothing will change that either." Lindsay reached for the door handle again and Blake stopped her.

"Are you telling me you're not a woman, that what happened between us meant nothing to you?"

"I'm telling you that the man I met, Bill Price, was a bit of a mystery, but he seemed to be a decent man, an honest man." She gave him a level look. "He wasn't. Now, if you'll take your hand off my car, I'm leaving."

"You haven't heard what I have to say. The whole story didn't come out in the deposition. I want you to hear the rest of it."

"Blake, don't you learn from your mistakes? You're talking to me about the lawsuit. I can't talk to you about that. If you want to discuss the case have Martin Blum call me."

"This doesn't just concern the lawsuit, it concerns us too."

Lindsay felt a swirl of strange emotion go through her. She had been sure she would never again be victim to this man's abundant charm, but in spite of herself, she felt a germ of sympathy for him deep inside. At the same time the pain he had inflicted and the jolt he had given her ego had left their scars. She bitterly resented him even as her heart ached. "I won't talk to you anymore, Blake. Please let me go. Please!"

His hand dropped from the door and her brief glance at him told her how black his emotions were. His face was flushed, though it seemed more from anxiety and frustration than anger. She pulled the door open and slipped into the car.

Blake just stood there in the street looking down at her through the window. He didn't move even when she started the engine. He was so wrought up that he seemed not to accept the fact that she was going. The expression on his face frightened Lindsay a little and as she put the car in gear only his half step backward permitted her room to maneuver the car into the street. Glacing in her rear-view mirror she saw him amidst the falling leaves, watching her go. She knew he could have been more adamant than he had been but she sensed that permitting her to go was his gesture of atonement. Still, it crushed her. With a final glimpse at him in the mirror before she turned at the corner, Lindsay felt her eyes well and tears began flooding. She was crying for both Blake Prescott and herself.

BY THE TIME Lindsay had made it safely to the sanctuary of her home, she felt totally spent, drained. Dropping her things on a chair in the living room she went into the kitchen, which was lit only by the fading light of day. When she pulled the refrigerator door open, light spilled into the room. Taking a half-empty bottle of white wine, Lindsay decided her day had entitled her to a drink. She took a large wineglass from the cabinet and poured out a healthy portion of the amber liquid.

Spying a lonely apple in a bowl next to the sink, Lindsay picked it up, examined the skin carefully as she had since childhood, and bit into the fruit, enjoying that unique gratification of the first bite. She then took a drink of wine, savoring the effect of the two flavors in her mouth.

A few minutes later she was climbing the carpeted stairs to her bedroom, feeling the weariness of emotional exhaustion. Lindsay's characteristic energy had abandoned her. She was tired. She would need a bath to reinvigorate herself before going to the Woodward's.

Whenever she was upset, Lindsay gravitated to her bedroom. The soft-blue carpeting, the blues, yellows and apricots of the bedspread and drapes soothed her. She went immediately to the large wicker chair in the corner with a polished cotton cushion and plopped down. Setting the wineglass on the small table beside her, she kicked off her shoes and leaned back, rubbing one foot on top of the other as she thought about the disaster that had befallen her that day.

Alternately sipping her wine and rubbing the tense cords in her neck, Lindsay relived the terrible moment when Bill Price had become Blake Prescott. The shock of it had been trauma enough, but the humiliation of having been so thoroughly deceived seemed the greater blow. She'd guessed that he'd been hiding something, but she'd been blinded by the man's charm and by the desire that burned inside her.

She had sensed from the beginning that something was not quite right, but she hadn't wanted to deny the joy he had brought to her life in the course of just two short days. She had turned a blind eye to his guarded answers, to the child's cup in his kitchen, the evasive explanation of his interest in her lecture. And the tires! That had probably been his doing as well.

If she were honest with herself, though, she would have to admit that Blake had seemed genuinely distressed at the car that afternoon. He seemed to regret the deception—and not just because he'd been caught. There had been nothing in his demeanor that suggested triumph.

Lindsay thought too of the urgent phone calls that morning. Undoubtedly he had been trying to reach her before the deposition. Obviously that would have saved some embarrassment but the fact remained—he had deceived her. She really didn't know the man.

Yet on paper she knew so much about Blake Prescott. He'd fathered Terry Moretti's child and now he was refusing to acknowledge her importance in his life. This image of the man—the facts she knew about him—seemed so contrary to her experience. Could the same man who had used Terry shamelessly have aroused her by the fire? Could he have held her in his arms and kissed her delicately and wonderfully on the mouth? She thought not. Blake Prescott, at least the Blake Prescott in her files, was not just Bill Price by another name. To be honest, she couldn't even imagine the Blake *she* knew as being attracted to a woman like Terry.

The confusion swirled in Lindsay's brain. The pieces of the puzzle didn't seem to fit. The Blake she had been attracted to was not the same man whose life she had carefully documented. Somewhere, amidst the confusion, was the truth.

Lindsay was afraid to admit it, even to herself, but she hoped her initial instincts about the man were true. If so, and if he really cared for her then...Then what? She didn't know.

She looked at her watch. It was after six and although Millicent's home was not far away, she knew that she would have to start getting ready. Listlessly, Lindsay went to her closet, hoping that the process of selecting her clothing for the evening would spark her energies.

A neat row of business suits and tailored blouses took up the bulk of her closet space. She turned her attention to her dresses. After some reflection she took an electric-blue cashmere dress with long sleeves and a jewel neckline from the rack. Stepping to the full-length mirror she held the dress up against her, examining it critically. The bright blue was a nice foil for her raven hair. Despite the fatigue on the face in the mirror, the image pleased her.

In a matter of minutes Lindsay had removed her gray wool suit and had hung it in the closet. She had undressed, selected fresh underwear from her dresser and began running water into the tub, anticipating with relish its effect on her tense muscles. A few minutes later she was easing herself into the hot water, drawing a deep breath, and feeling grateful for the caressing effect of the liquid that enveloped her body.

As she soaked, Lindsay wondered what would be said between herself and Millicent about Blake Prescott. She knew the subject would come up this evening, although the two women were perfectly capable of an evening together without discussing business. Still, she knew the purpose of tonight's invitation was in part to support and heal—for those qualities were deeply ingrained in Millicent's character. Also it was important that as partners they always be fully in tune with each other.

They had been through a lot the past few years and Lindsay was not concerned about the way they would handle this latest ripple. What did concern her was whether she ought to inform Millicent about her encounter with Blake on the street after work. She knew it was a sensitive issue—she had told Blake why she could not discuss the case herself—but something inside her said that the encounter was more personal than professional and that it should best go unmentioned this evening.

The mere thought of withholding something from Millicent made Lindsay feel strange, but she sensed that her secrets with Blake Prescott had a significance beyond their legal implications. As she sponged herself, Lindsay Bishop realized she was beginning to feel compassion for the man. That thought alone sent a tiny surge of hope through her body. It was the same feeling she had had two nights before when she let him take her to his house, hoping that she would be safe. Flirting with danger was uncharacteristic for Lindsay, but sitting in the safety of her tub, that was precisely her inclination.

CHAPTER TEN

THE GRAY-HAIRED MAN stood before the fireplace of the large room filled with French antiques of various epochs. He held a match to the bowl of his pipe, drawing steadily until a puff of smoke finally issued from his mouth. Flicking the match into the blazing fire, he turned to the young woman, his face cheerful and good-natured.

"Good to have a fire, isn't it?" he asked, his own delight apparent by the gravelly enthusiasm in his voice. "After a long summer I look forward to chilly autumn evenings when I can build a fire."

"It's wonderful, Kenneth."

The man dropped heavily into a big armchair next to where Lindsay sat. "How do you like the sherry?"

"It's delicious. Very smooth."

Kenneth Woodward took his own glass and sipped it, the pleasure obvious on his face. Then, as though a sudden thought struck him, he pulled back the cuff of his sleeve and looked at his watch, twisting his arm to pick up light from the fire. "I would say we must give Millicent another fifteen minutes to get ready. She only arrived a few minutes before you."

"Yes, poor thing. I feel dreadful that she got stuck at the office with an unexpected problem...and I went home early too."

"No need to worry, Lindsay. There's no problem too distressing for that woman." He chuckled aloud. "Not even me!"

Kenneth Woodward had been one of the pioneers of the electronics industry, virtually a founding father, a giant in corporate America. Nearly forty years earlier he had been an aspiring young entrepreneur and now he was enjoying his semiretirement, still owning the largest single block of stock of the company he had founded and built into a virtual empire. He sat on the boards of a number of firms and was revered as a patron saint of Silicon Valley.

Apart from his genius for business and innovation, Kenneth Woodward was ahead of his time in other respects. He was one of the first prominent businessmen in California to have a wife who had distinguished herself in her own right.

The Woodwards' relationship seemed ideal in so many respects. Each was a whole person in his own right and neither was dependent on the other. Their mutual respect and commitment created an atmosphere of support and tolerance. Lindsay had heard Millicent say on several occasions that the key to her relationship with Kenneth was a friendship built on mutual acceptance. "That *is* love," she had said to her young protégé one day, "the more insipid of the poets notwithstanding."

"So tell me, young lady, what exciting things are happening down at the offices of Woodward & Bishop these days, or is it already Bishop & Woodward?"

Lindsay laughed. "No, to the contrary, Kenneth. I'm still striving to live up to my status as junior partner."

He smiled benevolently. "Modesty's all well and good, but I know better—and that bit of information is from a very credible source, I assure you."

She smiled appreciatively and sipped her sherry. "Actually, today was one of the more notable in my legal career."

"What was so notable today—or is it part of those 'lawyer secrets' the rest of the world can only guess about?"

"Well, I suppose the safest course is to plead 'privileged information,' but I will say that Millicent and I did have a rather unusual man come into the office today—a man in your field as a matter of fact," she said. "Perhaps you've heard of him—Blake Prescott?"

"Blake Prescott! Yes, of course I know him, not well, but certainly by reputation. He's in telecommunications, started Converse Corporation here in the Valley several years ago." Kenneth livened with the advent of some gossip about the business world. "So, Blake Prescott is a client, is he?"

"No, not a client. He was in for a deposition. He's the defendant in a case where I represent the plaintiff. Actually, there's more to it than just a deposition." Lindsay hesitated. "I may as well tell you since you're family, Kenneth." Looking at the man, she suddenly felt a clutch of embarrassment. The subject was more difficult to discuss than she had expected. "I unwittingly got involved with Blake before I discovered he was a defendant in one of my cases. The details shall remain part of my 'lawyer secrets,' but the bottom line is that it has created an embarrassment for me—and for the firm for that matter. Millicent has joined me in handling the case."

"I see." Kenneth maintained a discreet silence.

"I don't know how much Millicent discusses her cases with you—I suppose the confidences of marriage supersede client privileges, but I'll do what's proper and not discuss the case itself with you. Not that you'd find it all that interesting.''

"I'll admit when you've been married as long as Millicent and I have, the only laws that count for much between spouses are the laws of God, but in all candor she rarely says much to me about her cases. The things we do talk about are more ideas and career events rather than details of her work.''

"I suppose what happened to me could be classified as a career event,'' Lindsay said laughing, "but to tell you the truth I do have a morbid curiosity about Mr. Prescott. What can *you* tell *me*?''

"Well, let's see...'' Kenneth looked into the fire. "Not much about him personally...I don't know him well. I know he's very bright, very aggressive. Unlike a lot of our young entrepreneurs these days, he seems not only to have ideas, he seems to understand business—that's rare, to have the aptitude for both.''

"Would you say he's rather mercenary, cutthroat?''

Kenneth smiled. "If you're asking whether he's unscrupulous I'd have to say probably not—one doesn't survive long around here with that sort of reputation.''

"Isn't it true though that some people are so driven they'll do anything to win?''

"Yes, there are people who take a shortsighted view from time to time, but they usually only survive until someone blind-sides them. You know the old saw about living and dying by the sword.'' He sipped his sherry. "But make no mistake, business is not charity work. What I'm saying is that there are rules in business life too, and the best people find they get further ahead with the help of others and not by using them.'' The old man looked at Lindsay like he must have looked at dozens of his own protégés over the years. "*That*, young lady, is the secret to success in the long run."

"I suppose that's true of life generally."

"I suppose it is."

Kenneth Woodward sat silently for a time puffing on his pipe. Lindsay looked into the fire feeling a modicum of contentment for the first time that day. She glanced at the kindly face of her partner's husband. There was a wan smile on his lips.

"Lindsay," he said thoughtfully, "earlier you said Millicent had joined you on this case involving Prescott. Does that mean she'll be dealing with him?"

The question took Lindsay a little by surprise. "Well, yes. Today she deposed him, as a matter of fact—or at least she did half the deposition. I did the first half. Why?"

Kenneth looked at her and sent a puff of smoke over his head toward the ceiling. "Is this discussion off the record?"

"If you like."

"Let's say—hypothetically—I was thinking of doing business with Blake Prescott. Something that would have a major impact on his company. Under your lawyers' rules of ethics what effect would that have on Millicent?"

"Well, the general rule is that an attorney can't have an undisclosed interest in a transaction affecting a client. To do so would be a conflict of interest."

"I suppose that applies to the business activities of the attorney's husband?"

"In most instances, yes. She stands to benefit, if only indirectly. You see, Kenneth, an attorney must abide by a very strict standard. There must not be even the appearance of a conflict of interest."

Kenneth looked at Lindsay intently. "But of course the lawyer won't have done wrong if she doesn't know about a conflict of interest. Correct?"

Lindsay could see Kenneth's questions were motivated by a good deal more than hypothetical interest. "For my sake and for yours and Millicent's sake, I don't think I should know exactly what you're getting at, Kenneth. But, let me warn you that just because Millicent doesn't know about something doesn't mean it couldn't be a problem for her. There's always the problem of proof. It wouldn't be easy to convince a jury that a professional woman didn't have the vaguest idea that her husband's business wasn't affecting her client in some way."

"I see." The man drank his sherry. "Lindsay, you said earlier that what transpired between you and Prescott was part of your 'lawyer secrets'—I believe that was the term we used."

"Yes."

"Well, businessmen have their secrets too. Might I suggest that this conversation be held in confidence by both of us? You've been vague and I've been hypothetical. Would you agree to a conspiracy of silence to keep things that way?"

"I think I would prefer to think in terms of a confidence between friends."

"Quite right. I prefer your formulation as well. And since we are friends I'll tell you what. I'll agree to pass on any gossip about Mr. Prescott that might be of interest, if you'd do the same for me—nothing improper mind you. What I mean is we might help each other to stay out of trouble."

A little smile on Lindsay's face sealed the compact.

"I think we're justified in the fact that we both have Millicent's welfare at heart." Kenneth winked when their private little chat was interrupted.

"Well..." Millicent's voice came from the doorway across the room. "Was that my name I heard being taken in vain?"

"Good Lord," Kenneth said in mock horror, "discovered again!"

THE CUP RATTLED SLIGHTLY in the housekeeper's bony fingers as she placed it in front of Lindsay. Taking a silver spoon from the tray she held in her other hand, the old woman placed it next to the cup on the fine white linen tablecloth.

"Kathleen, that was a marvelous meal," Lindsay said, looking up at the woman.

A slight twinkle passed over the old lady's blue-gray eyes. "Thank you, Miss Bishop. It was a pleasure I'm sure. Will you be havin' sugar and cream with your coffee, then?"

"No, thank you."

"Then I won't be bringin' it. Mr. and Mrs. don't use it either." Kathleen nodded politely toward Millicent and dismissed herself.

When Kathleen had left the room, Lindsay leaned across the table toward Millicent, who was wearing a mauve hostess gown. "She's remarkable, Millicent. How does she do it? She seems just to go on and on."

"Yes, poor dear. She's a little frailer, but she won't give up. Her job here is everything."

A few moments later the doorway from the kitchen opened and Kathleen entered the enormous dining room. The old woman's heels clicked on the hardwood floors until she stepped onto the beautiful rose colored Aubusson rug that covered much of the room. She made her way to the end of the huge antique Chippendale dining table where the three sat. The nine other places at the table were empty, but a sterling candelabrum at their end gave the setting a feeling of intimacy. The huge Waterford crystal chandelier above was dimmed, filling the room with a soft glow of light.

Without speaking, Kathleen poured coffee for the diners. Then, going to the buffet against one wall, she returned to Lindsay's side and placed a wedge of cheesecake in front of the young woman. "As I remember, this be a favorite of yours, Miss Bishop."

Lindsay's face lit up with delight. "Oh, Kathleen, your cheesecake! You must have remembered last time. How many pieces did I have? Was it two or three?"

"It was two, Miss. But you took one home, to boot."

Everyone laughed.

"Once again, Kathleen, an excellent meal," Millicent said. "Why don't you rest? Roberta can clean up in the morning."

"Thank you, Ma'am. There's some tidyin' I must do first, but then I shall." She headed for the kitchen. "Then I shall."

Lindsay sipped her coffee, enjoying the pleasant ambience of the Woodward home. In spite of having dined copiously on lamb, new potatoes, asparagus and a fruit salad, she managed to eat the cheesecake, which truly was special.

"So, Lindsay," Millicent said brightly, "did you have a chance to tell Kenneth about the interesting challenge we're facing in Mr. Prescott?"

"Yes, I mentioned he'd been in. We didn't really discuss the case, though. I did, however, give him a rather ambiguous account of my fall from grace."

All three laughed.

"Well, the whole thing sounds rather priggish to me," Kenneth said lightheartedly. "You barristers have a penchant for puritanism."

"In my case, unfortunately, not enough puritanism," Lindsay replied.

"Well, don't be hard on yourself," Millicent interjected. "The critical factor is avoiding any conflict of interest. By disclosing everything to Miss Moretti, you've put that issue to rest."

Lindsay and Kenneth Woodward exchanged glances.

Millicent turned to her husband. "Any interesting intelligence on Mr. Prescott you might provide, dear?"

"I was telling Lindsay earlier that he has an excellent reputation. He's a bright young man."

"Our information has it that he's a rather wealthy young man as well. Would you concur that he's been successful?" Millicent asked.

"To be blunt, Millicent, Prescott's at the point where he could make millions on that company of his."

"Figures," she replied, "it coincides nicely with his decision to toss out the woman in his life."

Kenneth glanced at Lindsay and then at his wife. "Your client, I take it."

"Yes."

"Tossed her out, did he?"

"She's suing for half of his estate," Lindsay explained.

"Divorce?"

"No, dear," Millicent said. "It's one of these modern things. You know mistresses have rights these days too."

"Oh? Now you tell me!"

Millicent playfully glared at her husband. "The girl's had a child by him, so it's hardly a frivolous relationship," she added, picking up her coffee cup.

In the silence that fell over the little dinner party, Lindsay thought of her questions to Blake that morning regarding his relationship with Terry and of his adamant denial that she meant anything to him. Lindsay had half believed him, but she also saw that with millions of dollars at stake it was a convenient position for him to take.

"Kenneth," Millicent said breaking the silence, "you said Mr. Prescott is on the threshold of something big with his company. What exactly did you mean?"

"Well, as you know, he founded his company several years ago and at that point it was worth virtually nothing. The founders of companies make their money one of two ways: they either sell their company to someone bigger, or they sell their stock to the public. Either way, their paper assets can overnight put many millions of dollars in their pockets. The trick is, of course, building up the company so that other people want to own it. It's like raising crops, actually. Farmers have been doing it for thousands of years."

Millicent began lightly drumming her fingers on the tablecloth. Lindsay looked up and saw that she was off in some creative corner of her mind hatching a strategy. There was silence while Millicent continued reflecting. Finally, her eyes focused on her young partner across the dinner table. "Lindsay, you said Mr. Prescott is adamant about not paying Terry Moretti a cent."

"Yes."

"Well, since our objective at this point is to force a settlement, and not to win at trial, it occurs to me that the fact that Converse is on the verge of this big development Kenneth speaks of may give us just the lever we need."

"What are you suggesting," Kenneth said wryly, "blackmail?"

"That's a rather indelicate way to put it, dear. What I'm suggesting is that if fabulous wealth is waiting just around the corner for him, he has a great deal of incentive to get this matter settled *before* the extent of his fortune becomes fully known."

"But this morning, at Terry's request, I offered to settle for $100,000. If he's so afraid she'll get part of his company, why didn't he settle?"

"Perhaps he feels he has time. Perhaps he feels we're not fully aware of his situation. Perhaps he's just stubborn. I don't know, but I suspect we can put enough pressure on him to bring him around."

"Blackmail," Kenneth intoned.

Millicent scoffed. "You say that, Kenneth, because you only have heard part of the story. What about the young lady who has lived with him for nine years, whom he tossed out like an old shoe?"

"Young *lady*!" Lindsay looked at her partner with a puckish grin. "Have you heard Jean on the subject of Terry Moretti? Her view of Terry is that she's an opportunistic woman out to make a killing on the guy."

"I guess that's why there are judges and juries," Millicent replied.

Kenneth touched Lindsay's arm. "You see, that's why I like business. We're not concerned with anything more philosophical than building a better mousetrap!" He gave Millicent a mischievous grin.

"Have your fun," his wife replied, "but just keep coming to see lawyers like us when you can't solve your disagreements amicably."

Outwardly Lindsay sat enjoying the pleasant banter, but in her heart she was feeling anguish, as though she were representing Blake Prescott and not Terry Moretti.

"Yes, Lindsay, I think I'm on to something," Millicent said enthusiastically. "I believe I should have a word with Miss Morretti. Perhaps $100,000 is unduly modest."

Lindsay loved Millicent Woodward as though she were her mother, but as she sat there contemplating the probability of Millicent's success, her heart began sinking. For the first time since she had known the woman she was not fully in concert with her. In fact, Lindsay now realized that at some level deep within her she was in league with Blake Prescott.

CHAPTER ELEVEN

IT WAS EARLY MONDAY MORNING and Martin Blum had to struggle to suppress a yawn. He scratched his balding head and looked at his client quizzically. "Blake, I'm confused. You don't want to settle, but you want a settlement conference. Why?"

"I've got my reasons, Martin. Just set up a meeting with Lindsay Bishop. I'll handle it alone. You don't have to be there."

"You might get the older gal, Millicent Woodward."

"I don't want to meet with her. Make the conference conditioned on Lindsay meeting with me."

The attorney tapped his pencil on a pad. "Okay, assuming I set it up, what do you want to offer them? They've asked for a hundred thousand."

"Right now, the money doesn't matter. That's not what I want to talk to her about."

Blum sighed with exasperation. "Could you give me a clue, Blake? I mean after all, I'm your attorney."

"Look," Prescott said impatiently, "I'll worry about that. Your job is to set things up."

"Okay. I'll do what you want, but if your objective is more social than legal why don't you take her out for a drink or something."

"I would, but she won't see me."

"All right, I'll call her. But give me a feeling for where you are on the case. What is it you want to do?"

"I'm not giving Terry a cent. She's a greedy, lying bitch."

"Right."

"So what else do we have to decide?" Prescott asked.

Martin Blum thought for a moment. "I've got an idea I want to run by you, Blake. The other side is making a big deal out of your son. Rusty knows the truth in this better than anyone. Why don't you let me bring him in. We'll shoot the plaintiff right out of the water!" The attorney laughed. "Lindsay Bishop would be so shocked she wouldn't know what hit her."

"No, Martin. I won't drag Rusty into this. I've gone out of my way to insulate him from this mess and I don't want to sacrifice him to save my own tail. I'd rather pay Terry the hundred thousand than hurt Rusty."

Martin gave Blake a soulful look. "If we don't settle and they take this to the wire you stand to lose a lot more than a hundred thousand."

Prescott's expression was incredulous. "You don't believe Terry can make this story of hers stick, do you?"

The other shrugged his shoulders. "Nothing is for sure in this business. I'll know better after I've deposed Terry but that won't be for three weeks or so. The point is they are talking settlement *now*."

Blake Prescott stood up and walked to the window of Martin's office. He looked down at the San Francisco Bay, dotted with sailboats. "Right now all I want to do is talk to Lindsay Bishop. Take care of it for me, Martin."

THE INTERCOM ON LINDSAY'S DESK buzzed and she picked up the phone.

"Martin Blum on line two."

She punched the button on the telephone. "Good morning, Martin."

"Hi, doll. How's the world's most beautiful opposing counsel?"

"Don't tell me. You've got another favor to ask, Martin."

"God, you're sharp, Lindsay."

"What is it you want?"

He laughed. "Whatever happened to the good old days where men were men and women were women?"

"They went out at about the same time most men stopped trying to use their masculinity for intimidation."

"You're right, of course, doll, but be honest, isn't there a part of you that wonders?"

"The only thing I wonder about, Martin, is when guys like you are going to give up. What do you want?"

"We want to talk."

"Settlement?"

"Let's just say we see some angles worth exploring."

Lindsay broke into a grin. She remembered Millicent's observations Friday night about the time being ripe to force a settlement. Perhaps Blake had come to the same conclusion. "When and where do you want to meet?"

"Blake is flexible, but he'd prefer soon."

"Blake? Why does he have to be involved? You and I can handle the negotiation without involving the clients, Martin."

"That's the way he wants it, doll."

"Well, I'll ask Millicent when she's available."

"No, Lindsay. He wants to meet with you. That's his condition."

Lindsay paused for a second. "Okay. Just make it clear to him I'm not interested in a personal discussion. Since he's represented by counsel, you'll have to be present. That's *my* condition.''

"Okay, let me discuss that with Blake. I'll get back to you.''

THE SOFT AUTUMN BREEZE drifted across the park sending bright colored leaves tumbling lazily from the trees at the edge of the bowling green. From her bench at the periphery Lindsay watched a group of elderly men gathering at one end of the green, chatting away in anticipation of their match. Most of them were in white pants and shirts though several wore sweaters and caps.

From a brown paper bag she took the tuna salad sandwich and small carton of milk she had purchased at her favorite deli, and settled back to soak up what tranquility she could from the relaxed mood of the bowling green. It was the sort of lunch Lindsay frequently enjoyed, particularly in the summer when the elderly participants came out in number. Watching them gave her a sense of peace, perhaps because they reminded her of her own father and the stabilizing force he had been in her life.

While several of the men were checking the condition of the various rinks after the heavy rains of several nights before, others were engaged in the amiable patter of longtime friends. As Lindsay munched on her sandwich she saw an elderly man and woman walk along one of the paths toward the entry to the green. They were holding hands and the man was dressed in white with a jaunty tam-o'-shanter on his head. The couple stopped at the gate and kissed before the man entered the green to join his comrades. The woman took a seat on a nearby bench to watch the match.

Seeing the little vignette Lindsay wondered if she would ever experience the quiet joy of companionship she saw in the elderly couple. There had been no one in her life with whom she had ever considered such a relationship. The love she had felt as a girl for Peter never included feelings beyond the immediate experience of marriage and perhaps children. The maturity implicit in a life of compatibility and companionship had not been part of her dreams.

Inevitably, Lindsay thought of Blake. She thought of the unique connection she'd had with him, the unity of spirit as well as the deep and instant attraction. Could those be the things enduring relationships were made of? Her brief fling with him had been the most exciting encounter she had ever had with a man—and it hadn't even been a real fling!

But how did Blake feel about her? *Really* feel about her? At her car on Friday he had said his feelings were genuine. And if that were true, were they strong enough for them to have a relationship sometime in the future when the suit was over? Lindsay knew the answer involved more than just their mutual feelings. *Who* they were was also critical.

The "who" of Blake Prescott involved other people in his life, like Terry Moretti. Lindsay was too mature to believe that broken relationships like Terry's and Blake's left one party innocent and the other at fault. There were always two sides to every story. Blake was not necessarily immoral for having had such a relationship with Terry and she was not necessarily bad in seeking compensation for the years she had devoted to him. Lindsay would be able to forgive Blake his past provided he hadn't mistreated or abused Terry. And it was that—the reality behind Blake's and Terry's relationship—that Lindsay found the most confounding of all. Eventually the truth would come out and eventually the lawsuit would be over. Lindsay would no longer be "plaintiff's attorney" and Blake would no longer be "defendant." That eventuality was really all she had to look forward to, if indeed there was to be a future for them at all.

The bowlers on the green had gravitated to the head of one of the rinks, and the first bowler, the lead, rolled the small white jack to the far end of the green. There was an exclamation of approval at his mark and the bowlers picked up their bowls and prepared to take their turns. Lindsay watched for a moment longer until the man in the tam-o'-shanter delivered his bowl to a point just inches from the jack. She saw the man's wife clapping and gesturing her approval from her vantage point on the bench and Lindsay got to her feet, feeling vicarious contentment. She turned away and silently headed back to her office and her career.

As Lindsay climbed the steps to her building, she wondered what further developments the afternoon would bring. It didn't take long to discover an even greater surprise than Martin Blum's call that morning. Jean had left a note on her desk.

Lindsay,

Martin Blum called just after you left for lunch. He said he'll be in court all afternoon and asked me to tell you that Mr. Prescott has fired him from the case and will be representing himself from now on. Mr. Prescott is anxious to have a settlement conference and will be contacting you to make arrangements.

Jean

Lindsay dropped into her chair in disbelief. Blake was apparently determined to see her at any cost. If he was acting as his own attorney, she would have no choice but to deal with him directly, unless of course, she withdrew from the case entirely.

The thought of being outmaneuvered annoyed her, but she also felt a spark of satisfaction. Blake's act was irrational but it also said something about his determination, and perhaps the depth of his feelings for her. However, good as his implied flattery felt, Lindsay knew that the underlying obstacle between them remained—the lawsuit. Having to deal with him directly might be more than she could handle.

After briefly considering dumping the whole mess in Millicent's lap, she decided not to run from the problem. No, she would face it head-on and carry the day by being professional and businesslike. That's the way it would have been if the Bill Price incident hadn't occurred, and Lindsay decided she would do her damnedest to make it that way now.

She opened her appointment calendar, then looked at her list of things to do, which she kept on a legal pad on her desk. She decided to begin by getting several letters out that she had been putting off. Taking a file from the rack on the credenza behind her, Lindsay reviewed the prior correspondence and notes she found inside. After a minute or so of thought, she reached for the dictaphone, dictated instructions to the typist and began her first letter.

When she had completed the backlog of correspondence, Lindsay looked again at her list, marking out the completed items. She glanced at her watch. Jean would be back from lunch now. She went to the door.

"Say, Jean," she said sticking her head out, "did those papers get typed this morning?"

"Do you mean the Myers's divorce or the final papers for Mrs. Betts?"

"Betts. She wants to remarry in a couple of weeks."

Jean shook her head. "My God. Where do these women find them?" she said more to herself than to Lindsay. "But, to answer your question, Betts is done. Myers is still in the typewriter."

"I want Myers filed today. Keep me informed, will you?"

"Sure...oh, Lindsay," she called before the other got away. "I got confirmation on your reservations for the speaking engagement in L.A. next month." She held out a neatly typed sheet of paper and Lindsay walked over to get it. "You'll be staying at the Century Plaza. The speech will be in the main ballroom there in the hotel."

"Good. Thank you, Jean." Lindsay started to turn away, then stopped. "By the way, was Millicent going to be in court all day?"

"She said she'd probably be back between three and four."

"Let me know when she gets back, will you, Jean? I need to speak with her."

"Sure."

Lindsay returned to her office and sat down at her desk just as the intercom buzzed. It was Karen.

"Lindsay, Blake Prescott is here to see you."

She felt her heart leap. "Here? He's in the office?"

"Yes, he said he came by to set an appointment."

Lindsay's mind started turning. She hadn't expected this. "Okay, tell him I'll be out in a minute." She hung up wondering why he had come by. He could have called. *Well,* she thought, *if the relationship is to be business-like, I may as well start now.*

Blake was standing in the reception area. The camel sports coat he wore was unbuttoned, his hand casually resting in his pocket. He looked up at Lindsay, the smile on his face gentle. His eyes brushed the length of her. Nothing that had transpired since Friday morning seemed to impinge upon his willingness to appreciate her frankly. He savored her a moment longer before speaking.

"Sorry to drop in on you unannounced, but I was driving down from the city and thought it would be just as easy to stop by as call."

"Well, I only have a few minutes. Come on back to my office and I'll check my calendar for a conference date."

They went to Lindsay's office. Blake closed the door as she went to her desk. "Please sit down," she said matter-of-factly and gestured toward a chair.

He dropped into the chair across from her. His demeanor struck her as unusually languid. Lindsay wondered why he would be so relaxed given the undercurrent of tension that she herself felt. When their eyes met his emerald gaze contained much the same message it had when she knew the man as Bill Price. Lindsay sensed that it would be up to her to keep the character of the meeting businesslike. She stole a glance at his wide mouth before speaking.

"Firing Martin seems like a rather extreme measure to have your way on this settlement conference you're proposing."

"It was important to me, Lindsay."

"Well, I hope you know what you're doing. I'd insist that any agreement that comes out of it be reviewed by an attorney. I'd be irresponsible and probably doing a disservice to my own client if I didn't insist on it.''

"We can cross that bridge later. First though, I'd like to apologize again for my poor judgment in the way I handled the situation last week."

Lindsay felt the impulse to react to Blake Prescott as she had to Bill Price. For the first time since the deposition she had a clear sense of him as one and the same man. The feeling alarmed her and she forced herself to think of him as the defendant in the case of *Moretti v. Prescott*. Her eyes trailed down from his face past the deep browny red of his tie to the calendar on her desk.

"When did you have in mind to meet to discuss the settlement, Blake?"

"It's important to me," he said ignoring her question, "that you know that my attraction to you and my feelings were genuine—and still are."

Lindsay could see she would get nowhere with him until she had made some concession. "I'll take you at your word."

"But do you believe me?"

She paused before answering, knowing his question was not lightly asked. It was in fact at the heart of the matter—his motives together with the truth about Terry Moretti. She almost wanted to say "That's what juries are for," but Blake was not addressing the attorney in her. He was talking to the woman.

"I believe it didn't turn out as you intended...and that you've been upset by what happened."

"But do you believe me?" he asked emphatically.

Lindsay felt anguish at that moment for both of them. "Please, Blake!" Her voice was almost pleading.

His eyes dropped with disappointment. "Look, I understand the conflict you feel. I respect your values and your professional ethics. I just want a few minutes with the woman, not the lawyer.''

"But Blake," she implored, ''don't you see that's impossible. I *am* a lawyer. This is a law office. There is a case. And *you* are the defendant.''

"Okay, let me ask you just one more question. When this lawsuit is settled and I'm no longer a defendant and you're no longer plaintiff's counsel, will you see me then?''

Lindsay looked at him, her violet eyes filled with surprise and uncertainty. It was the question she had asked herself at lunch. It was a question she didn't know how to answer. "Blake, I don't know.''

"Why not?''

"I don't know that either. It's not something I'm prepared to deal with right now.''

"But Lindsay, what do you *feel*?" he demanded.

"I'd like to say yes. I'd *like* to, but I can't deal with it now and I won't. All I'm willing to talk about is this case. So please, don't pressure me, Blake.''

She saw a gleam of satisfaction in his eyes. Lindsay knew it had been a concession, but it was also the truth. Yes, she'd like to say she'd see him later, after this was all over, but she was also afraid. Afraid this might be still another trick, afraid she might be in for still more hurt and rejection. Her eyes went to her calendar. "When shall we meet?''

"As soon as possible. Whenever you're free.''

"How long do you think we'll need?" She was skimming the pages of the upcoming days.

"I don't know. An hour?''

Lindsay looked for an appropriate block of time. "How about Thursday afternoon?'

"Okay, what time?" Blake was looking at his pocket calendar.

"Say three?"

"Fine."

Lindsay closed her calendar and rose to her feet. Blake rose as well and walked slowly to the door. Before opening it he stopped and turned to her as she came walking up to him.

"Lindsay?"

She looked up at the man towering above her. His physical presence assaulted her senses. She felt the emotion radiating from him.

"Trust me," he said in a half whisper. "I'll find a way to make things right."

Then in one gentle motion he lifted her chin with his hand and kissed her softly on the lips. Lindsay had not even breathed when he released her, opened the door and quietly stepped out.

CHAPTER TWELVE

LINDSAY SAT IN HER OFFICE in stunned silence for many moments after Blake left. That brief affectionate kiss had unnerved her as thoroughly as anything he had done to that point. It was not so much his act that was disconcerting as her own reaction to it. Her professionalism had completely dissolved under the touch of his lips, as though her body and soul cared nothing for the hours of indoctrination her mind had undergone. Blake's kiss had made a mockery of her resolve to be all business with him. Could that have been his intent?

Lindsay's reverie was broken when the intercom sounded.

"Hello, dear. Jean said you wanted a word with me." Millicent's voice sounded so calm, so reasoned. Lindsay yearned for the wonderful quiet strength of her partner and mentor.

"Do you have a minute now?" she asked.

Millicent Woodward was sitting at her antique mahogany desk when Lindsay entered her office. Removing her reading glasses she smiled at her young partner. "Sit down, dear."

The older woman in a black wool suit leaned back in her chair. The end of one earpiece of her glasses was at the corner of her mouth. "I understand that Mr. Prescott has removed Mr. Blum from the case. I take it that's what you wanted to talk about?"

"Yes. I suppose you heard that Blake was in this afternoon. We set an appointment for Thursday afternoon to talk settlement."

"Jean said he was by." Millicent looked at Lindsay for a long time. "What do you make of it?"

"I don't know what he's up to for sure."

"Seems rather strange that he'd fire his attorney *before* a settlement conference. Do you suppose he's so arrogant that he thinks he'd do better than Mr. Blum?"

"No, to be honest I think he wanted to arrange things so he could deal with me directly."

Millicent eyed Lindsay. "Curious behavior for a defendant, though not necessarily for a man."

Lindsay felt her cheeks flush and she hoped Millicent didn't notice. "Granted it's an unusual gesture, but I'm not taking him very seriously."

"Is that the objective analysis of an experienced trial lawyer, or of a vulnerable woman?"

Lindsay's eyes flashed.

"I didn't mean to be unkind, Lindsay, but you must ask *yourself* that question. It's important I know exactly upon what that you are basing your impressions."

She knew Millicent meant well, nonetheless it seemed to Lindsay that her judgment was being questioned. On reflection, she realized that this sort of candor had always been possible between them, though this particular question struck a sensitive nerve.

"I don't think my feminine vulnerability has totally neutralized my powers of reason, Millicent."

"Of course it hasn't, and that's not what I was implying. It just strikes me that Mr. Prescott may be pursuing lines of attack that are more promising to him than legal ones."

"That's occurred to me as well, and after what he's already pulled, I've hardly let down my guard." Lindsay thought of Blake kissing her in her office and cringed inside. She could see already that she was beginning to lead two lives in this case.

The earpiece of Millicent's glasses went to the corner of her mouth again, and she sat back in her chair. Finally, she leaned forward and looked at her young colleague. "So what do you think, Lindsay? Where are we in this case?"

Lindsay reflected, trying to think of Blake Prescott, the man in her legal file. She tried to picture him in terms of the facts contained in the interrogatories, depositions and pleadings. But instead, the feel of his touch, his masculine scent, the remarkable jade color of his eyes crowded into her consciousness. "I suppose I'll find out Thursday, Millicent."

"Do you think he's serious about settling?"

Lindsay thought of Blake's question, whether she would see him after the lawsuit was over, and thought that he, like she, wanted the business over and done with. But, did reason tell her this or was it the vulnerable woman Millicent had referred to earlier? "I thought your argument at dinner Friday evening was rather compelling. If Blake is on the verge of making big money with his company he clearly has the motive to settle now, before Terry…we…get wind of it."

"But we have gotten wind of it!" Millicent added triumphantly. "And that's where I think we've got him." She grimaced slightly. "We do have a bit of a problem, however."

"What is that?"

"I think our information is a little too general to be used effectively in a negotiation. I think what we need is

something specific, some hard evidence we can scare Mr.
Prescott with.''

"Like what?" Lindsay asked, feeling trepidation deep
inside.

"That's just it, I don't know. I thought about it over
the weekend. I even asked Kenneth some questions to get
a feel for the kind of information that would frighten Mr.
Prescott…''

"And…''

Millicent looked at Lindsay rather sheepishly. "I'm
afraid Kenneth wasnt very helpful.''

"Why's that?''

"I don't know. Whenever I asked him specific questions he got evasive. Finally I asked about it directly and
he told me he felt uncomfortable discussing people in his
industry with the aim of undoing them over a personal
matter having nothing to do with business.''

Lindsay recalled her little conspiracy of silence with
Kenneth and realized that he had an interest in Blake
Prescott that he'd hinted at to her, but had not disclosed
to his own wife. Considering the couple's close relationship, Lindsay suddenly had a funny feeling, a discomfort that put a further wedge between her and her
partner.

Millicent shrugged. "Perhaps I should accept it as one
of the foibles of the business world—I guess they have
their ethics and standards just as we have ours—but, to
be honest, I was a little surprised at Kenneth's attitude.
On the other hand it was a first for us. Given the nature
of my practice I've never had a case that touched on
Kenneth's domain before. Of course, I've handled di-
vorces where he knew the people personally, but the inner workings of the high-tech world were never at issue
in any of those instances.''

Lindsay couldn't help feeling a little sympathy for her mentor. Strangely, for a moment or two, they had reversed roles and it was Millicent rather than Lindsay who had experienced the clash of personal and professional lives. "I suppose," Lindsay said, "Kenneth has a reputation to maintain, and probably doesn't want to be thought of as his wife's Trojan horse."

"Yes, you're probably right." She smiled at Lindsay. "Well this doesn't solve our problem of intelligence on Mr. Prescott, does it?"

Lindsay could see Millicent's mind at work. She chuckled after a moment. "Judging by that expression on your face, you've got a solution."

Millicent grinned. "As a matter of fact an idea had occurred to me."

"Yes?"

"Max Bender."

"Who?"

"My old gumshoe friend from the days before no-fault divorce."

"A private investigator?"

"Yes, with the change in the law he's moved on to do a lot of industrial security work. He still does an occasional job for me, and it occurred to me he might be ideal to check up on Mr. Prescott. He knows the electronic industry well and has done a lot of work with high-tech companies. He may already be familiar with Mr. Prescott and Converse Corporation."

Lindsay felt a sinking feeling, but she saw that Millicent's blood was up for the hunt.

"Why don't I call Max and have him come over for a chat? I don't know if he can get us anything useful in time for your meeting with Mr. Prescott on Thursday, but then I doubt we'll get this totally settled in less than several weeks anyway. A juicy piece of intelligence to spring on him at a critical juncture just might put a good deal more money in Miss Moretti's pocket.''

Millicent was beaming and Lindsay was beginning to feel like a traitor. She couldn't tell her law partner about the confused state of her feelings about Blake Prescott, about the effect the man continued to have on her, or even about Kenneth Woodward's hypothetical interest in Converse Corporation. Lindsay lamented her plight, realizing that in less than a week both her personal and professional life had been thrown into complete turmoil by a perfect stranger.

THE TIME FROM MONDAY to Thursday of that week was an eternity for Lindsay. She sat anxiously when Millicent gave Max Bender his marching orders Tuesday morning. Max was both friend and enemy, much as Millicent herself had become. Lindsay saw the situation through different eyes all at the same time. The lawyer in her reveled at the prospect of furthering her client's cause. The human being in her felt hypocritical for having accused Blake of duplicity when she herself was hiring a detective to gather information on him. But the woman welcomed the prospect of ending this dispute that stood between her and the man who had moved her so deeply.

Lindsay found herself feeling progressively more isolated, having no one with whom to share her hopes, misgivings and sorrow. When Kenneth Woodward called her Wednesday afternoon, she realized that in him she had the closest thing to what might be termed a confidant.

''Per our understanding,'' he said in the same conspiratorial tone he had used in his living room the week before, "I thought I'd pass on the information on Blake Prescott that's come my way."

Lindsay tried not to sound as eager as she was. "What's that, Kenneth?"

"Well, it seems your Mr. Prescott has a reputation for being quite popular with the ladies."

"Oh?"

"Nothing unsavory, mind you, but he's considered quite a catch. Seems he takes a pretty low profile most of the time, although some of his activities have caught the public eye."

"Like what?"

"I hear he was dating a congresswoman from Southern California a year or so ago. Guess it made a gossip column or two."

"I see."

"All in all though, he doesn't seem like the sort of young man that a father would hate to see his daughter bring home. Just the opposite in fact. Frankly, Lindsay, you could do a lot worse."

"Me?"

Kenneth laughed. "Hypothetically speaking, of course."

"Glad you qualified it, Kenneth."

"Speaking of the hypothetical, how long do you think Millicent's going to be tied up with this business with Prescott?"

"If we're lucky, the case will be settled in a matter of weeks. I guess the way to put it is that the ball's in his court. I'm meeting with him tomorrow. We should know better where things stand then."

"Sounds rather indefinite."

"Hypothetically speaking, Kenneth, I wouldn't do anything that might embarrass Millicent for a while longer."

"Yes, yes," he said impatiently, "I see your point. Look, would you mind keeping your ear to the ground and let me know if Millicent moves off in some direction that might prove embarrassing to *me*?"

"Such as hiring a private investigator to see what Blake is up to with his business?"

"Yes..." His voice was hesitant.

"Consider yourself warned."

Kenneth sighed. "My God, that woman's unrelenting, isn't she?"

"It says a lot for your character, Kenneth."

"Mine?"

"Yes, I don't think an unfaithful husband would have survived a week married to Millicent."

Kenneth Woodward laughed. "Until now the pragmatic aspects of my virtue had never occurred to me!"

LINDSAY BEGAN WATCHING the clock almost from the minute she arrived at the office Thursday morning. She woke up half an hour before her alarm went off and decided she might as well get up and go in early. As it turned out, her normally quick decision regarding what to wear had dragged out longer than usual and she changed her mind three times before settling on a black suit and tailored white silk blouse. The final decision to look a little severe was her way of telling Blake she was there for business and not stolen kisses.

Lindsay's hair had not turned out right so she wet it again and finally managed to get it to turn under the way she liked. By the time the image in the mirror was satisfactory in every respect that morning, she ended up leaving for the office five minutes before her usual time.

Lunch was a sandwich Karen brought from the deli, but most of it went uneaten. Lindsay felt as nervous as she'd been on her first day in court. Blake Prescott was having an impact far greater than he deserved. By the time Karen buzzed to say Blake had arrived, Lindsay had managed only one small item that day on her list of things to do. After keeping him waiting in the conference room for ten minutes, Lindsay got up and went to meet him.

PRESCOTT HAD ONCE CALCULATED the value of his time at ten dollars a minute, which helped him to make decisions about the best use of the time available to him. He had found it foolish to squander such a valuable resource, and everything he did from reading reports to company meetings to playing racquetball was carefully calculated into the larger equation of his professional life. Thinking about Lindsay Bishop that morning he had decided he had already spent more on her than most people earn in a year. Waiting impatiently for her in her conference room, he decided he would spend as much as it took to get the result he wanted.

When the door finally opened and she stepped into the conference room, the vision he saw was that of the woman who had captured his heart and robbed him of his reason that stormy night a week before. Her jet black suit mirrored the glossy raven black of her hair and the simple purity of her white blouse complemented the ivory of her skin.

He rose to his feet, and Lindsay, mumbling a greeting, went directly to the side of the table opposite him and sat down. The silk of her hair brushed her shoulders as she scooted the chair up under the table. She declined to smile, but neither was she hostile. When her hyacinth eyes engaged his, they neither rebuked, nor challenged. They waited with innocent poise.

His face must have betrayed his enchantment because she smiled more with a generous motive than from amusement. "How would you like to begin, Blake," she asked simply. "Shall we review our last offer, or do you wish to propose one of your own?"

The gentleness of her tone was so much more pleasant than when they last faced each other in the room that Blake found himself uttering the only sentiment that came to mind. "Thank you, Lindsay," he whispered.

Her voice was soft. "For what?" A mutual gaze swung slowly from eyes to lips and back again.

"For being gentle."

Her lashes dropped, covering the violet gems of her eyes. "It's not easy to sit across the table from you like this," she whispered, still looking down.

"Then come around to this side."

She looked up and the corner of her mouth quivered with both challenge and amusement. "It's not *that* difficult."

"I can't touch you if you're over there."

"That thought had occurred to me as well."

"I can see your preparation for this has been thorough," Blake chided.

"Experience," she whispered.

He sighed. "Sins of the past."

"Blake..." Her eyes implored. "Let's talk about the case."

"Okay. But I'll have to warn you, I did a little preparation of my own."

"Oh?"

"Yes. I have an opening statement I'd like to make."

Lindsay smiled and Blake saw her as she'd been at the Buena Vista in the candlelight, her white teeth gleaming, her creamy skin waiting to be touched. "With just the two of us, I take it the rules are a little more flexible?"

"Why?" she asked with a touch of concern. "What do you have in mind?"

"I want to tell you what you wouldn't let me tell you Friday."

Lindsay watched a mini-storm of passion grow, then ebb on Blake's face. There was an internal combat playing itself out before he could begin his speech.

"At the deposition on Friday," he began, "I was very careful to tell the truth, but a wrong impression was made anyway. I had no choice."

Blake's words struck Lindsay as foreboding and she listened with nervous anticipation. The handsome lines of his face were pulled into a pained attitude and he looked at her somberly.

"You made a big deal out of the paternity issue," he continued, "by the questions you asked."

Lindsay dropped her eyes, feeling shame, though only the tone of his voice suggested it be so.

"I answered that I had admitted paternity, which I did, and that my name is on Rusty's birth certificate, which it is. But the truth is, Lindsay, that I'm not his natural father."

The statement cut through her like a knife. The green of his eyes almost looked black as he stared at her, waiting.

"You're not his father?" The next words she uttered came almost automatically. "Then who...who is?"

"My brother, Russell, was Rusty's father."

"Brother?"

"Yes. Russell and Terry had a fling ten years ago. She got pregnant. They were just a couple of kids, teenagers, but they wanted to get married. Because of their age it took a while to arrange things. He was living with me, and our parents were still back East. He needed their consent to get married. Two weeks before the wedding Russ was killed in a boating accident."

Lindsay sat stunned, not believing what she was hearing.

"After Russ died Terry didn't want the child," he continued, "but it was too late for an abortion by the time she decided. She had no real family, just an aunt who didn't care much about her. Russ was my kid brother, they had both looked up to me, so she just naturally came to me for help."

As he paused, Lindsay could see relief on Blake's face. It was the relief of a man unburdening himself.

He pushed on, wanting to finish his story. "I made a deal with Terry before the birth. She wanted to give the child away, but it was my brother's child, part of me, all that was left of Russell. I couldn't let her give the baby up. I told her I'd take him, but under the condition that he grow up thinking of me as his father. I paid for everything. She stayed with me for eight or nine months after Rusty was born, but then she left. Terry wanted to be a singer, not a mother, so I helped her get started. She began traveling but came back regularly to see the baby. She wanted to see him, but she didn't want the responsibility of raising him. We had an agreement and we've both kept our word to the letter, even with the law suit."

"Blake, I had no idea. Does Martin Blum know this?"

"You're the only one who knows besides Terry and me. I've never told a soul and so far as I know, neither has she."

"But surely someone…"

"Oh, my parents and her aunt knew and I suppose there were friends of hers and Russell's who knew. Maybe half the school was aware she was pregnant for all I know, but that was ten years ago and they were all pretty young. I'm sure they've long since faded away. I didn't know any of them anyway."

"Why hasn't this come out before, Blake?"

"There was no reason why it should. The fact that I'm not really Rusty's father never made any difference to me until Friday when you were grilling me about my relationship with Terry. I told you the truth. I've never slept with her. We've had no relationship except for the arrangement we have for her to come and visit Rusty. But my name on the birth certificate became damning in your hands, Lindsay. How was it you put it when I denied ever having slept with Terry—'except for that crucial first time'?"

Lindsay's eyes dropped and she felt dreadful. "But why didn't you just tell the truth about not being Rusty's father?"

"For Rusty's entire life I've been his father and I'm not going to do anything to throw a jolt into him now, not to save some lousy money. Perhaps some day he'll know, but not now, not as a means to beat his mother in a lawsuit."

"Would he have to find out?"

Blake shrugged. "So far Terry has had the decency to play it straight with the boy. If I don't make an issue of paternity then I don't see any reason why she would. The suit has nothing to do with Rusty. As you said at the deposition, the question is whether I've met my obligations to Terry."

Lindsay cringed at hearing her own words in Blake's mouth. They had been asserted at the deposition so self-righteously, with such certainty. The indignation of her tone was echoing with embarrassing absurdity in her mind, though there was no way she could have known the truth at the time. "Blake, what you're telling me is that Terry has been using your agreement over Rusty as leverage in this palimony suit, and that she knew she was safe because you'd never deny you were the boy's father."

"Basically it's come down to that, but I don't think that was her intent at the beginning. In the past I've given her money when she's been in trouble, then during the past few years she's tried to hit me up for big bucks. I think my growing success and all the publicity in the news about ex-mistresses suing and winning cases put an idea in her head. She apparently decided that if she could convince some attorney that she'd been my mistress, she'd end up with a whole lot more than an occasional handout. Frankly, I ignored the whole thing until I was served. Even then I didn't take it seriously. Martin told me that with you on the case it had to be treated as a serious matter, but I didn't fully appreciate that advice until Friday."

"Blake, if this is true..."

"It *is* true, Lindsay," he said emphatically.

"Then you've got to say so, you've got to let Martin challenge Terry with it."

"No. I can't. Rusty means too much to me."

"Then I have to talk to Terry about this. If she's lied to me, I've got to know it."

"No, Lindsay. I didn't tell you this because of the lawsuit, that will have to take care of itself. That wasn't my purpose in telling you."

"Then what was your purpose?"

"I wanted *you* to know the truth about me. I didn't want to be the man you believed me to be at the deposition. It was a false image. It's important to me that you know the truth."

Lindsay felt agony even more strongly than she felt relief. "But Blake. I can't just sit here knowing this without doing something about it."

"I don't expect you to do anything but understand me and believe me. That's what matters to me."

She could see that he had freed her from one burden even as he saddled her with another. "I suppose you expect me to keep this in confidence."

"Yes. I was speaking as a man, not a defendant and I was telling the truth to Lindsay Bishop, not the plaintiff's attorney."

She looked at him with anxious, longing eyes. "Blake, we've just traded one problem for another. What am I supposed to do now? This is supposed to be a settlement conference. What about the case? What do we do about that?"

"Tell Terry I'll give her enough to pay her legal expenses. I'll give her ten thousand dollars."

Beside Millicent Woodward's grandiose expectations of hundreds of thousands of dollars, Blake's offer seemed ludicrous and naive to Lindsay. Yet, considering the story he had just told her, he was generous at that.

She looked at his face, knowing he was unaware that she and Millicent were preparing a trap for him, but at the same time knowing that he had made it difficult or impossible to continue with the case. Suddenly a dreadful thought occurred to her. What if Blake had made up this whole story about his brother? What if this was just another trick to neutralize her? What if he was lying?

"By your expression you don't think Terry will settle for ten thousand."

Lindsay realized her emotions must have been all over her face. "I don't know how she'll react. All I can do is pass on your offer. The decision is hers, not mine."

"What do *you* think, Lindsay?"

The question was probably innocent enough, but Lindsay read into it all sorts of insidious motives. Now that he had neutralized her emotionally, was he testing to see whether she would carry his banner? On the other hand, everything he said could be true and Terry might not be deserving of a cent. Lindsay could see matters were rapidly coming down to a question of his word against Terry's. She felt trapped.

"What I think doesn't matter, Blake. As long as you insist on keeping the paternity issue secret, I have no choice but to ignore it—at least in my role as plaintiff's counsel."

"You know that's the part I care least about. What you think of me is what matters."

Lindsay wanted desperately to believe him, but she was frightened and torn. The look on his face was the look of a man seeing a woman. She knew that if it weren't for the table separating them he would have taken her into his arms. Part of her would have liked that, but part of her wanted to escape him. She knew that she had to get away where she could be alone and think.

Lindsay stood up and tried to tell him with her eyes what she had been thinking. There was disappointment on his face, but he seemed to sense that she needed distance. "After I've met with Terry I'll call you, Blake."

"Okay."

"It may not be until next week. It's not always easy to get ahold of her."

He was standing now too. "I understand."

"Thanks for coming. I'll be in touch." She glanced at him a final time and walked quickly from the room.

CHAPTER THIRTEEN

AT SEVEN-THIRTY the next morning it was sunny and the temperature was already climbing to an unseasonably warm level. Lindsay walked up University Avenue glancing in the windows of shops that would not open for a couple of hours. There was some traffic moving up the street, but few parked cars. Lindsay was early for her appointment and well ahead of the crush that would jam the business district later in the day.

At the corner she came to a restaurant, The Good Earth, where she would be meeting Max Bender. It was the only place for blocks where there was much life. Entering, she found the place crowded. Men in business suits read newspapers, students and academics from the university read paperback books or chatted over coffee, merchants, working people or unclassifiables like Lindsay herself made up the balance of the clientele.

After a few minutes she was shown to a table amidst the hubbub and clamor of the busy establishment. The smell of coffee, pastry and bacon filled the air. Lindsay felt comfortable with the high energy level of busy people at the beginning of their day. The waitress arrived almost immediately with a pot of coffee, but Lindsay ordered tea and a bran muffin. She watched for Max Bender to enter the restaurant.

As she waited, Lindsay thought about her decision to ask the private investigator to meet her for breakfast. It

had been a precipitous act. The day before she had agonized about her conversation with Blake for hours after
he had gone. Millicent had left the office early and
Lindsay had only a brief conversation with her, passing
on the gist of Blake's settlement offer, but saying nothing about his story regarding Terry and his brother Russell. Afterward Lindsay had sat alone torturing herself
with doubt and uncertainty over Blake's story, believing
him with her heart, but fearing the truth with her mind.
Finally, she had decided that she had to know the truth
and called Max, asking that he meet with her the next
morning.

The night had been a restless one for her and no
amount of rationalization let her feel comfortable with
the decision. Not only had she not consulted Millicent;
Lindsay knew in her heart that it wasn't Terry Moretti's
interest motivating her. It was her own need to know
about Blake—whether he was the decent and honorable
man he presented himself to be.

The waitress brought Lindsay her tea and muffin just
as she saw Max Bender enter the front door. It was exactly seven forty-five. Max was punctual to the minute.

She managed to catch his eye and as the private detective walked toward the table, Lindsay felt a sudden crisis
of confidence. Although Max had seemed good-natured
enough when she had met him in Millicent's office earlier in the week, there was a quality about him that told
an observer he viewed the world with skepticism. He was
the sort of man who seemed to look right through a person, engendering guilt even when there was no cause.
Seeing the slight, but guarded, smile on his face Lindsay
felt as though he knew all about her even before she'd
said hello.

"Well, good morning, Miss Bishop. I see you're early."

"Yes, I try not to keep people waiting." She gestered to him to take a seat and he sat down opposite her, carefully moving the place setting aside so there'd be room on the table for his beefy hands.

Max Bender was a stocky man in his early sixties with a thick head of gray hair, which he wore as he must have for the past forty years. It was shaved closely on the sides and neck so that you could see as much skin as hair fully halfway up his head. His eyes were blue and his face rather ruddy, though his general demeanor was relaxed. He betrayed virtually no emotion.

Max watched the waitress pour coffee into the cup before him, but declined a menu with a gesture of his hand. He looked at Lindsay with alert though inexpressive eyes. "You said on the telephone you had some further requirements regarding Mr. Prescott."

Lindsay looked down at her hands wondering whether that might be a sign of guilt to a trained eye. She looked up again but there was no indication on the man's face, only passive observation. "Since you met with Millicent and me," she began, "some additional information has come to our attention."

He waited silently.

"We believe that our client may have known Mr. Prescott's brother before she knew him, though the relationship is unclear at the moment. The brother, whose name was Russell, was killed in a boating accident somewhere around here about ten years ago. I'd like that information verified if possible."

Max took a small notebook from his inside pocket and scribbled several brief notes and looked again at Lindsay.

"Also," she continued, "we think Terry Moretti may have had an aunt that she lived with about that time. We'd like that verified as well."

He was sipping his coffee. "Do you know her name?"

"No."

More notes.

"Anything you can discover that might clarify or explain the relationship of the parties at about that time might be useful, too."

"Anything else, Miss Bishop?"

"No. Not unless you've got something of interest for me."

"Well, our investigation of Mr. Prescott has just begun and I normally don't report things piecemeal—unless its perishable intelligence or requires timely response."

"I see."

"But I can say nothing remarkable or unusual has turned up yet." He drank his coffee.

"We talked at the last meeting about Mr. Prescott's personal life in only the most general terms—" Lindsay hesitated "—has anything of interest come up along those lines?"

Max looked at her but didn't speak for a moment. Lindsay was afraid her face had the whole story written on it, and she struggled not to look down at her hands.

"My understanding was that the personal side was secondary," he finally said. "We've been focusing on the financial issues."

"Oh, I understand. I was just curious."

"No apparent homosexuality or sexual perversions, if that helps." He grinned halfway. "Of course, I don't know which you'd prefer."

"Oh, it doesn't matter."

Max's grin broadened and Lindsay bit her lip.

He put the small notebook in his pocket. "How urgent is this, Miss Bishop?"

"Not terribly urgent. I mean you don't have to alert Interpol yet...."

Max laughed.

"But as soon as is practical."

"Okay. I'll get someone on it and let you know as soon as we have something."

"Fine. Feel free to call me at the office or at home—it doesn't matter." She took a business card from her purse, wrote her home number on it and handed it to the man.

"I take it this is to be directed to your attention, not Mrs. Woodward's?"

"No, either of us is fine. The questions came out of a meeting I had and Millicent's been tied up with other things."

There was a slight smile on the detective's face. "I understand, Miss Bishop." He looked at his watch. "Well, unless you have anything else, I'd best be on my way." He hastily drank his coffee before pushing the cup and saucer away.

Lindsay looked at her watch, too. "Yes, I'd better run as well."

Max had already risen to his feet. "Looks like you lost your appetite," he said pointing toward Lindsay's untouched muffin and tea.

Another surge of guilt went through her.

Max tossed a dollar bill on the table. "Would you mind if I left you to get the check?"

"No, not at all. I intended it."

Max briefly saluted and walked with an even, erect bearing to the door and out into the street. Lindsay was sure she had made a dreadful mistake.

MILLICENT WOODWARD LOOKED at Lindsay with a thoughful expression on her face. "Well, dear, if you have doubts about Miss Moretti's veracity, then why don't we have her come into the office for a little talk? It wouldn't be a bad idea if I met her and formulated some impressions of my own."

"Yes, I think you should, Millicent. We don't want any surprises if the suit isn't settled and we have to go to trial."

"The whole business has become so murky, it's probably a good thing we're both on the case. Perhaps together we can maintain our objectivity."

Lindsay knew it had become apparent that she had lost her own objectivity, and she decided that Millicent was probably humoring her by letting her stay involved in the case. The truth was that if her sympathies tilted in any direction, it was toward Blake Prescott. The wise thing to do would probably be to admit this to Millicent, but Lindsay's pride and her doubts kept her from saying anything. Then, too, there was this mysterious interest of Kenneth's in Converse Corporation, which seemed a potential problem. Lindsay knew she was the common link with all of them, Blake, Terry, Millicent, Kenneth. It was incumbent on her to stay involved, at least until the dust settled.

"Maybe we'll have a better feel for where things stand next week," Millicent said, voicing Lindsay's thoughts. "After I've spoken with Miss Moretti and we've heard from Max Bender, it should be a good deal clearer."

Lindsay recalled her meeting that morning with Max and wondered whether she should mention it to Millicent. If it were to come to Millicent's attention some other way, it might make Lindsay look bad. On the other hand, it might be difficult to explain the business with

Terry and Russell without betraying Blake's confidence.
Telling Max was one thing—he didn't know the case and
the legal issues—telling Millicent would be another.
Lindsay decided to keep her silence at least for a while.
The conversation drifted on to other cases, other topics
and eventually to the decision to go to lunch together.
Lindsay was glad for the chance to be with Millicent
without talking about Blake Prescott, and the two
women managed to avoid talking about their law practice altogether.

Millicent and Kenneth had been laying plans for an
antique-buying trip to England and France the following spring, and the older woman shared some of their
ideas for the trip with Lindsay. They had decided on
taking a leisurely week of relaxation after the shopping
but couldn't agree on where. Millicent preferred Corn-
wall, Kenneth wanted the south of France. They had
shelved the decision until they could do more research.

By the time the two lawyers had returned to their offices Lindsay was beginning to feel good about her relationship with Millicent again. Her own duplicity was
nearly forgotten and the ties of their long-term friendship had reduced Lindsay's anxiety.

The afternoon went more quickly than those of the
previous week. Lindsay had an initial conference with the
wife of a wealthy real estate executive who had decided
to sue her husband for divorce when she discovered he
had been having an affair with one of the female execu-
tives at work. The couple lived on the same street in Palo
Alto as the Woodwards, but Millicent had asked Lindsay to handle the case since she had been close socially to
both husband and wife.

After the meeting Lindsay attended to some routine
paperwork, and when five o'clock came and the staff

began leaving, she decided that since it was Friday she would go as well. Clock-watching was not normal for Lindsay. She was usually surprised when the end of a workday came. Often it was seven or eight before her stomach told her it was time to go home.

When Lindsay descended the steps of the old Spanish-style building it was still pleasantly warm. The early evening air was heavy with the feel and scent of Indian summer. Walking in the fading light to her car, she breathed deeply, and savored memories evoked by the pungent earthy smells. But she was restless. As she walked, she began conjuring up some small adventure she could indulge in that evening to use up her surplus energies.

She was contemplating eating out rather than fixing a solitary meal at home when coming upon her car she saw the familiar figure of Blake Prescott. He was leaning against the vehicle as he had the time before. As she approached she saw a bouquet of tiny yellow roses in his hand. He had a relaxed, pleasant expression on his face. The brown suede sports jacket he wore was unbuttoned, and the tie, loosened at his neck, gave him a casual air.

"The defendant doesn't expect to hear from the plaintiff's counsel until next week, but Blake wanted Lindsay to have these," he said holding out the flowers.

She considered admonishing him, repeating the argument she had been making every time they had met, but she didn't. She walked up to him, told him with her eyes that he was incorrigible and took the flowers, sniffing them delicately.

"No rebuke?" he asked.

"No, I should, but no."

"There's a message with them."

She looked up at his green eyes and the lazy curl of his wide mouth. "What's that?"

"I wish I were free. Free to enjoy your company."

Lindsay searched for a response but every one that came to mind could only be taken as encouragement to him and was therefore censored. Finally she decided simply to acknowledge the gesture. "Thank you, Blake. You're very thoughtful."

He looked at her for a long time, apparently trying to glean a special meaning, a clue to her attitude. After searching her eyes for a moment he took a deep breath and looked up at the sky. "It's a beautiful evening." Looking at her, he saw that her expression betrayed no hint of her thinking. "Be a shame to let it go to waste..."

Lindsay knew he was waiting for her to say something—either a rejection or a word of encouragement. Instead she continued to look at his magical green eyes, mute, noncommittal, searching her heart.

"Nice evening for a walk...."

The corners of Lindsay's mouth turned up in amusement with the situation. She had had a similar conversation standing in front of her house with a boy when she was in junior high. She looked down at her feet as she had some eighteen years earlier.

Finally he took her by the arm. "Come on, let's walk."

Once again, despite her better judgment, Lindsay found herself following the man. As she walked along she turned and looked up at Blake from time to time, trying to make sense out of the inner turmoil, trying to find something appropriate to say. Finally, she sighed deeply in frustration. "You know I can't see you, Blake."

"Yes, I know," he said walking steadily, his hand still on her elbow.

"Where are we going?"

"I don't know. We're just walking."

"This won't do any good," she said plaintively.

He didn't answer, he just walked along. He didn't look at her.

Suddenly Lindsay stopped. She turned and faced him. "This is crazy. We can't just walk around aimlessly."

"I know. I haven't figured out a justification," he said with a smile.

"There is none, Blake."

"Hmmm...I see we've got a dilemma. Tell you what, why don't we walk up University Avenue, find a nice quiet little restaurant and see if we can figure this out."

She gave him a disapproving look.

"Really," he said. "I'll come up with proposals for solving the dilemma and you can shoot them down."

"Blake, I can't. Look, I'd really like to see you, I'll admit that. But I can't."

"Well," he said brightly, "that's progress!"

"No, it's worse actually. It'd be easier if I hated you."

Blake sighed, beginning to feel annoyed. "This is silly, Lindsay. We won't talk about the case; couldn't you just have dinner with me?"

"Not now."

"How about if we sit at different tables?"

She laughed.

Blake looked down at Lindsay, who was still smiling and holding his bouquet in her hands. They walked along without speaking. She, lost in thought, bringing the blossoms to her nose and taking in their fragrance; he, contemplating her raven hair and the soft yellow of the roses. The blossoms and silky strands were in stark contrast to each other, both lovely, feminine images, compellingly beautiful, arousing his manly instincts.

This diminutive creature, so full of the feminine graces, so taxing to his masculine energies, had rendered him spellbound again. He was unable to let go of her, unable to consider her with any attitude but desire. Being with her was wholeness. Nothing mattered beyond the autumnal envelope of time that held them together.

She too seemed suspended in some blissful fantasyland between the cruelty of reality and the blessedness of this encounter. She smiled still, caressing the fragrance of her roses, walking along because walking together with him was to deny the reality of their conflict.

When he touched her arm she didn't object, when he took her hand she acquiesced. She knew she didn't have to resist; time would rudely end the moment soon enough.

Prescott didn't like being passive toward fate. There was justice in what he wanted, justice in more than this moment of togetherness. "We don't have to surrender to this thing, Lindsay. We're free agents."

"Not as free as you think," she rejoined, softly.

"Look," he said with determination, "this is Friday—a weekday. You've been playing lawyer all day. Tomorrow is Saturday and you'll be just plain Lindsay Bishop, the girl up the street. I'm going to take my kid on a picnic. We're going to hike in the redwoods, a last outing of the season. Now, I can't think of any reason on God's earth why you can't go along. What could be wrong with a lady meeting a man's boy and spending a pleasant afternoon with them?"

Lindsay drew a breath to respond, but before she could speak Blake put his finger to her lips.

"Before you say anything, I want you to think about it. I'll walk you back to your car, then I'll call you tonight, okay?"

She gave him a skeptical look.

"Please, Lindsay, just think it over. I'll tell Rusty I have a very nice friend who makes wonderful brownies or whatever, who *might* be coming along tomorrow on our picnic. But you just let me know when I call tonight what you've decided." He looked at her longingly before they both slipped into a pensive but companionable silence.

It was nearly dark when they got back to Lindsay's car. Blake took her hand and squeezed it affectionately. "I'll call you tonight," he said.

Lindsay didn't object when he leaned down, kissed her softly on the cheek and walked away.

CHAPTER FOURTEEN

SHE HAD TOSSED HER CLOTHES on the bed and was slipping into a navy-blue terry cloth bathrobe when she realized she had no choice but to decline Blake's invitation. Her career, her professional integrity, even her relationship with Millicent could be on the line. It wasn't worth the risk. Besides, the whole thing could be over in a few weeks if they agreed to settle. On the other hand, if they went to trial it could drag on six months or a year. The timing of any future relationship with Blake Prescott was clearly up in the air.

Lindsay descended the stairs to her living room, put on some mellow music and sat down on her sofa to stare blankly at the opposite wall. She was anxiously waiting for the phone to ring; she simply didn't know how to handle Blake. What did she really want to say? What was causing all this consternation? Wasn't it clear what she had to do? She tried playing devil's advocate and wondered what justification there could be for *accepting* Blake's invitation. Would it be so terrible if she did go on the picnic? Did it *really* matter? Clearly she would not be violating the *spirit* of the code of ethics. Her relationship with Blake had nothing to do with Terry Moretti, and besides, she'd probably never lay eyes on the woman again.

Lindsay's frustration grew. She decided to lay out all the pros and cons of going on the picnic in her mind as she frequently did when faced with a difficult decision. The reasons "why not" didn't need much elaboration. They could be summed up in the person of Millicent Woodward. The reasons "why" were far more subtle, and in an emotional sense, compelling.

This man, Blake Prescott, had an effect on her like no other man had before. By refusing to see him when he called she might not see him again for six months or a year. Would the magic she felt in his presence last that long? Could she really take that chance? Lindsay knew that timing was so important in relationships and time could be cruel, especially with fragile, new love. She sensed deep in her heart that doing the prudent thing could cost her happiness. Could she take the risk?

Suddenly over the soft music the phone rang. Lindsay froze momentarily where she sat. Then she rose and went to the kitchen.

"Hello?" she said expectantly.

"Miss Bishop, this is Max Bender."

Lindsay felt her heart drop to her stomach. "Hello, Mr. Bender."

"We've gotten some of the information you requested this morning and I thought I'd pass it on."

"Yes…"

"We've confirmed the death of Mr. Prescott's brother, Russell. There was a boating accident at Anderson Reservoir with several witnesses present, including Terry Moretti."

"You mean Terry was *with him* at the time?"

"That's my information, yes."

Lindsay felt her heart soar. Blake's story was true!

"About the aunt, we haven't turned anything up yet, but that could take a while. We started with the newspapers and public records."

"Any information regarding their relationship?" Lindsay held her breath.

"The newspapers' account of the boating accident identified Miss Moretti as Russell Prescott's girlfriend."

Lindsay beamed, glad the detective wasn't there to see her face. "I see."

"That's about it. Thought you might want to know."

"Yes. I appreciate the call."

Lindsay bounced back into the living room, clapping her hands excitedly and squealing with glee. The news seemed just the palliative her indecision required. When the phone rang several minutes later she knew exactly what she'd say.

THE NEXT MORNING when the doorbell rang Lindsay took a last swig of orange juice, grabbed a paper sack and her shoulder bag from the kitchen counter and headed for the door. She was wearing a pair of faded jeans, some old white tennis shoes and a long-sleeved blue cotton blouse with tiny pink stripes and a button-down collar. She had thrown a bright-red Stanford sweatshirt over her shoulders and tied the sleeves loosely at her neck.

"Good morning, Blake," she said. His eyes seemed as bright to her as the new day.

"Hey, you look terrific," he replied with a broad grin. "Are you ready?"

She lifted the paper sack in her hand. "Brownies!"

"Great, let's go."

They descended the steps of Lindsay's town house.

"Rusty's so excited, he's been dressed since seven. The last three hours have been like Christmas morning."

They walked jauntily toward the street. Lindsay felt exhilarated and free.

"Hope you don't mind riding in a Jeep. We like to take it on excursions."

She gave Blake a look of uncertainty.

"Don't worry, it's covered. Just like riding in the Porsche, only higher and slower."

"The slower part sounds good."

He laughed, and it was the same full-throated laugh of the day they had met.

As they approached the Jeep parked just up the street, Lindsay saw a little head with a reddish mop bouncing in the back seat.

"His engine's running," Blake said laughing.

As the man opened the door, the boy popped his head between the seats and peeked at Lindsay.

"Hi there!" she said climbing in, "I bet you're Rusty."

The boy leaned back, suddenly shy toward the strange woman.

"You ready for a picnic?"

Rusty nodded and looked at Lindsay, his expression that of a bashful little elf.

Blake had gone around the vehicle and opened the door on the driver's side. "This is Lindsay, Rusty. Have you said hello?"

The boy nodded and smiled at the two adults looking over the seat at him.

"I didn't hear you," Blake chided.

"Hi," he said quietly.

Lindsay reached back and patted the boy on the knee. "Your dad told me you have a big appetite so I brought you a special treat!"

Rusty's face brightened and he sat up straighter.

Blake chuckled as he turned to start the vehicle. "I think you have his number already."

Lindsay took the paper sack from the seat beside her, opened the top and peered in. She inhaled deeply then looked at the boy. "Want to see?"

"Yeah!" he said energetically.

She reached back holding the sack open for him. Rusty looked in, his eyes widened.

"Can I have one?"

"Oh, not yet," she exclaimed. "They're for after you've walked miles and miles and you're really hungry."

"I'm hungry now!"

"Hey, young man," Blake said as he pulled into the street, "you didn't finish your eggs this morning, how could you be hungry?"

"That's different!"

Blake and Lindsay laughed. "I know," the man rejoined, "that's the problem."

"I don't like eggs."

"You've got to eat the healthy food too," Blake said, sounding very parental.

Lindsay winked at the boy. "Don't worry, Rusty. Brownies are healthy too. They've got nuts and eggs and lots of good things."

"Eggs?"

"Oh don't worry, you can't see them or taste them."

"Like vitamins?" the boy asked.

"Yes, like vitamins."

Blake glanced over at Lindsay. "Nine-year-olds know what's going on."

"Yes, I can see I need to brush up a little."

They rode through the streets in silence for a while.

"Do you work in a jail?" Rusty asked. He was now sitting forward, his hands on the backs of the seats.

"A jail?" Lindsay said in surprise.

"Yeah, Dad said you help bad guys, killers and things."

"No, Rusty," Blake interjected, "I said that *some* lawyers did that, but Lindsay is a different kind of lawyer.... I was telling him about you on the way over," Blake explained.

"On television lawyers work in jails sometimes," the boy said.

"You're right, Rusty, sometimes they visit jails if they have a client there," Lindsay said.

"What's a client?"

"It's like a person you work for. Someone who comes to you for help."

"Oh." He looked at Lindsay. "Like the people that go to doctors."

"Well yes, but they're called patients."

"We're at the age where semantics have become important," Blake interjected.

Lindsay laughed. "Yes, I can see that."

They exchanged smiles. Blake looked happier than she had ever seen him. "I'm really glad you agreed to come along, Lindsay. It's a wonderful day for a picnic."

Lindsay looked at the man's strong, even profile and the rich color of his hair. He was more rugged-looking this morning in jeans and a bulky white fisherman's sweater. His heavy hiking boots gave him the air of a true outdoorsman, an image he carried as comfortably as that of a successful businessman. Watching him, Lindsay decided she had made the right decision. She was glad she had come.

Forty minutes later the Jeep was twisting through the final curves of the narrow asphalt road leading into Big Basin State Park. They had gone some twelve miles from the ridge to this low basin in the Santa Cruz Mountains, filled with groves of giant redwoods and traversed by several streams. Although not far in distance, the park seemed remote from the crowded urban sprawl that rimmed San Francisco Bay.

As they wended their way toward park headquarters, the bright sun of the clearing and meadow ahead could be seen through the trees. Lindsay was looking forward to getting out of the Jeep and escaping the pitch and throw of their ride down the mountain.

"Are we almost there?" Rusty asked for the fourth time in ten minutes.

"Almost, son."

"That's what you said before."

"It was true before, too, only less so." Blake grinned at Lindsay.

"Are we going to stay overnight and sleep in a tent?"

"No, Rusty, we didn't bring the sleeping bags."

"Ah gee, why not?"

"Hey, tiger, this is a hike and a picnic, remember? No complaining now."

Blake turned to Lindsay. "Do you go camping?"

"Only in Holiday Inns and Howard Johnsons."

The man laughed. "Don't like the great outdoors?"

"Oh, the great outdoors is all right. It's just that I appreciate the facilities of modern civilization."

"Dad, what are facilities?"

"Bathrooms."

Lindsay blushed.

"You don't need bathrooms when you go camping," Rusty explained. "The whole place is a bathroom!" He giggled.

"It's not the size that concerns me," she said dryly.

"There are lots of bushes to hide behind."

"Yes, but there aren't toilets and basins and tubs behind the bushes."

"Gee, Lindsay, all you do is dig a hole..."

"That's enough, Rusty," Blake said firmly. "Lindsay can get the necessary instructions another time."

"Wow, a log cabin!" the boy exclaimed as they pulled up in front of the headquarters building. "Can I get out, Dad?"

"Sure, just stay off the road."

Rusty climbed between the front seats and was right on Blake's heel as he got out of the Jeep. He immediately charged after a blue jay perched on a rail fence next to the building.

"I'll get a picnic permit," Blake said to Lindsay. "Want to stretch your legs?"

She opened the Jeep door to the welcome scent of the forest. There was mostly deep silence, but occasionally one could hear the sounds of birds, a child's voice, or a car door slamming. From a long distance away Lindsay heard wood being chopped, a sound that seemed to echo deep in the woods, giving her a sense of the vastness of the nature surrounding her.

ALTHOUGH IT WAS ONLY a little after eleven, Rusty wanted to start the picnic—he was hungry. The boy proceeded to put Blake's resolve to the test. Lindsay finally intervened in the battle of wills between father and son with the suggestion that they compromise with a brownie to tide Rusty over till lunch.

Having gained satisfaction the young zealot cheerfully charged off down the trail. They had decided on a short walk in the woods before the picnic and the loop trail they followed took them through a grove containing the oldest and largest trees. It was a leisurely stroll, a pleasant interlude that permitted the man and woman to focus on each other for the first time in what seemed a long time.

Lindsay took a deep breath of air that was saturated with a panoply of fragrances from the abundant displays of nature surrounding them. The air was damp and cool and was earth-scented, making one feel vibrant in spite of the serenity of the still, towering trees overhead. She glanced at the man who silently accompanied her. Like the woods in which they walked, he exuded a calmness, a peacefulness that put her at ease, that made his presence comforting and reassuring.

"This is magnificent, Blake," she said looking up at the patches of blue sky above the massive trees. "There's an incredibly majestic feeling, almost like a Gothic cathedral."

"I like it too. These trees *are* incredible, but to tell you the truth I enjoy any little corner of the woods just as much."

Lindsay looked up at Blake who seemed even taller to her, "You're really an outdoors type, aren't you? You seem really at home, at peace."

"Yes, I guess so. When things press in on me a bit I like to come out to a place like this. That's why I wanted you to come with me today. I knew it would feel good here with you."

Lindsay took pleasure in his simple candor. "I'm glad I came, Blake."

Later on they selected a table in the picnic ground that was off by itself, sitting in an open spot where the sun brought them warmth. Just below was a stream. While Blake and Lindsay set up the picnic, Rusty was down at water's edge throwing pebbles and twigs into the briskly flowing water.

"There's enough food here for an army," Lindsay exclaimed. "Did you make all of this?"

"Oh no, my housekeeper Elena did it. She's a great cook. But the way Rusty eats we won't be feeding any of this to the bears."

"Bears!" She looked around anxiously.

"Don't worry, I'll protect you."

"But who's going to protect me from you?"

"Think you need it?"

She nodded slightly, her eyes showing she relished the prospect, though she dared not say so.

A BUTTERFLY FLUTTERED out of the dark of the forest into the sunlit glen where they sat. Hovering momentarily over the foil wrapper on the potato salad, it pulsed its wings slowly three or four times, then flew off on its erratic course into the cool woods.

Rusty was down at the creek, having put away generous portions of fried chicken and potato salad, two pickles, several carrot sticks and a soft drink. "He'll be hungry in ten minutes," Blake had said as the boy had scampered off.

The two adults relaxed after the meal, enjoying the warmth of the sun in the cool air. They sipped the last of the wine they had had with lunch and watched the child at play. Blake sat up, his eye on the boy, when Rusty started crossing the creek on a large log. Lindsay watched the man as he concentrated on the boy's precarious movements. Seeing the intense expression on Blake's face as he watched the child gave her pleasure. The man in his role as father had a peculiar effect on her. It somehow made his already comforting demeanor even more wholesome and safe.

When Rusty reached the far shore Blake leaned back and turned to Lindsay, smiling. The pleasure was still on her face and he realized in an instant she had been watching him.

"I hope my parenting isn't too boring. I know other people's children can be tedious."

"Not at all. I was rather enjoying watching you in the role." The corners of her mouth wrinkled impishly. "It's quite different from your Academy Award performance as Bill Price."

Blake searched her eyes. "You aren't resentful still?"

Lindsay reflected on his question. They were seated side by side, their backs against the table. She became aware of his nearness when he slipped his arm behind her, his fingers touching the ends of her glistening hair. Looking at him, she saw that he was appraising her both critically and adoringly. She tried to think again of his question. Was she resentful? Blake's hand slid across her back to her shoulder where it rested warm and large on her small body. Was she? He was leaning toward her. Was... His eyes caressed her lower lip just before his mouth touched hers. Lindsay melted into his embrace.

Blake's warm scent and the heat of his body surrounded her, mingling with the fresh smells of the outdoors. He was protection, shelter, affection, warmth, engendering a womanly craving in her to merge and blend with his masculinity. Man and nature conspired to fire Lindsay's elemental longings. The heaviness of his breathing and his increasing arousal sparked her own desire for submission.

"Hey Dad," Rusty called from across the creek, "watch this!"

They looked up, snatched from their private world of mutual awareness, to see a large rock plummet into the water, sending a crash echoing through the woods.

"Terrific! But enough for now, Rusty," Blake called to the boy. "Why don't you come back to this side."

"Okay."

Once again Blake saw Rusty safely across the log. Then he returned his attention to Lindsay, squeezing her shoulder with his strong arm.

"You enjoy being a father, don't you?"

"Yes," he said simply.

"He's a good kid, Blake. Really a sweet child...and the family resemblance is obvious."

"Actually, he looks just like Russ."

"You were close to your brother, weren't you?"

"Yes, considering the age difference. In a way I was like a second father to Russell too."

Lindsay thought about Max Bender's report on the accident. "You took his death hard?"

"Yes."

"What about Terry? She must have been devastated"

"Yes. She was there—witnessed the whole thing. It about killed her. It's a wonder she didn't lose the baby."

Lindsay sank into silent reflection, feeling more and more secure in her belief in Blake Prescott.

"Hey, Dad," Rusty called from the creek, "can I have a brownie?"

"You'll have to ask Lindsay, son. That's her department."

The child came walking toward them, dragging a little. He stopped in front of the woman and gave her an imploring look. "Can I have a brownie, Lindsay?"

"*May* you have a brownie? Yes, you may."

Rusty's face lit up and Blake reached out and squeezed the boy's shoulder affectionately.

"You going to let *me* have one, tiger?"

"Sure, Dad."

The man reached over and pulled the child to him, giving him a hug.

"Look at this, Rusty Prescott," Lindsay said taking the boy by the wrist. "These hands could use a trip to the facilities!"

The child wrinkled his nose in disgust. "All ladies think about is bathrooms," he said to Blake. "I'm sure glad only *boys* go camping."

"Brownies don't come from heaven, young man. You've got to learn the importance of treating girls right!" Blake grinned at Lindsay mischievously.

She gave the man with the laughing green eyes a coquettish look, then slowly extended a brownie toward his mouth.

ON THE RIDE HOME they had decided to drop Rusty off at Blake's house in Saratoga where Elena could fix him dinner, affording the adults time for a more leisurely drive back to Lindsay's place in Palo Alto. The Jeep twisted and turned, up through the hilly streets of the town, finally coming to a stop in the long circular drive of Blake's sprawling, Spanish-style rancher.

As Blake unloaded the picnic gear from the back of the Jeep, Rusty ran up and was about to open the door when someone beat him to it. A short, heavy-set woman with gray hair and a round happy face greeted the boy, who spilled out the day's events exitedly. Blake handed her the basket, explained that she was to go ahead with dinner, then returned to the Jeep. The woman nodded compliantly, smiled at Lindsay and turned to her young charge.

"Rusty seems right at home with your housekeeper," Lindsay said as they retraced the route back down the hill.

"Yes, she's a wonderful woman. Very bright and loving. I feel fortunate to have found her."

"By the way, Blake, where were Elena and Rusty the night you took me to your house?"

"They were at her niece's place. It's a large family with kids Rusty's age. Elena often takes him along when she visits, especially when I'm tied up."

Lindsay recalled the cup. "She must be a fabulous housekeeper. The night I was there I didn't see any evidence of a child living in the place except for that cup I saw in the kitchen."

"Well, Elena *is* a good housekeeper, but you didn't see the family room or Rusty's bedroom. I think you'd have believed he lived there after that."

"Clever of you to have kept me at the other end of the house," she chided.

"Delicate situation."

Lindsay's look was admonishing. "Anyway, I *am* pleased Elena is there. It's important that you have someone you trust and that he likes."

"Yes, Elena's virtually a surrogate parent. He gets the maternal input from her that he doesn't get from Terry."

"Is Rusty close to his mother?"

"He loves her. She gives him what she can, and he accepts it. Kids are amazingly flexible."

"But what does he think of your relationship with Terry?"

"We told him as soon as he was old enough to understand, that we weren't married and that we each had our own lives. We've told him we are friends and that since his mother has to travel all the time he lives with me, but that she will always visit when she's in town. We've never been hostile in front of Rusty, but we've never pretended to be more than what we are...or were.''

They were nearing the entrance to the freeway and Lindsay looked out the window without seeing. ''I guess this lawsuit has really changed lives, hasn't it?''

''Yes, I consider it tremendous good fortune.''

She turned to him in surprise.

''I wouldn't have met you if it hadn't been for Terry's greed.''

Lindsay was pleased but she also was aware that the good in what had happened to them couldn't erase the bad. A wonderful day in the woods with Blake Prescott didn't change the problems they faced and the obstacle between them.

An image of Millicent Woodward came to Lindsay's mind. She thought of the deadly plan her partner had hatched to undo Blake. She looked at the man beside her and felt a clutch of anxiety. She wanted to tell him about Millicent's thoughts and plans. She wanted to warn him, but she couldn't. Blake was very nearly a lover and at the very least a friend, but she was unable to alert him to the danger he faced.

''Are you okay?'' Blake asked with concern. ''I know I shouldn't have brought up the case. I'm sorry if I upset you.''

Lindsay looked at him appreciatively. ''It's tough being in the middle, Blake.''

''I know it is. I'm sorry.''

In the silence that followed, Blake sneaked several glances at his companion. ''You know, I bet that long face of yours is because you're hungry. Could I interest you in some pizza?''

Lindsay looked at Blake realizing she didn't want to say goodbye but she didn't want to be seen in public with him either. What she really wanted was to be alone with him. She felt an impulse and jumped at it before she had time to talk herself out of it. ''Why don't we go to my place and I'll fix you something to eat?'' she asked.

Blake looked like a man given a reprieve. ''I'd like that. I'd like it very much.''

Lindsay knew she had thrown caution to the winds, but she didn't care.

CHAPTER FIFTEEN

BLAKE PULLED THE CORK from the bottle of chilled wine Lindsay had taken from the refrigerator and set it on the counter. She looked at him and smiled.

"Wineglasses are in the cabinet to the left of the sink," she said.

He fetched the glasses, poured them each some wine and carried one over to Lindsay. Her hands were in the salad bowl tearing leaves of lettuce.

"Thank you, Blake. Just set it there."

He put the wineglass down beside her and tweaked her on the nose. Lindsay gave him a flirtatious grin and he felt a surge of desire for her. He leaned against the counter, sipped his wine and watched her working on the salad, his eyes ranging appreciatively over her tiny but vuluptuous body. Her jeans were just tight enough to reveal the nicely rounded curve of her buttocks without being too provocative. The full swell of her breasts under her blouse reminded him of that first evening when he had caressed them under the bathrobe. The memory intensified his yearning to hold her in his arms again.

She saw the look on his face. "What are you thinking about?"

"You wouldn't want to know."

"What makes you so sure?"

"Take my word for it."

She looked at him with acceptance and affection. "Okay."

Blake watched Lindsay moving around the kitchen, her movements graceful and efficient. To his eye her routine was almost a choreographed erotic dance—motion designed to entice and intrigue her male observer.

"Do you like to cook?" he asked.

"Not for myself. Too dull. At home I cooked a lot though. I was the only girl."

"You have a brother?"

"*Three* older brothers, plus two sisters-in-law and an assortment of nieces and nephews—five and one-to-be, to be exact."

"Parents?"

"Two. My dad is a retired Superior Court judge in St. Louis. The whole family's back there."

"What brought you to California, Lindsay?"

"I came out to Stanford for law school, fell in love with Palo Alto and never went home."

"How about your mom? Did she work?"

"With four kids? You bet she worked. Now she's working for the next generation—she's baby-sitter for my two married brothers." She looked at him. "Were there other children besides you and Russell?"

"No, just the two of us. That's why Rusty means so much to me. Our parents were a lot older and were living back East in New Jersey when Russ died and the baby came. They couldn't have taken Rusty on—it was up to me."

"Do you see them much?"

"Rusty and I go down several times a year, usually around the holidays. They come up occasionally, too." Blake drank some wine. "You'd like them, Lindsay... and they'd like you."

"I'm sure I would like them." She pushed the filled salad bowl to the side and picked up her wine. Looking at him over the rim of her glass, she saw the same sparkle in his eyes that she had seen in Bill Price's.

She knew Blake wanted her. By the expression on his face she could tell their lighthearted banter, the talk of family and past, was over and done.

Perhaps the die had been cast when she invited him to eat with her. Deep inside, she herself wanted the innocence of the day to end and the promise of the evening to begin. Perhaps her eyes now told him this.

As they stood in her kitchen drinking wine, Lindsay understood that to make the fantasy of that first night possible again they had needed a day grounded in reality. Was that why Blake had wanted her to be with him and the child, to commune in the unpretentious natural surroundings of the woods? In order to experience his magic again, she first had to experience him in his candid simplicity, in his boots walking among the trees, talking about the daily concerns of life.

Whether it had been necessary, whether it had been Blake's intent, the result was now unfolding. Their relationship had elevated to a new, even more exciting plane. The spark he had struck as Bill Price was smoldering once again. The difference was that this time, she would know the man in her arms.

LINDSAY STUDIED THE CONTOURS of his face in the flickering light of the fire. He was stretched out on the floor, propped up on one elbow, a wineglass resting in his hand. His boots had been removed and his plate pushed aside, the meal completed.

She was lying on several pillows, the side of her face supported by her hand and arm. She looked alternately into the fire and at him. He gazed steadily at the dancing flames.

"If you could be anywhere," he said wistfully, "doing anything, where would you be?"

"I sort of like it right here, with you."

He turned to her. "Yes. That's how I feel too."

Lindsay saw an unspoken statement playing in his eyes. This was where they both wanted to be. There was much more than mutual desire at issue. Being alone together was what mattered.

Blake reached over and took her hand, rubbing the creamy satin of her skin with his thumb. Her slender fingers were clasped in his palm until he opened it like a chrysalis opened for a butterfly. But before she could escape he pulled the hand toward him, kissing her knuckles and fingertips with gentle lips.

Bringing over a pillow for her head, Blake eased Lindsay back so that he was beside her and above her, his leg and hip now flush against hers, his hand touching the vulnerable flesh of her neck. She sensed his desire and the restraint he put on his powerful body. His touch was careful, as though she were a kitten instead of a woman. Lindsay felt her throat pulsing against his fingers with each beat of her heart, the rhythm quickened by his proximity.

She looked deeply into his eyes, wanting to know as much as possible, seeking reassurance. His nostrils flared slightly with a calming breath and he continued to hold back the urgency of his desire. His green eyes contained a message of calm and adoration. His lips were full and soft, his face tender.

Lindsay had no doubt about her vulnerability. Control had passed quietly and certainly from her hands to his. Her only fear was the unknown, the way his emotion and his physical passion would blend. The melody of his personal lovemaking was an unfamiliar composition. She waited, silently.

Blake felt the latent force of her passivity under his fingertips. Her slightly rounded eyes were dark and apprehensive in the flickering light of the fire. She was watching him, clearly mistress to his will, yet still an unknown partner, a female being with a soul-force and spirit far greater than he knew. He touched the swell of her lower lip with his finger. Her mouth greeted it with a silent kiss.

"You're lovely," he whispered.

Lindsay wanted Blake nearer then and invited him to come closer with her smile. He dropped down so that the warmth of his breath touched her cheek. He kissed it. Her heart began racing. Blake ran his lips along the slender arch of her neck. Sensation seared her spine, and her breasts leaned spontaneously against his chest.

His teeth gently took the soft flesh below Lindsay's ear and she reached up, grasping the back of his broad, strong neck with her hand. She held him against her, coaxing him to loosen his restraint. Blake's tongue slid up the side of her neck with feathery sweeps of fire and ice. She moaned and he pulled back to see the pleasure playing on her face.

Enjoying the desire in her pansy-colored eyes, he slowly fell upon her mouth, taking it fully, completely, with unrestrained determination. Lindsay let him take her, capturing her, claiming her lips and teeth and tongue.

Blake's affectionate but powerful kiss was for Lindsay the catalyst of release. He had been a forbidden fruit and untouchable love object. Now she embraced him, submitting to the elemental desires that ruled her.

His mouth covered hers, both taking sweetness and giving it, probing intimately and coaxing deliciously. He broke free and fell hard against her, taking her breast in the cup of his hand. "I want you," he said into the black thickness of her silken hair. "I want you, Lindsay."

She kissed his fiery skin, purring softly as his thumb circled the hardening nub of her breast. Blake's fingers went to the buttons of her blouse, swiftly unfastening each in turn until he could pull the garment open, exposing the soft full breasts swelling from her bra. His moist lips fell on them, teasing the flesh along the lacy fringe of the undergarment.

Lindsay slid her fingers into the coarse tangle of his auburn hair, resisting the temptation to crush his face against her. Blake interrupted his kisses long enough to unsnap the clasp between her mounds and lift away the filmy fabric. He savored the naked fruit before he took one nipple between his lips, entwining it with his tongue until it stood taut and erect in his mouth.

She moaned her pleasure, grasping the thick locks of his hair and heaving her breasts so that he might take in the fullness of her. Blake's tongue ran across her rosy patch to the tip of her pulsing nipple, then down the other side, sending charges through her body. While her heart raged in her chest he went at the other breast and plied it with his tongue and lips, stimulating it also to turgid heights.

Lindsay felt her body filling with excitement from every nerve ending to the center of her feminine core. She had been in bed with a man before but she had never been so aroused. Even the ultimate act had not produced a fire storm like that now ablaze in her body.

Her eyes were closed so that no perception but the sensation of his touch could enter her brain. She was

aware only of his tongue, his lips, his fingers tracing
lightly over her exposed skin. She didn't notice when he
unfastened the waistband of her jeans. She felt his strong
fingers pull open the snaps then peel the tightly clinging
garment from her hips and thighs.

Through half-open eyes she watched him remove the
pants from her legs, pull off her socks, then run his large
warm palm up her leg. Lindsay quivered as his hand
trailed over her thigh to the full curve of her hip.

Wanting to be free of her clothing she sat up and removed her blouse and bra. Then feeling sudden shyness,
she grasped her knees, pulling them up against her chest.

Blake was kneeling in front of her, his broad chest under the bulky sweater as wide as the length of her arm, his
shoulders twice the width of her own. He smiled, touched
by the shy and vulnerable woman nearly naked before
him. Reaching over with his hand he pushed strands of
her silky hair from her face, letting the raven skeins slip
through his fingers.

"You're so beautiful," he said, his eyes laughing with
delight.

"I love it when you touch me," she said. "No one has
ever touched me like that before."

Blake leaned over and kissed her on the nose.
"Touching a woman has never given me such pleasure."

Lindsay encircled his neck with her arms and pulled his
large body down upon her. He felt like a great living
eiderdown, the soft nubby fabric of his sweater rough
against her naked breasts, the lean muscular trunk of his
thighs pressed against hers. She received his mouth, now
familiar with the sweet melody of his kiss.

Their lips welded together during a long breathless
embrace. Then Blake rolled to his side, freeing his hand
to roam down her naked flank to her hip and the band of

her panties. While his mouth still nibbled at her lips, his finger slipped under the edge of her lingerie, then half-way across her stomach.

Lindsay's heart raced like a trip-hammer knowing his intimate touch was near. She yearned for his hand to slide down between her legs but somehow she also feared it.

"Don't touch me yet," she whispered. "I want to feel your skin."

Blake rose to his knees once more looking down at her, wanting her more than ever. Her nakedness had aroused him to a fever point of passion. The swell of his sex was constricted by his clothing and he wanted to be free to take her, to penetrate her.

He pulled the fisherman's sweater off in one deft move exposing the matted wall of his chest to her and to the crackling warmth of the fire. Below him the woman was bathed in firelight, its mellow glow awash on alabaster skin. He smiled when she reached up and touched his chest, letting her fingertips glide along his firm warm skin.

Then he rose to his feet, unbuckled his belt and re-moved his pants, kicking them away so that he stood over her unencumbered. He felt like a giant, a conqueror, master of a captive princess. There was fear as well as admiration in her eyes.

"Come hold me, Blake," she said extending her hand to him. "I'm afraid."

He dropped to one knee beside her and she held his hand with both of hers, searching his face for reassurance. He kissed her lightly on the lips then stood again, removing his shorts so that he was completely naked in her sight. Lindsay lay back against her pillow observing with awe his prodigious masculinity.

Blake stood there over her for only a moment but the image of him burned into the fibers of her brain for eternity. He was a ruddy giant of a man, his fiery hair a crown, his nakedness a regal cloak of firelight and shadow. His face was serene and genial, yet there was no doubt about his fervor for conquest. It was no accident that she should be the object of his will and aspiration. His desire for her was plain to see.

Again, she beckoned him with her hand. Again, he went to her side, stretching out beside her, gathering her to him with strong arms. Lindsay burrowed into the protection of his body like a chick into a nest. Her breasts were lost in the silky mat of his chest, his leg covered her like a blanket from waist to toe. She clung to him, less fearful of his touch than the sight of him.

Yet that male instrument of pleasure, his sexual essence, pressed against her, too. It entreated and tormented her by its being. She wanted it, but she wanted sanctuary from it. She craved it, but wanted protection against its awesome capability. Lindsay pressed her face into his neck, taking refuge so that he wouldn't yet do the thing she wanted most.

"It's been a long time, Blake," she whispered. "I'm afraid you'll hurt me."

"Are you protected?" he asked stroking her hair.

"It's okay, I'm safe now," she replied in a barely audible voice.

"Then don't worry. I won't hurt you, my darling. I won't hurt you." And he kissed her delicately to seal the pledge.

Before long his fingers toyed expectantly with the edges of her panties, the last garment between them and primal circumstance. Blake drew his hand up and down her thigh, growing impatient with the adagio of their love dance. He chafed, but was determined to grant her the tempo of her choosing.

By the way her hips rose to meet his touch he could tell the fever of her excitement was mounting. She pressed against him, a low purr gurgling from her throat each time his hand approached her intimate place. When finally he drew his hand up the velvet length of her inner thigh, she took his wrist and guided his touch to its ultimate destination.

Beneath his palm and the thin film of the fabric, Blake found the dewy caldron of her femininity. The discovery left him weak with desire. All his energies seemed focused for the moment in his aching loins.

His hand slipped under the band of her panties, through the soft triangle of down, to the fecund recesses of her womanly being. She moaned under his touch, her body arching in yearning need of him. As she lifted her hips, Blake pulled the lacy panties down, over her slender legs and off her feet.

He cupped the bare skin of her buttocks with his hands, as if to claim the prize he had uncovered. She trembled. Leaning down he kissed her breast, the flat of her stomach and the downy fringe of her most private place until she quivered. Her fingers dug into his back and arms as if to measure his masculine force. He dropped down upon her so that the full length of their bodies pressed one against the other. Feeling her, small and voluptuous beneath him, he swelled in expectation.

"Oh God, Lindsay I have to have you."

The tiny cry of pleasure from her throat told him she was ready. He kissed her again. He ran his hand up and down her body. Her breathing became staccato bursts of air. His finger probed her. She writhed in a spontaneous undulation of desire.

"Take me," she moaned through clenched white teeth. "Oh God, please take me."

He parted her legs. Her knees lifted and she opened herself for him to take her. Lindsay felt her breath wedged in her throat as her body arched to accept his penetration. As he lifted himself above her she felt him rigid and hard against her thigh.

She gasped. With several gentle thrusts he took her, his invasion fulfilled. The man—his essence—sank to the utter depth of her core, filling her in ultimate conjugation.

The bubble in her throat burst and a cry of joy emitted from her. Lindsay surrendered completely, opening herself and receiving him. Then in an exquisite dance their bodies moved in unison, he alternately entering and withdrawing. The pace was slow at first, slower than the pulsing storm inside her, but the rhythm soon quickened.

The heave and crush of his body heightened the waves of her excitation, sending her tumbling before them. In an instant her pleasure gained momentum of its own. Her hips rose forcefully to meet him. Strength surged through her in a ripple of sensation and energy.

Blake's own excitement had risen to a white heat of fury. He was gasping frenzied breaths into the pillow, his body rushing to its ultimate fulfillment, moderation long forgotten.

Lindsay was so overwhelmed by his furious tempest that she found her body experiencing more excitement because of his involvement. As Blake built toward explosion she was swept up with him, her cries in counterpoint to his, his thrusts becoming hers, her pulse indistinguishable from his.

Suddenly she was filled with the sensation of expectant eruption. She felt as though her loins would burst. "Oh now!" she cried. "Please now!"

And then he did. Life force surged from him, sending the waves of her own passion over its bounds. She, like he, exploded in a cataclysm of uncurbed, unqualified release. Wave after wave of pleasure consumed and plundered her body until she was spent and exhausted. All at once he collapsed into her and she received him again, this time the conqueror and mistress of his body.

He lay heavily upon her in miraculous and harmonious union, a fallen giant mellowed by her. Lindsay lay still, her body alive with aftershocks of her subsiding pleasure. Still joined with him, she felt complete and whole. The man in her arms, lost as in a drunken sleep, had been her fulfillment. She clung to him, not wanting to lose the unique sensation that continued to throb inside her. It had been a miracle, though natural and right as life itself. Until this night, with this man, she had never known such physical passion.

Blake finally stirred, lifting part of his weight from her, permitting her to breathe more easily. He kissed her forehead, smiling through the stupor of their sexual drug and eased his weight onto the carpet beside her. Lindsay felt the coolness of the air on her skin, moistened by the heat of their bodies. She sighed deeply, welcoming the feathery touch of his fingers on her breasts. She put her hand to his face, which glowed in the shimmering light of the fire.

"You're wonderful," she whispered.

Blake kissed her fingertips, then gathered her into the protection of his arms, holding her tightly as though he feared she might escape.

CHAPTER SIXTEEN

THE WORD PROCESSOR CLATTERED softly in the outer office. From time to time a phone would ring and she would hear Jean's voice. The hum of work filled the air just as it always had, but Lindsay Bishop wasn't part of it. She was hopelessly adrift in the pleasures of her weekend, out of touch with the familiar world of work around her.

By Monday morning Lindsay was awestruck at just how forcefully Blake Prescott had changed her life. He had given her an awareness of herself she had never had before. The incredible sensations she had experienced under his touch revealed a dimension to life that prior happenings had only hinted at. A whole new woman had blossomed from the old.

She pictured Blake's face vividly in her mind. She saw it in firelight and in shadow and rumpled by the soft morning light. After the fire had burned down they had climbed the stairs to her bedroom and there she spent the night in his arms. She recalled his kisses and the wonderful feeling of waking up with him at her side.

He had fixed her breakfast the next morning, then they sat together on the couch reading the Sunday paper, her feet snuggled under him. There had been quiet affection and companionability between them, a delight that Lindsay hadn't fully expected. The warmth of that quiet time together made the wonders of the night before all the more special. Afterward when he had gone she felt certain there would be other Sundays just as enjoyable and that she would spend them with Blake Prescott.

But there was another side to Blake that Lindsay had seen as well. On the picnic she saw him as a family man and father. The hours the three of them had spent together in the woods had been a happy time. Rusty was a delight and Lindsay had felt a fondness for him from the moment she had seen him in the Jeep. She had sensed a strong chemistry among the three of them. Her rapport with the child and Blake's love and attachment made a balance and harmony that pleased her. Seeing father and son together greatly increased the sympathies Lindsay already felt for the man.

The real world she had found at the office that morning seemed also to have changed over the weekend. The lawsuit looked less ominous given her greater sympathies and depth of feeling for Blake. She had gleaned a spirit of optimism, believing that Terry Moretti's duplicity would be exposed and the matter soon disposed of. Lindsay was cheered by Jean's news that Millicent had arranged for Terry to come in that afternoon to discuss the case. If Millicent saw through Terry too, as Lindsay expected, Blake's offer to settle for ten thousand dollars might look good to everyone.

With the lawsuit becoming more an annoyance than a millstone, Lindsay felt free to look to the future and the prospects of Blake Prescott playing a significant part in it. She was reliving the feeling of his arms around her when a voice surprised her at the door.

"Well, good morning, dear. You're certainly looking blissful for a Monday morning."

"Oh! Good morning, Millicent!" Lindsay snapped her vagrant mind into gear. "Guess this file inspired me into a daydream—really interesting stuff."

"I know the feeling. Have a nice weekend? You look a lot more relaxed than you did on Friday."

"Very nice. Got some rest...and exercise..." Lindsay blushed at the thought of her exhaustion in Blake Prescott's arms. "How about you, Millicent?"

"Kenneth enticed me to a very dull business cocktail party Saturday night, but we went to a very pleasant little concert of baroque chamber music Sunday afternoon."

"One for two's not bad."

"Maybe not for baseball players, or football players—whichever it is—but believe me, dear, spouses have to do better than that. Kenneth is always telling me seventy-five percent is the minimum degree of compatability for a successful marriage and that we consistently do eighty-five percent or better." Millicent smiled broadly. "I think he's right actually, even though I find the use of a formula a little clinical."

"You have a wonderful marriage, Millicent. I hope someday I'll find a man like Kenneth."

"He'd be awfully pleased to hear that. Of course once in a while he hears it from me...but not *too* often," she added with a mischievous smile. "Men are easily spoiled you know. Anyway, dear, we shouldn't discuss the poor creatures during working hours when more often than not they're the enemy. We've got our little flock of clients to worry about by day, our Miss Moretti being a case in point. I assume you'll be sitting in on our talk this afternoon?"

"Yes, I plan to."

Lindsay had thought about the meeting with Terry and had agonized over whether she dare bring up the matter of Russell Prescott and his death. She was leaning toward it but knew she'd have to alert Millicent first. She looked at her partner and, on an impulse, decided to raise the issue. "By the way, Millicent, I don't believe I mentioned this last week, but at my conference with Blake the subject of his brother came up. Apparently he had been a friend of Terry's too."

"Oh? What's the significance?"

"I'm not sure but it struck me as strange that Terry never mentioned it to me. If you don't mind, I thought I'd discuss it with her this afternoon."

"No, do as you think best."

"As a matter of fact, I was so curious I asked Max Bender to verify the facts."

"Max?"

"Yes, I hope you don't mind but he looked into it for me and did verify the information Blake gave me."

Millicent was silent and Lindsay could see that her initiative was being given critical evaluation. "What's your purpose in questioning Terry on the matter?"

"I'd like to feel comfortable that she's giving us a full and accurate account."

Millicent nodded but Lindsay knew she was troubled at some level. Undoubtedly Lindsay's motives were being questioned. She wondered if Millicent was about to challenge her regarding Blake and was relieved when she didn't, letting the matter drop.

"Well, if she does pass the test I think we'd better begin our campaign against Mr. Prescott. Applying pressure is what's called for. We certainly want to spring our trap before he gets away, don't we?"

Hearing her partner speak of hurting Blake that way left Lindsay heartsick. There was no way to ignore the terrible conflict that had been plaguing her. All she could do now was hope the unpleasantness would be over quickly.

AT FOUR O'CLOCK that afternoon Lindsay sat in Millicent Woodward's office next to Terry Moretti, listening to the young woman and watching her intently. For fifteen or twenty minutes Millicent had been questioning Terry on material that had been covered in Blake's deposition. She also talked in general terms about the possibilities of a settlement, telling Terry about their supposition that Blake was about to become a good deal wealthier than Terry had thought him to be.

Lindsay saw mild surprise on Terry's face but no particular elation at the news. She watched the singer intently, looking for signs of duplicity, clues that her story was fabricated, that it was the greedy, money-grabbing scheme Lindsay had come to believe it was. But, if Terry was a liar, it wasn't at all obvious. Terry said no more than she had to, but she answered Millicent's questions with no noticeable discomfort other than a vague uneasiness, particularly when they talked about the prospects of a settlement.

Millicent had suggested before the meeting that Lindsay question the young woman about Russell Prescott and also relate the news of Blake's offer of ten thousand dollars to settle. First, however, Millicent wanted a go at Terry.

Lindsay listened carefully to Terry's comments as Millicent was bringing her portion of the session to a close. Terry had crossed and uncrossed her legs several times, fiddled with a ring on her finger, but otherwise remained calm.

"Miss Bishop met with the defendant last week," Millicent was saying, "and will fill you in on developments there."

Terry turned to Lindsay with an expression that Lindsay thought was more wary than expectant. The attorney looked into the woman's eyes in search of signs, but found none. "Before we get into my meeting with Blake, there are some loose ends I'd like to clear up with you first, Terry."

The other waited.

"We've retained a private investigator to help us gather information that would be useful in the case, and..."

"What sort of information?"

For the first time Lindsay thought she detected a telltale sign of concern. Or was she just looking for it? "Information on Blake's finances, mostly," she replied. "But in the process he turned up some curious information that hadn't come up before. I'm not sure what bearing it has on the case, but the last thing we need is an embarrassing surprise later."

Terry waited. Lindsay felt her heart bump.

"Terry, the investigator told us that before you became involved with Blake you'd had some sort of relationship with his brother, Russell."

Terry's face went blank for an instant but she didn't flinch. "So?"

"Well, the information concerned us because it didn't come from you. If we're to represent you we'll have to know everything that might bear on the case, particularly if it's something the defendant might know about and use against us."

"Well, I didn't mention Russell because I didn't see how it mattered."

Lindsay smiled, trying to maintain her bedside manner and not betray the well of emotion inside of her. "That's what Millicent and I are paid to do, Terry, decide what's relevant and what's not."

"Okay, what do you want to know?"

"Tell us about Russell Prescott if you would please."

"I met Russ when I was in high school. He was ahead of me but we were friends. Actually, we were dating when I met Blake." She laughed, glancing at Millicent a little self-consciously. "It was like one of those things, you know...older man and all that."

"You mean you stopped seeing the young man and began a relationship with Mr. Prescott, the defendant?" Millicent asked.

Terry shook her head. "No, not exactly, Mrs. Woodward. Russ liked me a lot and Blake didn't want to hurt him so we saw each other secretly."

"So you were seeing both of them at the same time?" Lindsay asked.

"Well, in a way."

Lindsay chafed at Terry's vagueness. "Let me be a little more specific. Were you sleeping with both of them?"

Terry grimaced, obviously annoyed.

"What Miss Bishop is getting at," Millicent explained, "is that when you're deposed or on the witness stand in court, questions of this nature could come up. We should know your answer in advance if we're to do the proper job as your attorneys."

"Blake's Rusty's father, he's admitted it, so I don't see how it matters," Terry replied. "But I'll answer your question, I don't mind. Russ and I were just friends. I never slept with him. I had an affair with Blake but it was secret so that Russ wouldn't be hurt. I saw Russ all the time. Some people might have thought we were going together, but we weren't really. As a matter of fact, I was with Russ the day he died. A group of us went to the Anderson Reservoir and Russ drowned waterskiing.'' Terry bowed her head, rubbing her fingers together nervously.

"Were you pregnant at the time, Terry?" Lindsay asked.

"Yes, but Russ didn't know."

Lindsay bit her lip, wanting to scream at Terry Moretti, wanting to tell her what Blake had told her, wanting to confront her with the truth, but she knew she couldn't. She already had taken it to the point of breaching Blake's trust. Instead she looked at the singer whose head was still bowed. Lindsay felt antipathy for her, but there was also pity. Terry's day of reckoning would come soon enough.

Lindsay sighed. "Well, I'm sorry to bring up painful and unpleasant things, Terry, but Blake's lawyer would, so you may as well hear these things from us first."

"It's okay," Terry said softly. "I understand."

"Actually, I'm not sure when and if you'll have to face his lawyer. At the moment he doesn't have one. He fired Mr. Blum."

Terry looked up, her expression indicating she was perplexed, as though the significance wasn't clear to her.

"If this goes much further I imagine he'll get someone else to represent him," Lindsay went on to explain, "but for the moment he's representing himself. I did meet with him on Thursday, however, and he's made a counter-offer to our offer last week." Lindsay looked squarely into Terry's eyes, not knowing what to expect. "He's willing to give you ten thousand dollars to settle."

Terry looked shocked. "That's nothing."

"True, it's considerably less than the hundred thousand you've asked for."

Terry turned her head back and forth between Lindsay and Millicent. "I can get more than that, can't I?"

"Depending on what our investigation turns up," Millicent replied. "Mr. Prescott's estate may be worth several million dollars."

"So what would I get?"

"Conceivably half."

Lindsay's stomach clinched and she hated Millicent for a brief moment, wanting to scream out that Terry was a liar and wasn't entitled to a cent.

"Blake would never agree to that," Terry said shaking her head.

"Conceivably not," Millicent said. "Certainly not without being forced. And then of course, there's no guarantee we'd win a trial if we tried to force the issue."

"I don't want a trial," Terry insisted. "Can't we make him pay more than ten thousand without a trial?"

"I would certainly hope so," Millicent said. "This was only his first offer. Hopefully he'll reconsider and offer more."

"Why are you willing to settle for one hundred thousand, Terry?" Lindsay asked. "Why not insist on your full share?"

Terry groused. "I'm not trying to rape him, Miss Bishop. We weren't married and fair's fair. I didn't know he had millions, but that makes one hundred thousand even fairer to him, doesn't it?"

Millicent leaned forward, pulling the arm of her glasses from the corner of her mouth. "You mean you still will settle for one hundred thousand?"

Terry thought for a second. "Yes, if he'll give it to me."

Lindsay and Millicent exchanged looks.

"Listen, Miss Moretti," Millicent began, "we'll do as you wish, but I'd like to suggest you hold off until we've had a chance to pressure Mr. Prescott a little. He just may be willing to give you more than what you're asking. Will you give me a few days to find out?"

Terry twisted her mouth with uncertainty. "I don't know, Mrs. Woodward..."

"But surely a few days can't matter."

Lindsay saw an opening. "Terry, is there something you're afraid of?"

The singer looked at Lindsay and flipped her long blond hair off her shoulder. "Yes, as a matter of fact. I'm afraid of Blake."

"Afraid of what?" Millicent interjected.

"That he'll hurt me."

"Physically?"

Terry lowered her eyes. "Yes, he's violent."

"*Violent,*" Lindsay exclaimed.

"Well, he's threatened me."

Millicent rapped her knuckles on her desk to give emphasis to her thought. "*How* has Mr. Prescott threatened you?"

"When I saw him the first time after the suit was brought he really got angry and said all sorts of things. He has a bad temper. I thought he was going to hit me."

"Why didn't you tell me this before?" Lindsay asked.

"I don't know. I guess I thought it was the normal thing for a guy to do."

"That depends," Millicent said. "What sort of threats did he make?"

"Well, you know, that he'd hurt me. Whenever he gets mad he...sort of says things like that." Terry watched

Millicent Woodward lean back, the arm of her glasses in the corner of her mouth.

Lindsay felt the same sinking feeling she had felt at the dinner party at Millicent's house. She wondered whether this was more of Terry's lies.

"What difference does it make?" Terry asked.

"It certainly doesn't make him look good, and that sort of behavior could hang him if we go to trial. Besides, the more we've got on him now, the harder we can squeeze."

Millicent and Terry were looking at each other, both thinking. Lindsay was beginning to see that her life was moving again toward a precipice and she felt a sudden urge to get up and walk out. More than anything she would have liked to have Blake's arms around her just then. She needed his reassurance.

"WELL, WHAT DO YOU THINK?" Millicent asked after Terry had gone.

"What do *you* think?"

"That young woman may not make the best witness in the world, but she's tough and she's a good deal smarter than she looks. I think we might wring several hundred thousand out of Mr. Prescott, maybe more."

Lindsay winced inwardly. "It sounds like a hundred thousand is all she wants. I don't think she has the heart for a fight."

"I must confess her attitude toward the settlement perplexes me a bit, but it may just be a matter of conditioning. Some people feel guilt or fear and let that inhibit them even when they know they're entitled to compensation."

"Terry doesn't strike me as motivated by either."

"Perhaps not, but we'll see. That business about Prescott threatening her did surprise me though," Millicent said lifting her chin as she thought. "He didn't strike me as that sort of man."

"Maybe it was a lie."

Millicent looked at Lindsay, who could almost see the older woman's thoughts rolling through her mind. She was sure Millicent was wondering about her sympathies for Blake. A silent moment passed between them.

"Well, dear, let's wait and see what we hear from Max Bender, then shall we talk about this again?"

Lindsay was relieved that Millicent had decided to drop the matter without challenging her. A few minutes later she left, feeling guilty about her role in the affair and somewhat of a traitor.

For the next hour or so Lindsay sat in her office thinking about Blake and Terry and Millicent. She could almost hear Millicent's thinking through the walls, but she knew it was silly. It was her own guilt she heard.

For a time Lindsay considered the notion of walking into Millicent's office and confessing everything, of telling all, but her pride and her unwillingness to admit weakness held her back. Besides, the truth would soon come out—though maybe not as quickly as she had hoped—and her sympathies for Blake would be vindicated. Was that really all? Lindsay wondered if she harbored any doubts about Blake, whether she was holding back out of fear of being made the fool.

She asked herself if Terry could possibly be telling the truth and if Blake could be the liar. Lindsay searched her mind and her heart. She pictured Blake sitting in the conference room telling her that he was not really Rusty's father. She pictured Terry admitting a relationship with Russell, but insisting she had a secret affair with

Blake. Was Terry's story possible? Lindsay had to admit it was. She also knew that Terry had a reason to lie. Her case against Blake would lose its emotional sting if the truth about Russell were known. Blake would become a more sympathetic figure, just as he had become for Lindsay.

But what about Blake? What motive could he have to lie? It wasn't the money—she knew that—because he refused to bring the story out into the open. If he had lied, he did so to influence her. On the one hand it struck her as flattering that he might care enough to fabricate a story about Russell and Terry. On the other, it would still be a lie. The Bill Price episode continued to trouble Lindsay at some deep emotional level. She had mostly forgiven Blake the earlier incident, but it continued to haunt her, and the possibility of further lies was more than she could bear.

By quarter to six Lindsay and Jean were the only two people left in the office. Everyone else had left for the day. Lindsay was clearing off her desk, exhausted by the emotional ups and downs of the afternoon, when Jean came to her door.

"Lindsay, Max Bender is on line two. He asked for Millicent, but when I told him she had left for the day he asked for you."

Lindsay looked at Jean quizzically then reached for the phone. "Lindsay Bishop," she said into the receiver.

"Miss Bishop, this is Max Bender," he said in his measured tone. "I was wondering if you and Mrs. Woodward would have a few minutes to meet with me in the morning."

"Well, yes, I think so. I'll be in and I believe Millicent will as well.... Is there something wrong?"

"Not exactly. I've turned up something that I think you ought to know about."

Lindsay felt a sudden clutch of panic. "Is it a problem concerning the case?"

"Yes, but I'd rather not discuss it over the phone. I'd prefer to tell you about it in person."

"I see. When do you want to come in?"

"Is first thing all right? Say eight-thirty?"

Lindsay glanced at the calendar lying open on her desk. "Yes, that's fine with me. Let me just check Millicent's calendar. How long will we need?"

"Oh, not long. Fifteen or twenty minutes should be plenty."

"Okay. I'll check." Lindsay pushed the hold button. "Jean!" she called through her open door.

"Yes?"

"Would you see if Millicent has half an hour on her calendar tomorrow beginning at eight-thirty?" While she waited Lindsay became worried and perplexed. Could this have anything to do with her and Blake? She shuddered at the thought. Surely if it did, Max wouldn't be including her, he would go straight to Millicent. On the other hand, maybe he only had a suspicion and was trying to flush her out. Lindsay chastised herself for her own paranoia. There was no reason for him to suspect. Besides, he was investigating the past, not the present.

"She's clear at eight-thirty, Lindsay. Nothing till ten," Jean called from the other room.

"Okay. Would you call her at home and tell her that we have a brief meeting with Max Bender at eight-thirty tomorrow morning?"

"Sure."

Lindsay pushed the blinking light. "Mr. Bender?"

"Yes."

"Millicent's free. We've confirmed the meeting for eight-thirty here at our offices."

"Good. See you then."

Lindsay hung up the phone and wondered whether fate had still another rude awakening in store for her.

THE HOUSE WAS DARK AND QUIET when she arrived home. Nothing in her cupboard inspired her, and Lindsay regretted her decision to pass the supermarket after leaving the office. The freezer contained only some vegetables and one frozen lasagna, which seemed too heavy for her tentative appetite. She finally settled on tuna fish.

Lindsay put some water on for tea and looked in the vegetable crisper for something to eat with the tuna. There was a small overripe tomato, which she sliced up, throwing away the softest portions. Taking some unsalted crackers from a box in the cupboard she prepared her salad plate and poured some boiling water over a tea bag in a mug. She placed a paper napkin, a knife and fork on the counter and pulled up a bar stool to eat her meal.

Acutely aware of her loneliness, she glanced at the spot where Blake had stood Saturday night. There was no mark, no sign of him, nothing left except her memories to remind her of that night. A deathly stillness seemed to pervade the house. The clock in the living room ticked somberly and the entire place had an eeriness about it.

Putting down her fork, Lindsay went to the living room, turned on a light and the stereo, but the improvement was only marginal. The floor in front of the fireplace seemed strangely indifferent to the momentous event that had transpired there. Feeling a clutch of fear that the memory of Blake making love to her that night might be the only such memory of him she'd ever have,

Lindsay quickly retreated to the kitchen and her lonely meal.

When she finished eating it was seven-fifteen. Blake had said he had a late meeting but that he would try to call her when he got home. She wondered if he were there yet. It would be nice to hear his voice because his cheerful optimism made things seem better. Over the weekend he had dispelled her worst fears and she needed his assurance again. She considered phoning him, but told herself to be patient and wait for his call.

Lindsay began puttering around, trying to occupy herself, but nothing seemed to work for more than a few minutes. She glanced through a fashion magazine on her coffee table but wasn't distracted for long. Blake kept returning to haunt her. She saw herself with him by the fire, at breakfast, in the woods. Her mind was unrelenting in its obsession.

When she began pacing the floor she decided that it wouldn't hurt to try to reach Blake. Just making an effort to contact him would relieve her tension, she thought as she went to the phone and dialed his number. It rang and she waited. Finally a woman answered. By the trace of an accent in her speech, Lindsay decided it must be Elena, the housekeeper.

"Is Mr. Prescott there?"

"No, he is working still."

"You don't know when he'll be home?"

"Only that it is late."

"I see."

"Is there a message you wish to give?"

"Yes, please. Could you tell him that Lindsay Bishop called?"

"Yes, miss."

Lindsay hung up feeling a little better for having made the effort. She decided to retire to the comfort of her bedroom. After double-checking the locks and turning off the lights, she went upstairs, undressed, then put on a nightgown and a cozy old bathrobe.

In her sewing box on the night stand next to her bed Lindsay found some needlepoint that had gone untouched for months. She picked it up, examined the piece and decided that doing constructive but mindless work would calm her ruffled nerves. Propping up some pillows, she climbed into bed and began work.

Lindsay had lost track of time when the phone beside her bed rang. She looked at her watch; almost ten o'clock. She grabbed the receiver.

"Lindsay, this is Blake. Elena said you called. Are you all right?"

"Yes. I just wanted to hear your voice."

He chuckled. "I'm sorry I'm late in calling. I just got home. How was your day?"

"Okay, I guess."

"Anything wrong?"

"No, not really. I guess I just miss you." Lindsay felt a little embarrassed at her own faintheartedness. She also knew she couldn't tell him about her conversation with Terry. "How was your meeting?"

"Tiring, but productive. Unfortunately I've got an executive committee meeting first thing in the morning—no rest for the weary."

"Poor thing. I should let you go. Did you get to eat?"

"Yes, we had some sandwiches brought in."

"Sounds exciting," she said dryly.

"It was just fuel. Our minds were on the meeting."

"I hate eating like that."

"I don't like it either." He paused. "I miss you, Lindsay."

Her heart raced. "I'm glad." She wondered if he were as truly happy as she.

"What are you wearing?" Blake asked.

"A bathrobe. Why?"

"Is that all?"

She wondered what he was up to. "No, I've got a nightgown on too. Why do you ask?"

"I just thought if it sounded irresistible I'd do something foolish and irresponsible like drive over there."

"Well, I'm pretty ordinary tonight, not irresistible. Anyway, you've got an early meeting and so do I." She thought of Max Bender and shuddered.

"I don't think you could be ordinary if you tried," he said softly.

The calm resonance of his voice raised goose bumps all over her arms. "I would like to see you," she admitted, "but we've got to be practical."

"Whatever happened to romance?" Blake chided. "Modern women are much too practical!"

Lindsay had to chuckle to herself. If he only knew what he had done to her life. "Experience," she retorted.

"Well, far be it from me to complain. When can I see you?"

Lindsay suddenly felt brash. "I didn't bring my calendar home with me, Blake."

"Let's make it tomorrow. Shall I pick you up at work?"

"God no! I'm not even supposed to be seeing you. We're in the work week now. I'm no longer the girl up the street, I'm the lawyer, the one suing you, remember?"

"As far as I'm concerned you're a lovely creature in some tempting nightgown that would drive me crazy if I could see you."

"It's flannel and buttons to my neck."

"Perfect. I'll be right over."

"Blake!"

"Okay. I'll meet you at Henry's on University Avenue after work. How about six?"

Lindsay hesitated, but she knew there was no way she could say no. "All right. Henry's at six."

CHAPTER SEVENTEEN

By MORNING the weather had turned blustery and cold. The brief Indian summer had ended and the wind came roaring out of the south—the direction of most foul weather. Drops of rain splattered the windshield as Lindsay drove to work.

Max Bender was sitting in the reception area when Lindsay arrived at the office. His face and speech told her nothing of what his message might be. There were no clues as to what he thought of her, whether he knew of her complicity with Blake Prescott. As Lindsay sat down with Millicent and the private investigator she felt like a traitor. She was holding on to her self-respect by her fingertips, hoping that soon the truth would bail her out.

"Well, Max," Millicent said in a businesslike tone, "what have you got that brings you out on such a foul day?"

"You indicated last week that timeliness was critical to your strategy," Max began soberly, "so I felt I ought to give you an interim report." He looked at Lindsay. "First, as regards *your* interests, Miss Bishop...

"Terry Moretti's aunt, we've discovered, died about three years ago. We did confirm that Terry was living with her at the time of the accident, but I'm afraid nothing more. I'm sorry."

Lindsay was disappointed, knowing the woman wouldn't be able to help establish the truth, but she was also relieved that Max showed no signs of knowing about her relationship with Blake.

Turning to Millicent he continued. "I've learned, Mrs. Woodward, that Mr. Prescott's company, Converse Corporation, is on the verge of a major announcement."

"What sort of announcement?" Millicent asked with interest.

"The company has developed a new product with unique applications for the space program. Apparently major government contracts involving tens of millions of dollars are just over the horizon."

"My God!" Millicent exclaimed sinking back into her chair. "If I'm not mistaken, the value of Converse Corporation will explode overnight. Defense or space contracts are like gold. They firmly establish the value of a company, a fact that appeals to investors." She turned to Max. "Are you sure of this?"

"My source is very reliable."

Lindsay felt bewildered. "What source? Who would tell you a thing like that?"

Max shook his head. "I'm sorry, Miss, I can't reveal the source, but I will tell you the person is in a position to know. This is direct information."

Millicent was beaming. "This is marvelous news. Just marvelous news!"

Lindsay was looking at her partner quizzically.

"Leverage," Millicent pronounced. "More leverage. Mr. Prescott won't want this lawsuit hanging around his neck when an opportunity to sell comes along. They say the best time to sell is on the heels of a big announcement or development of this sort. I'll wager he'll want to buy us off. And we need not go cheaply either."

Lindsay felt sick. First she felt badly for Blake. He was—as Kenneth had said—being blackmailed. Also, he had been betrayed—probably by someone in a position of trust. Secondly, she felt badly for herself. The news Max had relayed was something Blake obviously had known for a long time but had kept from her. One could hardly expect a defendant to tell the plaintiff's attorney damning information of that sort, but then he had confided the truth of Rusty's paternity. Why not this?

The revelation she had just heard left Lindsay with a strange feeling. She realized how much still stood between herself and Blake Prescott. And, it was not as if the holding back was his doing alone. She had slept with the man but she hadn't told him of Millicent's plans to squeeze him dry. The realization made it clear that they really had no business being together at all. Feeling dreadful, Lindsay was glad when the meeting was over and she could be alone in her misery.

Later that morning Lindsay was forcing herself through the motions of her work when a call came in from Kenneth Woodward.

"Tell me, young lady," he said in his gravelly voice, "do you have time for a hypothetical lunch with a tired old businessman?"

Lindsay laughed. "Hypothetically, yes."

"Would you mind waiting for me on the corner so I don't have to come into the office?"

"Dear me, Kenneth, if we're seen people will think you're having an affair with your wife's partner."

"I don't want to have to explain to Millicent why I'm taking you and not both of you...and I don't think you want to explain to her either."

"Well..."

"On the corner at twelve then?"

THE ANCIENT SILVER-GRAY BENTLEY turned off University Avenue onto the side street and stopped at the curb in front of Lindsay, who was standing under her umbrella in a light rain. She got in.

"The least you could have done was come in a plain dark sedan," she teased.

Kenneth chuckled. "To hell with them, let their tongues wag."

Fifteen minutes later they were being seated in Kenneth's favorite restaurant, Dal Baffo's in Menlo Park.

The waiter, dressed in formal attire, handed each of them a menu. "Would you care for a cocktail this afternoon, sir?"

Kenneth glanced at his companion. "Lindsay?"

"Will I need one?"

He looked at the waiter. "Two vodka martinis."

Lindsay groaned.

When they each had had their first sip of their drinks, Kenneth leaned across the table. "Tell me, my dear, what are we going to have to do to turn that woman off?"

"Millicent?"

"Yes."

"You mean turn her off Blake Prescott?" she asked.

"Precisely."

"Good Lord, I feel like Judas Iscariot." Lindsay looked at Kenneth Woodward's candid blue eyes and wished she could tell him how she was already up to her ears in duplicity and double-dealing. The last thing she needed was to break further trusts with unauthorized disclosures to him.

"I just need advice, Lindsay."

"But I'm in a rather delicate situation, Kenneth. I can't disclose to you what Millicent is doing. If she wouldn't tell you, how can I?"

"I'm not asking for you to tell me any privileged information. I just need to know what it would take to end this business with Prescott. I'm not at liberty to discuss just why, but time now is of the essence."

Lindsay thought of the meeting that morning with Max Bender and shuddered. "It would take a settlement agreement between the plaintiff and the defendant."

"Is that likely?"

Lindsay thought, choosing her words carefully. "They've each made offers to the other, but Terry wants ten times what Blake offered. Millicent wants even more."

Kenneth grinned. "Doesn't surprise me in the least." He studied Lindsay's face. "Could you be more specific? How much money are we talking about?"

"What I've already told you could cost me my license—or at least a reprimand."

"I see." He reflected. "What would it take to get her to quit the case?"

"Probably a full explanation from you."

Kenneth rolled his eyes. "I value my hide more than that."

Lindsay was sipping her cocktail though she didn't normally drink martinis. "I wish this suit was settled myself."

Kenneth sighed. "Far be it from me to give advice, Lindsay, but you've been helpful to me and I owe you a little warning." He lowered his voice. "Millicent is worried that you have let Prescott mar your judgment."

She watched him drink his martini. "It doesn't surprise me. Millicent's no fool. I should probably have a talk with her."

"Well, you'll have to keep your own counsel, but it might be worth holding off a while to see how this thing evolves first."

Lindsay wasn't sure exactly what Kenneth was getting at, but there was an authoritative tone to his voice. "Thank you," she said.

The waiter returned. "Would you care for the wine list before you order, sir?"

"Not necessary," Kenneth replied. "I know it by heart."

IT HAD RAINED off and on all afternoon. Lindsay watched it from her window until five forty-five when she took her trench coat and umbrella and left the office. She decided to walk the few blocks up to the business district where Henry's was located. Darkness was falling and the streets were jammed with traffic. Lindsay, walking under the protection of her umbrella, managed to keep pace with the slow-moving line of cars stretched bumper to bumper up the street. She wondered if the rain and rush hour traffic would make Blake late.

Lindsay shivered a little against the cold and damp of the evening as she walked, but the freshness of the air was a pleasant contrast to the closed atmosphere of the office. The numbness she had felt during the long afternoon disappeared in the crisp air of the outdoors. She was eager at the prospect of seeing Blake.

After meeting with Max and talking to Kenneth, Lindsay realized that the relationship evolving with Blake was impossible to maintain. She had decided to tell him so, but her need to see him and be with him was great. All that mattered was the comforting presence that she now associated with him. Blake was both her salvation and her damnation.

When she arrived at the door of Henry's Lindsay saw that the lively after-work crowd had already gathered. Walking through the doorway she was enveloped by the happy revelers, many with drinks in hand.

Lindsay made her way to the long mahogany bar with its fat, brass foot rail to a spot where she might look for Blake in the crowd. The patrons were mostly younger businessmen and a smattering of women. Some were playing liar's dice to determine who would pay for drinks and others were into socializing and singles' encounters.

Blake saw Lindsay before she saw him. In her trench coat, the image she presented was similar to the woman he had first seen the night of the lecture. She was not soaked as she had been that night in the storm, but he saw the same violet eyes, the same full lip as the woman who had instantly captivated him. Then she had been a stranger, now she was comfortable in his arms. Blake waved his hand and tried to call her name over the din.

Out of the corner of her eye Lindsay saw a beefy man with a mustache starting to sidle up to her when she heard her name being called. Looking into the crowd she saw the auburn hair and the handsome even features of Blake Prescott.

He was waving his hand. "Lindsay, over here."

Squeezing past the interloper who had not yet managed to get out his first words, Lindsay made her way toward Blake.

"You look beautiful," he said taking her hands and kissing her on the cheek.

She looked up at him happily, feeling the warmth of his large strong hands as he kneaded her slender fingers in his palms.

"Your fingers are like icicles," he said. "Let me get you a drink to warm you up."

Lindsay smiled gratefully, enjoying his touch, enjoying the luxuriant warmth of his eyes that bathed her with affection.

"What would you like?" he asked as he slipped his arm around her shoulder and stepped with her toward the bar.

"Sherry would be nice."

Blake called to the bartender over the heads of customers sitting in front of them. "Harvey's Bristol Cream, straight up and a vodka tonic with a twist."

It was too noisy to talk easily so while they waited for their drinks Blake helped Lindsay out of her trench coat. "Let's try to find a table in the back where it's quieter," he said into her ear.

Blake took the drinks from the bartender, paid him, then led the way toward the back room where a hostess greeted them.

"Will you be dining this evening?" she asked.

Blake turned to Lindsay. "Would you like to have dinner?"

She had been thinking in terms of a frank conversation over a drink before heading for home, but she would have to eat eventually so she reluctantly nodded her acceptance. They followed the woman to a quiet corner table.

"I want you to know I'm playing hooky tonight to see you," he said smiling.

"Why's that?"

"Passed up a Cub Scout meeting."

"Oh," Lindsay said frowning her disapproval. "Was it something Rusty was counting on?"

"No, this wasn't a pack meeting involving the boys. It was a parent meeting, so he's not even aware of my dalliance."

"We could have met tomorrow," she said.

"No, I'm glad for the excuse. I'm afraid I don't do well at that sort of gathering."

"Why's that?"

"Impatience, I suppose." He sipped his drink. "Let me put it this way. I joined the P.T.A. and at my first meeting they spent an hour debating some silly budget item of several hundred dollars. I got so impatient I finally stood up and asked if they would accept my check for the difference and move on to the next item on the agenda."

Lindsay laughed. "Blake, that wasn't very nice."

"No, it wasn't. The chairwoman was miffed. I tried to make amends by making a donation, which they accepted." Blake's teeth gleamed as he grinned at Lindsay. "It was my last P.T.A. meeting."

"I can see why."

"Well, I suppose I'm not cut out for the community aspect of parenting." He looked at Lindsay with suddenly serious eyes. "Are you?"

The question took her by surprise. "I've never had occasion..."

"Well, maybe I'll have you go for me." He saw the surprise on Lindsay's face. "Put you on retainer or something," he quickly added.

Her eyes dropped and Blake reached over and covered her hand.

"You're so lovely tonight."

She returned his gaze shyly as his eyes drifted over the chocolate-brown raw silk dress she wore. The shirtwaist, though conservative, was a departure from the usual business suit, but she had wanted to affect a slightly more feminine look for him when she had dressed that morning.

"I like your outfit."

"Thank you."

Blake squeezed her hand. "You seem a little somber. Is there something wrong?"

The words struck her as cruelly ironic, though she knew Blake didn't mean it that way. *Is there something wrong?* Where could she begin to explain the utter frustration she felt? Terry's credible performance? Millicent's trap? Kenneth's intrigue? Her careening toward disaster? Her need for Blake? The utter danger he represented?

She didn't want to say the words but she knew it was inevitable. Her eyes fell from his, she couldn't look at him when she said it. "We can't see each other anymore, Blake. Not until this is over."

"But why? What's happened?"

Her lips were pressed together in anguish. She shook her head. "Don't you see? I can't even tell you why. Anything I would say would be a breach of my client's trust."

"Well, why don't you quit the case? Let Millicent Woodward handle it."

"That wouldn't help. I'm already in the middle of it. Besides, even if I did withdraw, my firm would be involved. I couldn't go running around publicly with someone the firm was suing."

Blake's face twisted with annoyance. "What's different now from this weekend?"

"I shouldn't have been with you then."

"But you *were*!"

Lindsay looked at him with pleading eyes. "I talked with Terry yesterday."

"You didn't tell her that I told you about Russell?"

"No, of course not. I kept my word. But I did ask her about Russell, using an excuse that his name had turned up in an investigation."

"And?"

"Blake, she should have been an actress not a singer. She hardly blinked. She did so well I didn't know myself whether to believe her or not."

His expression grew hard. "But you don't believe her."

"No, I don't. That's not what I meant."

Blake sighed deeply, rubbing his forehead with his hand. "Nothing's easy, is it?"

"No. I don't see any way out unless you let the truth come out about Rusty."

"It's out of the question, Lindsay. I don't want him to know, at least until he's older, much older. I don't want him feeling like an orphan and that what he gets from me is charity."

"Surely he'd love you just the same, no matter what."

"I can't do it to him. No amount of money is worth that."

"Terry *is* willing to settle," Lindsay replied.

"Yeah, for a hundred thousand dollars."

"Considering the value of your company, that's not so much, Blake."

"What do you mean?"

"Well…I mean…isn't…" Lindsay was suddenly flustered.

Blake was looking at her, his face black. "What do you know?"

She dropped her head. She had been talking out of school and let slip the fact that she knew more than he realized. It had been a terrible blunder. She felt foolish, trapped. She couldn't look at him.

"Lindsay, I want to know what you were referring to."

She sat mute. Her hands were in her lap, her head was bowed. She shook her head without looking up. "I can't," she half whispered.

"You know, then, about our new product and the government contracts."

She didn't move. By her refusal to react she knew she was giving him the answer he wanted, but it was too late now, it was too late. Finally she found the courage to look up at him. Blake sat stunned, frozen in thought. "Don't you see, Blake? This has been the problem, there's no way for me to avoid a conflict of interest." Her voice became plaintive, pleading. "It's torture for me to sit and watch them do this to you. It kills me!" Tears glossed over her eyes.

He still looked away, deep in thought.

"Blake, don't you understand? I...I care for you and this business is killing me!"

He turned toward Lindsay, a smile touching his lips. He opened his palm to her on the table and she put her hand into it. Blake pulled her fingers to his mouth and kissed them softly. Excitement, fear, anguish cavorted through her body.

He held her hand, pressing it between his large fingers, but his thoughts had captured his attention. He was staring into space even as he caressed her hand. His eyes engaged her. "Exactly what do they know, Lindsay?"

She looked at him with pleading eyes. "Don't you see? I can't tell you. That's the problem. I want desperately to tell you, but I can't."

LINDSAY REMOVED HER WET SHOES and spread out her trench coat on a kitchen stool. The anguish of their parting when Blake had dropped her back at her car was still gnawing at her. Sending him away had been the hardest thing she'd ever done. She felt totally bereft, ready to take to her bed.

She was at the foot of the stairs when the doorbell rang. Lindsay peered through the peephole. It was Blake. Shocked to see him, she opened the door.

"Sorry to bother you, ma'am," he said, "but I have a couple of flat tires and thought perhaps I could borrow your shower."

Lindsay's brow was furrowed in both anguish and amusement. "Oh, Blake." She stepped back, permitting him to enter.

She watched as he removed his coat. His hair was wet and she was reminded of the night he had rescued her in the storm. They stood in the entry looking at each other, she in stocking feet, diminutive, he erect and tall. Her face was that of a wounded doe. "What now Blake?"

"That, my darling, is the easy part." With that he bent down and swept her into his arms. She looked at him tentatively. His head dipped toward her and he kissed her tenderly on the mouth.

"You know," he said, "if it weren't for that lip of yours I probably could have resisted you." He kissed the fullness of it and then his own wide mouth stretched into a smile. "But, I couldn't just go home knowing it was here alone."

Lindsay's arms were around his neck and she pressed her face against him. "Oh, Blake," she whispered, "I don't know what to do."

He didn't respond, but went with her in his arms to the stairs. He started climbing, climbing as though she were no more of a burden than a newborn calf or a lamb. Suspended in the cradle of his arms she felt lighter than her weight, a waif, a child being snatched away, carried to some forbidden experience of his choosing.

The hall was lit by a single fixture but the bedroom was dark. The faint light from a lamppost in the street was coming in the window. Blake, still holding her, pushed the door closed with his foot and deposited Lindsay gently on the bed.

A moment later he had lit the candle on the bedstand and slipped off his jacket, tossing it on a chair. He removed the tie already loosened at his neck as she watched, transfixed. Then he sat next to her on the edge of the bed, stroking the raven strands of her hair, running his thumb over the softness of her cheek. "Will you put that nightgown on, Lindsay? The one that buttons to the neck?"

Her eyes widened, but she nodded and crept from the bed to her dresser, then retreated into the bath.

When she returned to the bedroom several minutes later Blake was in bed with a couple of pillows propped behind his head. His chest was bare and the sheet covered him to the waist. He watched her walk to the side of the bed where she stood looking at him through darkly beautiful eyes.

He extended his hand and she took his fingers, letting the energy flow between them by the simple touch. Blake let his eyes sweep over her, over the swell of her breasts under the flannel. The three tiny white buttons at the top of her gown were fastened so that she was totally covered to her neck. The suggestion of her body under the modest garment aroused him more that if she wore a filmy negligee.

They were frozen in that position for several moments, the tips of their fingers touching, their eyes engaged in a dance of entreaty and veneration. The candlelight played on their faces, hers framed by the glossy ebony of her hair and his by tousled burnt sienna.

Behind her the rain drummed against the windowpane, a cacophonous sound without rhythm or melody. Their desire filled the air.

"Come," he whispered, inviting her by a gentle tug with his fingertips.

She climbed onto the bed, her hair swinging and grazing her flanneled shoulders. Blake's fingers encircled one wrist just below the lace cuff of her sleeve and he pulled her over near his side. She knelt there, sitting on her feet, the hyacinth of her eyes gleaming in the flickering light as she watched and waited.

He twisted the corner of his mouth up in amusement at the passive wonder on her face. Her spirit was subdued and quiescent. She waited, observing him as he pulled her fingers to his lips. Touching the tip of each finger lightly with his tongue, Blake watched her mouth drop slightly open, teased by the sensation. Without taking his eyes off her he took each finger in turn between his lips, sucking it as he would her nipples, lightly, sensuously, until they tingled in the liquid air.

Lindsay felt a cavalcade of waves ripple from her womb to the periphery of her body. The skin of her back and buttocks began to tingle and her breathing nearly stopped. Her stomach tightened and her breasts arched under her gown. The sensations drove her to want to touch him so she leaned over and put her hand flat against the warmth of his chest. Lindsay drew her hand slowly downward so that his silky hairs tickled her palm and made her want to seize his meaty flesh and knead it like dough. Sinking her fingers into him, she found only the surface soft. Under it the taut fiber of his muscles lay like subterranean rock.

She heard a little sigh of pleasure emit from his lips and enjoying the response her touch evoked, she put her hand

at the top of his chest and drew it slowly down once
again. This time though, when her hand reached the sheet
lying discreetly at his waist, she let her fingers slip under
it and tease the thick tangle of hair below his navel. Again
he made a sound, more plaintive and beseeching, a moan
of pleasure.

For a moment her hand lay flat on his abdomen.
Blake's eyes were hungry as they waited, watching. He
craved her touch, she could see it. Letting her hand slide
farther down she came to his intimate place. A sound
coming from his throat urged her on and her fingers
inched ahead until they met the solid root of his
masculinity.

Lindsay's own heart surged and leapt at the encounter, inevitable but unexpected. He waited. Knowing his
desire, she let her fingers trail up the length of him, now
erect and hard with anticipation. Her small slender hand
seemed inadequate to the challenge, but she wrapped her
fingers around him and stroked him gently till the throb
beneath her touch was as eager as her own desire.

Blake's eyes were closed; he was lost in his pleasure.
The sheet still shielded him from her curious gaze but her
hand told her of his wonders. Soon the magic of her
touch, its results and implications, frightened Lindsay
and she withdrew her hand, dragging it back along the
route of entry.

He smiled in gratitude then reached over and took the
hem of her gown bunched at her knees and tugged at it,
beckoning her closer. Obedient to his request she scooted
nearer.

"Sit on me," he commanded softly.

After a moment's hesitation she lifted one leg across
his hips, which were still covered with the sheet, until she

sat upon him. The full swell of his masculinity was soon apparent to her through the thin fabric between them.

Now his hands were under the hem of her gown, touching her knees and moving slowly and in tandem up each of her thighs toward her hips. The progress of his movement was slow and excruciatingly delightful. Lindsay looked down at the billowing fabric of her gown, covering his arms to his shoulders. She shuddered with pleasure.

Blake's hidden hands had gained the rounded curve of her hips which were, like the rest of her, naked under the flannel. He squeezed the fullness of them in his large strong hands as though he were claiming the forbidden territory as his own.

After a moment his hands rounded the small of her waist so that between them he nearly encircled her. He gripped her thus as if to take possession. Then his hands loosened their grip and slid up her torso until they found the curve of her breasts. She moaned when he seized them, a plunder unseen by either of them, but acutely felt by both.

"Oh Blake, oh Blake," she whispered as her nipples hardened under his touch, aroused by unseen hands, stroked to pulsing erection.

Lindsay's head fell back so that he could only see the vulnerable curve of her creamy throat. Her arms hung loosely at her sides—she had submitted her body to the invisible hands that foraged beneath her gown.

Finally Blake pulled her face down to his so he could kiss her mouth. Lindsay felt the sheet under her being pulled free so that she was seated astride him without protection, and she felt his desire immediately. Her nightgown was still draped over them, secreting the intimate encounter, acutely felt but still unseen.

Blake's hands were on her hips and she felt his powerful grip as he virtually lifted her over his erect and prodigious offering. Lindsay felt its swollen pulsing warmth
at the port of her being. Slowly, his strong arms eased her
down so that he filled her to the very depth of her core.

"Oh God," she moaned, her face lifted toward the
ceiling, only her throat visible to his hunger-crazed eyes.

Taking her by the torso Blake lifted her up his shaft
then let her ease back down so that the sensation of penetration could be relived. With Lindsay moaning in ecstasy he repeated the dance then, again and again, until
her body found the rhythm and moved around the exquisite point of union without Blake's help. As her un-
dulations built in fervor, sensation raced about her body
and she felt the pinnacle of her excitement rapidly
approaching.

Blake's own excitement too had reached a fever point
and a warning of explosion gurgled from his throat.
Then, just when Lindsay knew it was coming, Blake
pulled her down, wrapped his arms around her and rolled
on top of her so that his body might take command of the
fevered pace. With great heaving sweeps of his pelvis he
sent her to the peak of her excitement and then with one
great surge he exploded into her, sending her soaring
from the pinnacle into the timeless sensation of
cataclysm.

Long after he was spent Lindsay was still struggling for
breath, her heart still hammering in her chest, and waves
of sensation still rippling across the landscape of her
body. Although her fulfillment was complete, she was
still excited by his weak but adoring kisses. When his lips
traced across her cheek to the shell of her ear she heard
the soft rumble of his voice as he whispered, "I love
you."

CHAPTER EIGHTEEN

HER RAVEN HAIR was loosely twisted at the back of her head and pinned into place. Her toes protruded from the foamy water at the other end of the tub. She stared dreamily at them, seeing instead Blake Prescott's face as it had been the night before on her pillow. The pleasure she had seen on his candlelit features gave her pleasure, both then and now. The softly whispered endearment, "I love you," still rang in her ears.

"Lindsay!" she heard him calling. "When can I start breakfast?"

His voice was drawing near, climbing the stairs to the bedroom. A moment later he was at the bathroom door, which she had left open. He peered in.

"Mmmm, maybe we should forget breakfast and I'll have a bath myself."

"But I'm hungry and you promised me more of your scrambled eggs."

"Why not both?"

She wrinkled her face with disappointment. "We don't have time. I'm due at the office in less than an hour."

"Well, I found a newspaper on your doorstep," he said holding it up. "Mind if I sit and read while you soak?"

"No. I thought I'd give myself five more minutes."

Blake smiled at her, noting the bubbles that covered all but her face and toes. "There's something about that body of yours, when I know it's there but it's hidden from me. It really turns me on."

Lindsay chuckled. "Yes, last night I got that impression."

"How do you feel?"

"A little sore," she admitted, "but otherwise wonderful."

"Did I hurt you?" His voice showed concern.

"Let's just say I'm out of practice."

Blake grinned mischievously. "Music to a man's ears."

"Not to mention his ego."

"Yes," he agreed. "That too."

Lindsay closed her eyes and Blake unfolded his paper, each of them content and happy to be together. While he read, using the only seat in the room, she relaxed her muscles, savoring the mellow glow that remained from their lovemaking the night before.

She opened her eyes from time to time to look at him. She had become very fond of that face and those emerald eyes that had mesmerized her from the moment she had first seen him.

Suddenly a frown crossed Blake's face. His mouth dropped open. "My God," he said.

Lindsay lifted her head. "What's the matter?"

"It's Terry," he said. "Somebody tried to kill her."

"Kill her?"

"Well, shoot at her anyway." He was reading.

"What does it say?"

"Let me read it to you.

Singer Assaulted. A San Jose area entertainer was shot at early this morning by an unknown assailant, according to San Jose Police.

Terry Moretti, 28, of Saratoga reported that several shots were fired at her from a vehicle in the parking lot of the Capri Club in San Jose at about 1:30 A.M.

Moretti, whose professional name is Terry Moore, reported that she was returning to her car after a singing engagement when the assailant opened fire from the window of his vehicle, then sped away.

Moretti, who was alone at the time, was uninjured in the incident but was unable to positively identify her assailant. There were no witnesses to the assault, but police report that several patrons of the supper club heard shots as they were leaving and went to investigate. Police were called and the incident is under investigation.

According to police there are no suspects, but Moretti's estranged lover is wanted for questioning. The vehicle driven by the assailant, a late model black Porsche Carrera, matches the description of a vehicle owned by the man sought by police.

A spokesperson declined to identify the man sought but indicated that he is suspected of having threatened Moretti and is presently the defendant in a civil suit brought by the singer. No other details of the incident are available and Moretti is reported to be in seclusion.

Blake looked at Lindsay who was sitting up in the tub, dumbfounded. "Blake, they think *you* did it!"

He looked back at the paper in his hands. "Yeah, I don't suppose there are too many other guys who fit the description."

"How could Terry say a thing like that? It couldn't be an honest mistake. She had to tell the police it was you."

"Yes. Undoubtedly." He looked up at Lindsay and smiled. His eyes drifted down to her bare breasts and Lindsay instinctively folded her arms over them. "At least *you* can't doubt my innocence."

Lindsay's mouth dropped as a thought struck her. "Do you realize that I'm your alibi?"

He looked at her and a pained expression gradually crept across his face. "Damn," he muttered angrily.

She watched him, feeling as though her life—or at least her career—was passing before her eyes. "We don't have any choice," she said. "You have to tell them you spent the night with me."

"Don't be ridiculous, Lindsay. That would ruin you."

"Yes, but the police are talking assault. That's nothing to sneeze at. We'll go down together. I'll tell them the truth."

"No!" he said forcefully. "I appreciate the gesture but I won't have some ridiculous incident ruining you. It can't be that serious. Obviously I'm innocent. What proof would they have against me?"

"I'm no criminal lawyer, but I know you have to take this seriously, Blake. What are you going to say when the police ask you where you were at one-thirty this morning?"

"At home in bed."

"Undoubtedly they've already been to your house and talked to Elena. If you're caught in a lie it'll only make you look worse. I've got to go to the police with you."

Blake stood up. "No, Lindsay, I won't let you. I'm going to call Elena and see if anyone has been there." He left the bathroom and went downstairs.

Lindsay got out of the tub, dried herself and got dressed as quickly as she could. She went downstairs and found Blake sitting on a stool in the kitchen. He looked up at her. "They were there at seven this morning," he said. "Elena is all upset. I told her not to worry. I called my office. A couple of detectives are there now."

"Blake..." she implored, but he cut her off.

"No, I'll deal with this myself."

"At least go with an attorney. That's the minimum I'll accept."

Blake smiled at her and extended his hand, beckoning her to him. "I like your spunk, counselor." When she drew near he wrapped his arms around her waist and pulled her against him, kissing her on the nose.

Lindsay slipped her hands behind his neck. "I've got a friend from Stanford Law School who does criminal law in San Jose. His name is Doug Childers, and he's got a great reputation. Let me call him and have him arrange for you to go in for questioning."

"Okay, but *I'll* call him. It's better that you not be involved at all. I don't want the lawyer to put two and two together when I conveniently forget who I spent the night with."

She gave him an anxious look but knew it was useless to protest. His eyes caressed her and she felt flooded by emotion. "Oh Blake," she whispered in a barely audible tone, "I hate seeing you hurt."

LINDSAY WAS LATE arriving at the office but the news had already preceded her. Jean spotted the article in the paper that morning and the office was buzzing with excitement.

"Gee!" Karen exclaimed. "To think that both of them have been right in this very office. Just imagine if it had happened here!"

"Blake Prescott hasn't even been accused," Lindsay said. "It could be a mistake."

"Or a lie," Jean added dryly.

Lindsay was beginning to appreciate the wisdom of her paralegal.

Millicent was shocked at the news, uncertain whether their case could be harmed or helped. If Prescott were convicted of assault, she reasoned, Terry's case would gain considerable sympathy. On the other hand, she knew that they wouldn't be benefited if the incident ruined him. She wanted him writing checks, not in jail.

Lindsay accomplished absolutely nothing all morning. She spent most of the time pacing the floor behind the closed door of her office. Blake had promised her he would call her at home that night, but she didn't know if she could bear to wait that long to discover his fate. She tried to remember what she could from her courses in criminal law and procedure in school, but didn't feel confident about anything she could recall. Since she knew Blake to be innocent and that there could be no evidence against him other than Terry's word, she thought it unlikely that he would be arrested. Still, the police would certainly take a dim view of his refusal to say where he had been at the time of the shooting.

By midafternoon Lindsay couldn't stand the uncertainty and decided to call Doug Childers's office. Doug was still out of the office, presumably with Blake. Lindsay had visions of the grand inquisition going on down at police headquarters. She explained to Doug's secretary that she had gotten his name from the police and was coincidentally an old friend. She told her she was representing the alleged victim of the shooting in a lawsuit and wanted a word with Doug. An hour later he called her back.

"Gee, Lindsay, a voice out of the past and a small-world coincidence in one phone call! How the heck are you?"

Doug was a sweet man and had been one of her favorite people at Stanford. "Concerned that the defendant in our suit will end up in jail. Will you manage to keep him a free man, Doug, or will we have to wait until he's paroled?"

"Not to worry. They're a long way from even bringing charges, let alone getting a conviction. I may be an impoverished criminal lawyer, but I'm not stupid."

"Then they didn't hold him?" she asked, trying not to sound too anxious.

"No, they grilled him forever, but no arrest. I finally had to tell them to fish or cut bait. Unless they were going to bring charges we were walking out."

"So you walked out?"

"We walked out."

"They must not have a case," Lindsay tossed out casually.

"They've got nothing except acute anxiety over his refusal to say where he was last night. If he'd just quit covering up for the woman he's protecting they'd already be looking for another suspect."

"Woman?"

"Yeah, I figure he's having an affair with a married woman and she'd be destroyed if he had to reveal he was in bed with her last night." Doug laughed. "So what are you on his tail for? Paternity?"

"No..." Lindsay hated to say it, knowing Blake was really the innocent party, "Palimony," she managed.

"I see. Well, the guy lives a colorful life."

"Yes. He's a fascinating man. What happens next, Doug?"

"Unless they find someone else to charge, or unless he tells them the name of his lady friend, they'll be on his tail for a while. I only hope he was straight with me. If they come up with some physical evidence against him, like a gun, he could be in trouble. Otherwise it'll be a game of nerves."

An hour later Lindsay was home, pacing the floor of her living room waiting for Blake's call. At six-thirty the phone finally rang. It was him.

"Blake, are you all right?"

"No beatings with a rubber hose if that's what you mean."

"Was it awful?"

"Annoying would be more descriptive. I'm trying to run a business and end up spending half a day going around in circles with a couple of detectives who think they're Mickey Spillane. By the way, your friend Doug Childers was a good man. He gave them plenty of slack and jerked the rope on them at just the right time."

"I heard about it. I called Doug this afternoon, but in the guise of Terry's attorney and didn't tell him I knew you."

"Well, they shouldn't be able to figure out where I was last night—short of torture anyway."

"I still think you're taking an unnecessary risk, Blake. I wish you'd let me talk to the police."

"Not until they're ready to haul me off to San Quentin."

Lindsay groaned. "What's going to happen now?"

"I guess I just have to lay low until they find whoever did it, or until they forget about it. I think I'd better stay away from you for a few days in any case."

Lindsay felt her heart sink though she knew she shouldn't be seeing Blake anyway. "I don't know when

I've hated a situation more. I miss you. I want to be with you and I'm not even supposed to be talking with you, let alone..."

"Speaking of which," Blake said with a laugh, "do you suppose anybody would be suspicious if I came over to your place tonight for a settlement conference?"

"Not unless you want me to go to jail right along with you."

"Couldn't be worse than this. It's torture knowing that lip and that nightgown are just fifteen minutes away."

"What lip?"

"The one on your face that I lust after."

"Oh Blake, you're torturing both of us. I should never have let you in the door last night—or gone on that picnic. If I had any sense I'd tell you goodbye until this thing is over. It was bad enough before, now the police are involved on top of everything else!"

"I love you," he said tenderly.

Lindsay wanted to cry and—in spite of her best efforts—she did.

After her call she went to her bedroom and continued to weep softly for a long time. She felt completely at a loss. For days she had been torn between her career and her feelings for Blake Prescott. Now his future with regard to both the lawsuit and the shooting incident seemed to have fallen in her hands. It was the most difficult predicament she'd ever been in and she didn't have the vaguest idea of what to do. No alternative made much sense. Should she confess all to Millicent and go to the police? Should she lay low and not see Blake until the mess was finally cleared up?

Lindsay realized the problem was that she had lost all perspective. Her judgment had been warped, totally distorted by fear, emotion, love. What she needed was the clear, levelheaded advice of someone who loved her, who had no involvement, who was both wise and understanding. She looked at the bedside clock. It was just after eight o'clock. That made it after ten in St. Louis.

Sitting on the edge of her bed Lindsay dialed the telephone number she had known since childhood and waited those long moments while a telephone rang in a familiar house halfway across the country. It rang several times and finally on the fourth ring she heard the voice of her father.

"Daddy, this is Lindsay. Did I wake you?"

"Lindsay! How are you, darling?" He cleared his throat. "Your mother and I were in bed, but I only just turned off the light. Are you okay?"

"Yes, Daddy. I'm sorry to call so late, but I've got a professional problem I needed to talk to you about. Would you be willing to put on your judicial robes again and give me a little advice?"

"Certainly, darling, I..."

Lindsay could hear her mother's voice in the background and her father saying to her mother that she was all right.

"Daddy...listen...this might take a while. Would you mind going to the phone in your study so we won't disturb mother?"

"Certainly, Lindsay."

"Good. Let me talk to mother while you get to the other phone..." She heard the mumbled explanation of one parent to the other. "Hello? Mama?"

"Lindsay, are you trying to scare me? Are you okay?"

"Yes, of course. I've got a legal matter to discuss with Daddy. I'm sorry to call so late but the time got away from me and I wanted to talk with him before tomorrow."

"You're all right then?"

"Yes, yes. It's only a little after eight here. Listen, I wanted to tell you that the camellia on my deck—remember the one you loved so much when you were out here last year?"

"Yes."

"Well, it's grown two feet and it's in full bloom."

"Oh, it must be lovely. It was a wonderful pink color, wasn't it?"

"Yes, it's a deep pink."

The sound of her father picking up the extension could be heard. "Yes, okay, I'm on."

"Okay, Daddy, let me just finish with mother.... How are the boys?"

"They're all fine. They ask about you.... I guess they don't get any letters from you either..."

Lindsay always expected that comment and never failed to get it.

"Matt and Sybil and the children are doing fine. So are Bill and Narda. Stacey and Melissa both have the flu and have been out of school for a week now."

"How about Alan? Does he have a girlfriend now?"

"Oh yes. Very sweet girl. Laura. They've been dating for six weeks or more."

"Sounds serious, for Alan. They usually don't last more than a month."

"Well, I think he's smitten with Laura, although I asked him and he just gave me a funny look. But you know your brother. He'll have children in school before he tells his parents he's married."

"Yes, Edris," her father interjected, "why don't you and Lindsay call each other on Sunday when the rates are low and catch up on family gossip."

"Oh, don't be so impatient Harold. I never talk to the girl, she's my only daughter."

"Yes, honey, I recall. But my feet are getting cold."

"Don't you have on your slippers?"

"Say, Mama," Lindsay cut in, "why don't I give you a call this weekend. I've been meaning to anyway. Let me talk to Daddy now."

"All right, Lindsay. I'll let you two talk. Why don't you send me a postcard now and then so I know you're alive..."

"Mother!"

"I'll let you go. Love you, darling." And she hung up.

"You there, Daddy?"

"Yes, I'm here. What's your problem—they offer you a seat on the bench?"

Lindsay laughed. "It's good to hear your voice, Daddy.... I'm afraid I'm in a pickle."

"No problem's too big for vigorous minds and constructive intentions, Lindsay."

She had heard him say that hundreds of times and it cheered her every time he said it. "Yes I know—that's why I called the best mind I know."

Her father chuckled appreciatively. "Let's have it then."

Lindsay started at the beginning, telling her father what had happened from the night she met Blake Prescott at her lecture. She left the details of her romance with Blake unstated, but told him enough that he would understand the scope of her dilemma.

Lindsay cherished the fact that she could speak frankly with her father and know that he would listen with an open mind, and without prejudice. He was the most nonjudgmental person she had ever known in her life. He freely gave his opinion when she asked for it, but he never tried to impose his point of view or his will. Was that a sign of her wisdom, or of his?

In her last year of high school when she considered marrying her boyfriend and foregoing college, her mother went into a fit and her father took her for a long walk. They talked over all sides of the issue, Lindsay uncertain at the end just where he stood, though she knew he had always been thrilled with her plans to follow in his footsteps and become a lawyer.

It was his final comment that he would support her decision whatever it was that caused her to realize she was really mistress of her own destiny. Maybe he had planned it that way, but it didn't matter because she knew in her heart that she could have elected to marry and forgo her education if she'd wished.

"You know, Lindsay," said the beloved voice from half a continent away, "there is in the end no right or wrong in this kind of dilemma, there are only priorities, penalties and rewards to balance."

"Sort of like when I was considering marrying Peter Bradley, isn't it?"

"I guess you could say that, yes. Happiness is the final arbiter. Only you know where your own personal, emotional and intellectual needs fit into the equation. Who but Edward VIII could say abdication was the right choice for him?"

"You're saying what boils down to is career versus love."

"Yes, Lindsay, that's what *his* choice ultimately came down to, but you can be darn sure that in making his decision to abdicate Edward had to take into consideration the welfare of an entire nation, not just himself."

Lindsay mused. "You're saying no man is an island, right Daddy? I can't just think about myself, I have to think about Blake and Millicent and Terry and Kenneth and God knows who else.''

''I don't know where that leads you, Lindsay, but yes, responsible people have to consider every aspect and every person affected in making a decision.''

Lindsay sighed. ''You know what, Daddy?''

''What?''

''You're the smartest man in the world. And I love you!''

CHAPTER NINETEEN

LINDSAY SLEPT BETTER that night than she had at any time since Blake Prescott had come into her life. She decided to tell Millicent Woodward about her relationship with Blake and the fact that he was with her the night of the shooting. She knew the decision was momentous—it might even ruin her career—but it would unburden her and it would enable everyone involved—Millicent, Blake and Terry—to protect themselves. If it was abdication, it was for them as well as herself.

Waiting for Millicent to be free to talk the next morning gave Lindsay a sense of what it must be like for a condemned man after he had had his last meal and was waiting for the fateful hour to arrive. She was calm, but knew the day of reckoning was upon her. When Lindsay finally went into her partner's office, Millicent had a foreboding look on her face, perhaps reflecting what she saw in Lindsay's grim visage.

"You have the look of a bearer of bad tidings," she said.

Lindsay sat down. "I'm here to make a confession."

Millicent waited.

"I've been seeing Blake Prescott," she said in an even tone, "and I've come to realize there's no more pretending that I can see him and meet my responsibilities to Terry Moretti and to you. I suppose my actions already constitute a breach of ethics and rather than let it go on so that others are hurt, I've decided to come clean.''

Millicent dropped her eyes and Lindsay saw that she was feeling shame for her. The older woman tried to remain calm and reasonable as she spoke. ''What exactly have you done?''

''I've met Blake secretly. I've slept with him.'' Lindsay's voice trembled ever so slightly.

There was a hint of disgust on Millicent's face, but she quickly masked it. The arm of her glasses went to the corner of her mouth.

''I know it doesn't exonerate me,'' Lindsay went on, ''but I'm convinced that Terry Moretti has fabricated her story from beginning to end and that Blake is an innocent victim.''

''Do you have specific evidence, Lindsay, or is it intuitive judgment you're basing your conclusion on?''

Lindsay thought about the deception regarding Rusty's paternity, but she had given Blake her word and she would honor that trust. Besides, she couldn't prove that either, not yet in any case. ''I believe Blake,'' she said simply.

''Doubtless you've discussed our case with him,'' Millicent said dryly.

Lindsay bowed her head. ''Actually I was rather discreet. Blake didn't put any pressure on me. He seems to care more about me than the lawsuit. I managed to keep my mouth shut. But there was one bad blunder. I inadvertently let him know we knew about his government contracts.''

Millicent seemed to crumple in her chair but said nothing. Lindsay wished that her partner would just scream her anger at her, but she didn't.

"I didn't say anything," Lindsay continued. "He guessed from my reaction to him. I realize it amounts to the same thing, but I want you to know I didn't intentionally do anything to hurt you or Terry."

Millicent's voice was low, almost weak. "I accept that, Lindsay."

They sat in silence. Millicent thought. Lindsay thought. "What do you want me to do?" Lindsay asked.

"We've got to worry about malpractice at this point. I don't know how badly Terry Moretti has been damaged, but our own exposure is considerable."

"Not if she's a fraud, as I believe she is."

Millicent's smile was almost a smirk. "We're vulnerable no matter what. You know the law holds an attorney to the highest standards. There can't be even an appearance of a conflict of interest. Besides, we can hardly base our defense on your intuitive judgment."

The words were harsh but Lindsay knew she deserved them.

"Then too, you may have problems with the Bar Association. This is not an uncomplicated situation, Lindsay."

"Yes, I know."

"Well, we'd better start shoring up our defenses. The first thing we have to do is disclose this to Miss Moretti. I don't see any way our firm can continue to represent her, unless she insists on it. But you personally will have to withdraw from the case."

"Yes, I agree."

"You know, Lindsay, there's still a problem with your relationship with Mr. Prescott. Until we get ourselves out of this one way or another, you ought to avoid further...society with him."

Lindsay felt like a schoolgirl being reprimanded for immoral behavior. She hadn't felt such humiliation in her life. "Yes, I understand."

They looked at each other, and Lindsay knew that the trust and respect that had always existed between them had just been dealt a severe—if not mortal—blow.

"There's one thing more, Millicent."

The other looked at Lindsay.

"Blake was at my place the night the shots were fired at Terry. He didn't do it. He was with me when it happened."

Millicent was already so numbed by Lindsay's revelations that she seemed to accept the latest blow with equanimity. "So, you're involved in that business too."

"Only to the extent I can vouch for Blake's innocence." Lindsay thought she detected skepticism on Millicent's face.

"What do you propose to do about it?"

"I plan to go to the police and tell them the truth."

"Mr. Prescott didn't?"

"No, he refused to let me go with him. He didn't want to hurt me."

Millicent was thinking again. "I don't really see the need for you to go to the police. After all, Mr. Prescott is not under arrest and it would be a further embarrassment to the firm."

Lindsay looked at her partner incredulously. "Millicent, how can I not go? He's an innocent man and I can vouch for him! To not come forward would be selfish and in utter disregard of the ends of justice. I may have been a woman who let her heart cloud her judgment, but I am a lawyer and I know my duty. I have an obligation to bring forth evidence that would clear Blake!" Lindsay's voice had risen and she was glad for the chance to feel a little self-righteous indignation. Till now she had been the goat.

Millicent had folded her hands on her desk and was looking at Lindsay. "You're right, of course. What I just suggested was as bad as anything you've done. I apologize, Lindsay."

The young attorney couldn't help smiling. "I'm the one who should be apologizing. I've brought disgrace on myself and the firm. I may have ruined my own career, but I couldn't bear to think I might have sullied your name, Millicent."

"Well, now we're becoming overly dramatic. It's a nasty situation but hardly the end of the world. We'll just have to put things right. I hope for your sake that Mr. Prescott is as innocent as you believe him to be."

Lindsay suddenly felt as though the weight of the world had been lifted from her shoulders. She could tell that Millicent had forgiven her.

AFTER GIVING HER STATEMENT to the police, Lindsay had only to tell Blake what she had done. She decided to go to his office directly and get it over with. The day had been one of the most difficult in her life and she concluded that she may as well do the hardest thing of all— tell the man she loved that she couldn't see him anymore, at least not for a while.

Lindsay drove directly to the Converse building in Sunnyvale, managing to get there before the doors were locked but after most of the employees had left for the day. She was relieved to see Blake's Porsche sitting by the walkway leading to the building.

Walking briskly to the front door, Lindsay began feeling fearful of Blake's reaction to her news. He had pretty well controlled things and had had his way from the time they met. Going to the police was contrary to his wishes, but it had been, in her mind, absolutely necessary.

Blake's secretary, a crisp and efficient middle-aged woman, came out to the reception area to greet Lindsay. They walked together through a maze of corridors in the low-rise, modern building, until they came to the executive offices. Most of the employees had left for the day, and hallways were nearly empty as they traversed the facility. With darkness falling, Lindsay saw a light coming from the door of Blake's private office. Other offices in the suite were dark. The secretary saw Lindsay to Blake's door, said good-night and left for the evening. The company president and the lawyer were alone.

Blake walked over to Lindsay and put his arms around her, sensing she had come with important news. He hadn't spoken. He was in his shirt sleeves and Lindsay pressed her face against his shirt. "Blake," she mumbled, not wanting to see his eyes, "I went to the police this afternoon."

She felt him stiffen. Taking her by the shoulders, Blake held her away from him so that he could see her face. His expression was one of concern, not anger. She felt like a contrite child.

"I couldn't deal with the hypocrisy anymore. I couldn't stand by and see you hurt. I had to do it, Blake." Her upturned face was filled with conviction. "I really had to."

"Oh Lindsay," he sighed, kissing the top of her head. "How will I ever live with myself if this ruins you?"

"You're not responsible, Blake. I am. I'm an adult. I knew what I was doing. You didn't kidnap me or force me into anything. What I did, I have to live with."

"But I pressured you, Lindsay. I took advantage of you from the beginning. Granted I had no evil intent. I could have let you handle this as you wished, but I didn't. I wanted you on my own terms."

His green eyes seemed to beg for forgiveness. She felt compassion and regret. Strangely, sadly, the mood between them was funereal. She wondered if he knew what her decision meant. "We can't see each other anymore," she said somberly. "Not until this is over."

He turned away, his broad shoulders somewhat stooped, his energies bridled. When he turned back to her, Lindsay saw his handsome face flush as the implications of what had happened seemed to hit him. "Have you told Millicent Woodward?"

"About us? Yes."

"Then why can't you see me? You're free now, aren't you? You won't be dealing with Terry anymore."

"No, but the firm is involved with her—at least it is unless she decides she wants other counsel. As a partner in the firm I have to avoid even the appearance of impropriety. I may already have exposed us to a malpractice suit and may be facing disciplinary action by the Bar Association."

"Because we love each other?" he raged.

"No, because of who we are, our roles."

Blake turned away and walked across his office and back again. He was angry but Lindsay knew it was over the circumstances, not what she had done.

"For God's sake," he fumed, "what kind of a world do we live in when what *we* have together is punished?"

"After this is over we can be together," she said, trying to calm him.

"But what could be more important than us?"

"Our self-respect is important too! What good is a relationship that costs us our careers, our integrity and livelihood? Both of us have worked hard for what we have. It's foolish to destroy it because of impatience and shortsightedness."

"Is that what we've had together," he shot back, "shortsightedness? Is that what brought us together, impatience? Is that all it means to you?"

"Blake, of course not. Please don't be angry. That's not what I meant at all!" She watched as he paced the room again, glaring.

"Look," he said finally, "this whole thing is my fault. I take full responsibility and I'll tell the court or the Bar Association, or wherever they hang you, that I forced you into this."

"Blake, that's absurd. It's no more your fault than mine. I've already said I take responsiblity for my actions. No one's to blame."

He stood facing her halfway across the room, his hands on his hips. She could see his anger, the face that was so dear to her had turned venomous. The body that had given her such pleasure, such wonderful, magical pleasure, was rigid with hostility. She stared at him, not wanting to believe that the man she had come to love had disappeared. At that moment she hated what had happened. She resented Blake, though she couldn't hate him. She wanted to reach out and touch him and quiet his anger, bring his love back again.

"Okay," he said with a resigned voice, "if integrity is what matters most to you, I have to respect that."

"I didn't say it matters most," she said imploringly. "I said we need that in our relationship, too. We can't ignore the rest of the world. I don't want to spoil what's beautiful and wonderful between us. I want us to be proud of what we have together."

"I understand that," he replied in a suddenly calm voice. "I accept that."

But she knew he didn't, not completely. "Do you doubt my feelings for you, Blake?"

He looked at her. "No. I just want us to want the same thing."

Lindsay wanted desperately for him to put his arms around her. "We do, Blake. I know we do." She walked over to him. His hands were still on his hips. She touched the end of his tie with her fingers. He didn't move. She looked up at him with shimmering violet eyes. "Do you want me to leave?"

His mouth widened into a reluctant grin. He took her narrow shoulders in his hands. "Lindsay Bishop, why couldn't you have been a nurse...or a go-go dancer...or a physicist?"

She laughed sadly. The thin film of tears on her eyes gathered at her lower lid, brimmed, then slid down each of her cheeks.

Blake brushed the tears away with his finger then kissed her on the forehead. "In my field we say what counts is results. I'm through talking now, Lindsay. I'm going to roll up my sleeves and do what I have to do." He took her by the arm and started walking with her out of the office, all the way to her car in the parking lot, saying nothing further.

Lindsay's heart was beating with anquish and dread. She wanted to ask him what he meant, when she would be seeing him again, whether he hated her, whether he no longer cared.

"I promise you this," he said as the cool evening air blew across them, fluttering his tie and the auburn locks of his hair. "I have my values, too, and one of them is never to be defeated—by anything."

Lifting her chin he bent down and kissed her lightly on the lips, then turned and went into the building.

From the lobby Blake watched the taillights of Lindsay's BMW disappear. He had hours of work left to do that night, but knew that his conversation with Lindsay would be preying on his mind for days. Her action had probably been fated from the beginning, but his stubbornness and the tremendous attraction he felt for her had made him try to buck fate. If only she had been a little more patient.

Long after Lindsay had disappeared from sight, Blake looked wistfully out the door into the darkness. It somehow seemed cruel that he had won her and captured her love only to lose her to circumstance. Thinking back to his insistence on seeing her, he knew he should have waited until after the lawsuit was over, but that would have been surrender and he never lightly surrendered to anything.

Sadly, he went back to his office, but the reports and documents on his desk seemed blatantly irrelevant to the thing that mattered most. Pulling a drawer open, Blake took out a file and opened it on his desk. Lindsay Bishop's lovely face was there before him, staring at him from Jerry Randall's photograph. The full lip he had come to adore, the hair, the eyes, they were all there for his longing admiration.

Blake knew he was torturing himself, but he also knew he wouldn't be able to lie in his bed at night without remembering her nakedness against him, the feel of her full, ripe breasts on his chest, the image of her astride him in her ecstasy. He was hopelessly in love with the woman's mind, her body, her soul.

Holding the photograph before him as though by doing so he might somehow bring her back to the room and into his arms, Prescott savored the image. Finally, in frustration he put the photo down and reached for the telephone. A moment later he had Jerry Randall on the line.

"Jerry, I've got another job for you.... No, not spring me out of jail. What's the matter, you believe everything you read in the paper...? Only if it's about clients? Well, how about *former* clients...? Okay, listen. I want you to find Terry Moretti for me. She's apparently making herself scarce, so it may take some doing. Yeah, the same broad, only it wasn't me that shot at her. That was a case of mistaken identity. I think she'll be interested in what I have to say, so tell her not to worry...and, Jerry, this is one of your double rate jobs. I want her found immediately."

CHAPTER TWENTY

LINDSAY PULLED her black wool coat across her chest as she descended the steps to her office. A cold wind gusted and swirled sending leaves tumbling along the sidewalk. In a matter of days the season had gone from summer to winter.

She had made it through her first day after telling Blake she couldn't see him anymore, but it seemed a miracle that she had. Every time the phone had rung she expected to hear his voice or Karen telling her that he was in the reception area to see her. It didn't happen.

Walking toward her car Lindsay thought of the previous week when she found him waiting with flowers in his hand. She remembered his face and the importance to him of her forgiveness. That's all that seemed to matter to him, not the lawsuit, perhaps not even his pride. She was all he seemed to care about.

Turning the corner to the side street where she parked, Lindsay searched the area around her car, almost expecting to see a tall man with auburn hair, but he wasn't there. No sad but hopeful face, no flowers, no quiet countenance determined to have its way. Blake Prescott wasn't there.

As she drove home, Lindsay looked in her rearview mirror, scanned the streets leading toward her house, unconsciously looked at parked cars, but saw nothing suggesting Blake. Rounding the corner near her town house she saw a vacant parking space outside her home, but no black Porsche. Walking up the steps she found the evening paper, but no note, no card, no flowers, no one sitting on the stoop waiting for her arrival.

Lindsay changed her clothes, fixed dinner and ate it without enthusiasm, but the phone didn't ring. She went over and over the events of the past few days, reassessed her actions and her words and asked herself hard questions. She tested her reasoning, reasserted her case to herself and realized she had done the right thing. Still, the phone didn't ring.

Sitting propped up in bed, Lindsay watched a silly television program, but her thoughts kept turning to Blake Prescott. She was uncertain of the message he intended by his silence. It was loud, very loud, but not clear.

Perhaps Blake had finally recognized the wisdom of her decision. Perhaps he too had accepted the necessity of being apart, of putting duty before desire. She recalled his bitterness, his unwillingness at first to accept what she had done. She hoped desperately that this was what his silence meant—that he had accepted the inevitable as well. But something deep inside caused her to fear, to doubt, to be mistrustful.

Silence is what she asked of him, but it was a double-edged sword, it confounded her as well. He did what she demanded, yet she resented his compliance—if only because she wasn't sure what it meant.

Lindsay thought about her plight with bitter irony. She had gone into law because of a belief in justice—the kind of justice her father meted out in his courtroom. But what kind of justice had the law given *her*? It had wrenched from her the one man in her life who made her feel like a whole woman, who seemed to match and complement her, word for word, feeling for feeling, touch for touch.

The words Blake had uttered to her in his office came to mind—*What kind of a world do we live in when what we have together is punished?* Now from the perspective of time, she realized how insightful those words were. Had justice become an enemy conspiring against them?

Lindsay arrived at the office the next morning and immediately began preparing to leave for Law and Motion court. She had two pleadings of her own to tend to and Millicent had asked her to handle something for her as well.

Millicent had taken charge of the Terry Moretti case and they had hardly discussed it since Lindsay had made her confession. The senior partner did tell her that she had been unable to contact Terry and had decided to send out certified letters to every address they had for the singer, asking her to come into the office to discuss the case.

The file Millicent had given Lindsay the night before to handle in court was on her desk. She paged through it idly, her brain numb from lack of sleep. She was thankful she would only have to make a court appearance and not try a case.

Later that day, while waiting for her cases to be called, Lindsay sat daydreaming. Some of the other attorneys around her took advantage of the idle minutes to work out of their briefcases, while others congregated in small groups just outside the courtroom. Lindsay stared blankly ahead, remembering her own long struggle to achieve prominence in the legal profession, remembering a speech she had given and the love affair with Blake Prescott that resulted.

At the office that afternoon there were a number of real-world problems waiting for her. She had to mediate a fight between Jean and the word processor, then there was a flare up in an old child-custody battle she had handled, followed by a hectic rush to get a restraining order against a husband who was physically threatening his estranged wife.

In the days that followed, Lindsay gradually eased back into the routine of work. She was grateful for the frantic, long hours because they kept her mind off Blake. Still, he was never far away, haunting her thoughts at quiet times like a tenacious demon.

It was particularly difficult at home during the evenings. She managed to keep her hands busy, but surrendered her mind to Blake. She walked to the market, but he followed her, an obsessive spectre. She watched an old movie on television, but Blake loomed up behind the faceless actors, insinuating himself into every corner of her consciousness.

Saturday night she went out to dinner. Sitting alone at a table she listened to the conversation of a young couple nearby and wondered if she and Blake sounded equally silly to a sober-minded eavesdropper. Afterward she walked down the street, but everything she encountered, from an eccentric-looking old man to the luminescent cast of the evening sky, evoked a thought or observation she wanted to share with Blake. She missed him so.

AT TEN-THIRTY Monday morning Millicent came to Lindsay's office. She was standing in the doorway, her face ashen.

"Millicent, what's the matter?"

"Max Bender was just in to see me and gave me quite a shock."

"What happened?"

"He's found Terry Moretti—I asked if he might help locate her."

"Yes?"

"I'm afraid, dear, that she's moved back in with Mr. Prescott."

Lindsay's mouth dropped open. "Moved in with Blake?"

"Yes, or at least she spent the weekend at his house. Max said she didn't leave."

"Well, maybe she was there visiting Rusty. Maybe Blake is on a trip or something."

"No. Apparently he was there as well—and that's what concerns me." Millicent looked at Lindsay with sympathetic eyes. "I'm sorry to bring you that sort of news, considering your feelings for Mr. Prescott, but I thought I'd better discuss the situation with you."

Lindsay was dumbfounded. It didn't surprise her that Blake might talk to Terry, but why would he have her staying at the house—after all that had happened?

"What concerns me," Millicent was saying, "is that Miss Moretti might be double-crossing us. I mean, it would be nice if they were able to work out their problems, but I worry that they might leave us hanging out to dry. Regardless of what they do, we still have the exposure of a malpractice suit. I guess what I'm asking is if you think Mr. Prescott capable of some malicious or vindictive act."

Lindsay was still having trouble believing what Millicent was telling her. "I don't know what's happening, Millicent. I can't believe Blake would do anything to be hurtful, no."

"Well, I hope you're right, but when you consider how much money is at stake in this business, you have to wonder if Mr. Prescott isn't looking at things pragmatically. Not to demean what he feels for you, Lindsay, but we *are* talking about millions of dollars."

"Yes, but what could he do that *we* have to worry about?"

"I suppose the worst he could do would be to encourage her against us, but that would be possible only if he was angry with you for breaking off with him...."

"No, I don't believe Blake would do that."

"There's the possibility that Mr. Prescott and Miss Moretti have reconciled, Lindsay."

"I don't believe that for a minute. They never had a relationship to begin with!"

"Forgive me for asking, dear, but would he be capable of taking up with Miss Moretti to avoid a major financial loss?"

"Absolutely not. And I doubt she'd be interested either. She's after his money, not him," Lindsay rejoined firmly.

"No, I shouldn't think so either, but we have to consider every possibility."

Lindsay was staring at Millicent but she was trying to imagine Blake and Terry in his house together. Apart from a mutual interest in Rusty, the notion of them together seemed absurd.

"Unless you have some objection, Lindsay, I'd like to try to contact Miss Moretti at Mr. Prescott's house and ask her to come in to speak with us."

"No, of course not."

"I take it his telephone number is in the file?"

"Yes."

"Perhaps I'll try to reach her now." Millicent left Lindsay with her thoughts.

Blake was up to something unusual, and she wasn't sure what. But why would he have Terry stay with him? The question haunted her. Could it have to do with Rusty? The possibilities suggested by Millicent made no sense, knowing Blake's feelings as she did, but he had proven himself capable of doing the unexpected. Then too, there was the excruciating week of silence that had passed. Could Millicent be right? Could he have felt resentful and written Lindsay off?

Several minutes later Millicent returned. "I don't like it," she said breezing into the office, "that girl's being terribly mysterious. But she did agree to speak with us. We've set a tentative appointment for Friday."

Friday! How could she possibly wait until Friday to find out what was going on? For Lindsay, this wasn't just another phase in the lawsuit.

As Lindsay was getting into her car after work, an impulse struck her. Instead of heading for home she headed toward Saratoga. Soon finding herself jammed up in freeway traffic, she regretted having succumbed to the temptation but was determined to see it through. She wasn't sure herself what she would do when she arrived at Blake's place, but she felt the need to confirm the bizarre story Millicent had recounted.

It was dark by the time Lindsay finally found Blake's house, having to consult her map several times when she became lost in the hills. She stopped across the street from the house and sat staring at it. There were lights on, but the drapes were drawn and she could see no one. There was no sign that Terry Moretti was there, nothing to tell her what was happening.

She waited in the darkness for something to happen, but she wasn't quite sure what. Did she expect to see them leaving or arriving? Perhaps loud voices—an argument? All that Lindsay could hear was the wind that howled through the trees and whistled around her car in the night.

She briefly considered going to the door and demanding to know what was going on, but dismissed the notion, realizing that it was simply a symptom of her frustration. No, unless Blake came to her first, she would have to wait the interminable days till Friday in order to discover what was happening. Lindsay started her car and somberly drove back to Palo Alto.

After she got home she realized that going to Blake's was the most foolish thing she could have done. Instead of relieving the tension, it only made it worse. By morning her doubts and suspicions mounted to a point where she felt as though she would burst. Lindsay realized that she had to see him and get his reassurance at any cost.

She struggled through the day, planning at first on going to his house again. But as the prospects of seeing Terry and the possibility of there being a scene occurred to her, she decided instead to go to his office. Lindsay left early that evening convinced that all she needed was to speak with him for a few minutes. She needed to look into his eyes, hear his voice, judge his feelings. A few minutes, nothing more.

Blake's secretary told Lindsay he was tied up in a meeting that promised to last well into the evening, but agreed to let him know she was there. The woman went into Blake's office and when she returned Lindsay was certain she would be sent away, but instead the secretary asked if she would mind waiting a short while.

Each minute seemed interminable. Although the door to his office was closed and the window drapes drawn, she heard the faint murmur of voices and the suggestion of figures moving behind the opaque fabric covering the glass.

Suddenly the door opened and a shaggy-haired young man in short sleeves and a tie walked out, followed by a heavy-set man in a sweater. Then Blake, also in shirt sleeves, appeared. "Let's reconvene in ten or fifteen minutes fellas, and why don't you try to reach General Mordstrom, Al. Find out what you can about timing."

The other men gave their assent and walked out of the suite and down the hall. Blake turned to Lindsay who had risen to greet him. "Hi. Sorry to keep you waiting. Come on into my office."

Closing the door he gestured for her to sit down. Lindsay searched his face for a clue to his attitude. She could see that he was tired and distracted. There was an uncharacteristic formality about him. She feared the worst. "Sorry to drop in you like this, Blake," she said as he sat down in the chair next to her.

He gave a sigh of fatigue. "No problem. I'm sorry things are so hectic. It's been a big day."

"I hope I haven't interrupted your meeting."

"No, don't worry, we needed a break." He looked at her, smiling finally, as though for the first time he was actually seeing her. He reached over and put his hand on hers. "It's good to see you."

Somehow she wasn't sure she believed him. "Is it?" His hand was warm, just as it always was, but something seemed different, missing.

"Of course, Lindsay. I didn't expect to see you, though, after our last conversation. Your decision didn't exactly thrill me, needless to say, but I understood what you meant.''

"Did you, really?"

"Yes, it was what you were saying all along. I just hadn't been listening."

"It's not what I want emotionally. Do you understand that?"

He nodded. "I understand. It's not what I want either."

Lindsay pondered her next words. "I suppose I'm here because it was important for me to hear that." Her expression became wistful. "Don't you see how hard the silence was to take?"

"I was trying to honor your wishes, Lindsay."

"Yes I know, but that didn't make it easier."

He stared at her, frustration and a hint of anger on his face now. "What would you have had me do?"

"I don't know. Is there another way, Blake, or was I right?"

"Right about what?"

"That we can't see each other again."

"No, certainly we can see each other again."

"But when?"

"Well, you were right, this is a difficult time for both of us. It's bad timing."

Lindsay was hearing the man's practical mind speaking. The passion was gone, the burning desire to see her, to be with her. Before, nothing could stop him. Now "the right thing to do" was all too clear, too easy for him to do. Tears glossed over her eyes, but she fought them back.

"It's very important to me, Blake, to know what you're really thinking, to know how you feel about me. I want to know whether things have changed."

"No Lindsay, of course nothing has changed. I've just come to realize you were right. We have to get this lawsuit behind us."

She looked at him and hated the reasonableness of his words. Between the lines he was telling her that his priorities had changed. She no longer came at the top of his list. She realized this clearly now, but there was no way she could say it to him.

Finally, she rose to her feet and he stood up beside her. It was the same handsome face she was seeing, but *he* was no longer the same. She had lost the man who had rescued her in the storm, the man who made love to her in front of the fire. The sadness she felt was overwhelming. Tears filled her eyes and flowed down her cheeks. She did not resist them any longer.

Blake took her hand and squeezed it in his. Then he took her by the shoulder and gently pulled her against him. There was comfort in his touch, but it was qualified by the communication that had passed between them.

After a long silent minute she looked up at him. "This has been terribly selfish of me to do this to you. I'm sorry. I hope you'll forgive me."

He chuckled and spoke with a little more energy, trying to lighten the mood. "Come on now. No long faces. It's always darkest before the dawn. You know that."

She let her head fall against his chest one final time. She inhaled the pleasant aroma of him that she had always found so erotic. She savored this final moment as though it would be the last she would ever experience with him.

At last she pulled away and looked at a damp streak on his silk tie. "Oh look, Blake, I've not only interrupted your meeting, I've ruined your tie!"

"Doesn't matter," he said lifting her chin with his finger and surveying her upturned face. "Trust me," Blake said, leaning over and kissing her softly on the lips.

His mouth felt so soft and warm on hers that she didn't want the kiss to end, but he pulled away nevertheless. She looked up at him, coveting the mouth that had given her such pleasure, wanting it back again, claiming her, taking her. But it hung above her instead, drawn now into a harder attitude, aloof, withdrawn.

"Just let me get through this, Lindsay. Will you?"

There was a hint of mystery in his tone, something of the unknown. Lindsay thought about Terry and wondered if she was behind the germ of hesitation in Blake. She hadn't asked him about Terry, and she wouldn't. They heard the voices of the men outside the door.

"I'd better go," she said softly.

Blake let go of her arm. "I'll walk you to your car."

"No," she said stepping to the door. "Finish your meeting. I can find my way."

One hand was on the doorknob. She was ready to open the door and leave, but it was a difficult thing to do. She glanced at him a final time and tried to smile. Blake was near her, but he, too, was holding back.

Lindsay touched the tear spots on his tie, a final contact before she opened the door and left.

CHAPTER TWENTY-ONE

AT FIVE MINUTES BEFORE ELEVEN Friday morning Lindsay sat in her office. In a few minutes Terry Moretti was due to arrive and the long wait would be over. She and Millicent would find out exactly what was going on.

Lindsay's feelings were a mixture of expectation and dread. She sensed this meeting somehow would involve the critical revelation, the denouement. She breathed deeply and waited.

When the intercom finally buzzed Lindsay jumped. She picked up the receiver. It was Karen.

"Lindsay, Terry Moretti and Charlotte Phelps have arrived. I've got them in the conference room. Millicent wants you to join them there."

"Who's Charlotte Phelps?"

"An attorney, I think."

"An attorney? Okay, I'll be right out." Lindsay picked up her legal pad and headed for the conference room wondering what this could mean. When she entered the room Millicent and the other two women were in the midst of introductions.

"Oh, here's Lindsay," Millicent said turning. "Miss Phelps, this is my partner Lindsay Bishop... Lindsay, Charlotte Phelps, an attorney with Pillsbury & Morrison in San Francisco."

Lindsay shook hands with the handsome woman in her late thirties. Charlotte Phelps had short blond hair, cut squarely, and was dressed very precisely in a business suit. Lindsay glanced at Terry Moretti, who was sitting at the table with a rather uncomfortable expression on her face.

"I know you weren't expecting to see me this morning," Charlotte said, sitting down next to the singer. "Let me apologize in advance for bringing the news to you in this manner, but I have been retained by Miss Moretti to represent her in her suit against Blake Prescott."

"I see," Millicent said perfunctorily. "You realize that..."

"Forgive me, Mrs. Woodward, I'm aware that the niceties of protocol have been omitted—again I apologize, but as we progress I think you'll understand why."

"Very well."

"You see, I was contacted last week by Mr. Prescott and Miss Moretti for the purpose of preparing a settlement agreement for them...."

Lindsay and Millicent exchanged glances.

"Naturally when I discovered that an action had been filed I advised Miss Moretti to contact you. For reasons I'll explain she said she could not."

"Do you represent *both* parties, Miss Phelps?" Lindsay asked in amazement.

"No, I only represent Miss Moretti. I explained to Mr. Prescott that given the nature and history of the suit I could not represent both of them. He accepted that and agreed."

"Why weren't *we* notified, Miss Phelps?" Millicent asked insistently.

"Because *your* firm was made a party to the settlement agreement."

"We? A *party* to the agreement?"

"Yes. That's why I'm here under these circumstances. Let me summarize for you what's happened."

"I wish you would," Millicent said, unable to hide her irritation.

"Before they contacted me, the two parties reached an agreement. They asked me to draft it. Of course, I wasn't going to do anything until I'd seen your file and had spoken with you. However, it soon became apparent that wasn't necessary when Terry admitted to me that she had...well...exaggerated the facts greatly in representing her case to you. To be blunt, the entire story was fabricated. There is no basis for the suit."

Millicent looked at Terry incredulously. "I see." Turning again to Charlotte Phelps she said, "And you say that Woodward & Bishop has been made a party to the settlement agreement?"

"Yes."

"How's that?"

"Well, first of all, Mr. Prescott was concerned that his relationship with Miss Bishop might have been the basis for a malpractice suit against your firm. Miss Moretti has agreed to release you from any liability in that connection."

"That's very considerate of Mr. Prescott," Millicent said, smiling at Lindsay.

"And secondly," Charlotte continued, "there's the matter of the conflict of interest implicit in the purchase of Converse Corporation by your husband, Mrs. Woodward."

"The *what*?" Millicent exclaimed.

"The purchase of Mr. Prescott's company by your husband. You were aware, weren't..."

"My God!" Millicent gasped.

"Oh, dear," Charlotte said. "I thought surely he had told you."

Lindsay looked at Millicent who was ashen. Her lower lip was quivering with shock. Lindsay suddenly saw the reason for Kenneth's keen interest in Blake and his concern about Millicent's involvement in the case. She knew something had been afoot, but had had no idea his role was so pivotal in the whole affair. "You mean," she asked, "that Kenneth and Blake have been negotiating with each other over the sale of Converse?"

"Yes. My understanding is that they've been deeply involved in a business relationship for the past few weeks."

"I'll kill the man," Millicent said, her voice quivering with shame and rage. "I'll kill him!"

Lindsay and Charlotte Phelps exchanged looks.

"I am sorry to have brought you the news this way," Charlotte said, "but Mr. Prescott and Mr. Woodward were looking out for your welfare. That's why Mr. Prescott included the release of your firm in the settlement agreement. Perhaps Mr. Woodward intended to tell you himself. You see, I haven't dealt with him at all, only Mr. Prescott. Your husband may not even have known I was coming here today."

"Actually, he probably found out this morning," Millicent replied in a somewhat calmer voice. "I had several urgent calls from him in the past hour, but I missed them."

Lindsay remembered Bill Price's frantic calls the morning of the deposition—Blake's urgent desire to let *her* know in advance about his deception. The irony struck her as rather amusing.

Looking over at Millicent, Lindsay noted the older woman blushing with embarrassment. It was the first time she could ever remember seeing Millicent in a truly compromising situation.

"So, what is the present status of this settlement agreement, Miss Phelps?" Millicent asked, recovering.

Charlotte lifted her briefcase from the floor and opened it on the table. "I have copies of the agreement for your review. Miss Moretti and Mr. Prescott have both signed. Once you've agreed, the matter will be resolved."

Charlotte's last words struck Lindsay. It hit her for the first time that the document the woman held in her hand represented an end to the cloud that had been hanging over her and Blake. It represented freedom from the bittersweet torment that had been so much a part of their relationship.

Lindsay took the document that Charlotte handed her. Both she and Millicent read in silence. She skimmed over the recitals and legal verbiage. The heart of the agreement was rather brief. It provided that Blake would pay Terry fifty thousand dollars in exchange for a full release for himself and for Woodward & Bishop.

After reading the document Millicent removed her glasses. "The man is certainly generous." She glanced at Terry Moretti. "Is this agreement acceptable to you? Is it what you want?"

"Yes, Mrs. Woodward. I just want it over with. I'm sick of the whole thing."

"Lindsay?"

"I don't know what to say. I'm shocked."

"Yes, I'm flabbergasted myself."

"I don't know what more we could expect. Blake has ensured everyone's satisfaction," Lindsay said.

"He certainly has," Millicent agreed.

Charlotte addressed both Millicent and Lindsay. "Would you care to sign? I'll file the necessary papers with the court and have everything wrapped up as soon as possible."

"Yes. I'd like to run through it again, if you'll give me a minute."

Lindsay glanced up at Terry Moretti. She was preoccupied with her hands, her face screwed up as she concentrated intensely on her long pink fingertips. Lindsay watched her, unseen, marveling that this woman had been both a benefactor and a cause of torment in her life. But for her, Lindsay would not have met Blake. But for her, she could have been happily with him these past miserable days.

Terry slowly chewed gum, oblivious to Lindsay's curious observation. Charlotte had said in a polite way that Terry had lied, but what exactly had she lied about? Had Blake been totally honest, or had Terry only exaggerated the nature of her relationship in several critical areas for the sake of her lawsuit? In a few minutes the meeting would be over, Terry would leave, and Lindsay would never have another chance to find out what Terry and Blake's relationship had been like. She thought for a moment and decided to speak with Terry. She couldn't be sure how truthful the woman would be, but Lindsay knew she had to ask.

"I find this to be satisfactory, Miss Phelps," Millicent said and turned to Lindsay. "What do you think?"

"Yes, it's fine, Millicent."

"Good. Let's be done with it then." She took out her pen and began signing copies of the document.

Lindsay followed Millicent's lead, her mind on how she might approach Terry. As Charlotte organized the papers and Millicent got to her feet, Lindsay leaned across the table toward Terry. "Would you mind if I spoke with you for a moment, Terry, about a personal matter?"

The singer looked up with a vacant stare, her mind finally focusing on Lindsay's words. "Sure. I don't mind."

Charlotte Phelps, like Millicent, had risen to her feet. "Why don't I wait for you outside, Terry?"

The other two women left the room and Lindsay and Terry remained seated at the conference table, opposite each other.

Terry finally broke the silence as Lindsay was searching for the right words. "I hope you didn't take this personally, about Miss Phelps and all."

"No. Not at all, Terry. That's not what I wanted to talk with you about." She dropped her eyes downward, trying to summon the courage to ask her question. "Now that this is settled, nothing that's happened matters. I mean, in a way the truth doesn't even matter. But, I did want to ask you something that *I* care about."

Terry was looking at Lindsay with a skeptical, uncertain expression.

"It concerns Blake...the truth about your relationship with him."

Terry smiled when Lindsay's point finally became clear. "You really like the guy, don't you?"

"Yes." Lindsay knew a request for candor required candor.

"Well, I'm not surprised. He made such a big deal out of protecting you in the settlement I figured he either had something going with you or he was back into saving people again."

"Is that what Blake did for you, Terry? Saved you?"

The other bowed her head briefly then returned Lindsay's look. "Yeah, I suppose you could call it that."

"He helped you because of Rusty?"

"Yes."

"And Rusty's not his child?"

"He told you?"

Lindsay nodded.

"No. Rusty was Russell's. Neither Blake nor I ever told anyone, even with this lawsuit. Blake didn't ever want anyone to find out.... I guess he must really like you, if he told you about Rusty."

Lindsay couldn't help but beam. In her heart she had known it was all true, what Blake had told her, but hearing it from Terry was the indisputable confirmation. "Thanks, Terry, I appreciate your telling me."

The woman shrugged. "Well, it doesn't really matter to me what you know. If Blake doesn't care, it's nothing to me."

"Still, it's a gift, Terry...more than you could possibly know."

Terry Moretti got to her feet. "I hope the two of you will be really happy," she said flatly. "Any more questions, Miss Bishop?"

"What about Rusty, Terry? What are you going to do about him?"

The young woman shifted her weight from one foot to the other. "I still want to see him. Blake said I could just like before, but it's not easy. He's getting bigger now and a mother's not as important as before. I figure he'll understand if I don't come as much...he's still mine...I love him and all, but..."

"I understand."

Terry Moretti made an awkward exit from the room, leaving Lindsay alone. After she had left, Lindsay ran directly from the conference room to her office to call Blake. His secretary said he had left for the day and wouldn't be back in the office until Monday. She telephoned his home, but Elena said he had gone away for the weekend. Lindsay was crestfallen. She wanted so badly to see him now that they were free, but he had disappeared.

She wondered if he had really gone away, or if he would be coming for her, first. But if he were going to pick her up, would he come to the office or go to her home? She dreaded the thought that she might not know for hours.

Within half an hour a florist's delivery van arrived at the office and Lindsay went to the reception area in response to Karen's urgent call. There she found a mountain of flowers and a little note. It read, "I'll be waiting. Get away as soon as you can. Love, Blake."

Millicent walked in and on seeing Lindsay with her flowers broke into a broad grin. "Well, dear, it looks like all's well that ends well."

Lindsay laughed happily.

"Heavens, why are you bothering to stick around here? Why don't you go and find your young man?"

"I *was* thinking of leaving," Lindsay admitted.

"Good. I've told the girls all to take an early weekend and I'm leaving myself. In fact," Millicent said, "if you don't mind, I plan on making it a four-day weekend."

"No, of course not. What's up?"

Millicent held up an envelope and handed it to Lindsay. "Have a look."

Inside Lindsay found a note and some airline tickets.
The note read:

Dearest, at 5:00 P.M. I'll be at the airport. If it is in
your heart to forgive me please meet me there and
bring these along.

Love, Kenneth.

Lindsay looked at the tickets. "Paris! On the
Concord!"

"Yes. Well, it's a start," Millicent said dryly. She
squeezed Lindsay's shoulder affectionately and headed
back toward her office.

Five minutes later Lindsay quickly descended the steps
of the office and headed toward her car, her arms overflowing with her flowers. When she rounded the corner
he was there waiting.

Blake was leaning against the car as he had that other
time. In his hand was a bouquet of yellow sweetheart
roses. She ran to him.

"Looks like you have a secret admirer," he said casually as she drew near.

She was gleeful. "No longer secret!" She edged toward him, her face upturned.

"I brought you some flowers," he said holding up the
roses.

"How lovely." She tried to juggle the enormous bun-
dle she already carried in order to take them, but couldn't
get a hand free.

Blake leaned over and kissed Lindsay sweetly on the
lips. "Those are a bit inconvenient," he said nodding
toward the flowers. "Come on, let's toss them into the

back of my car. We're going to my cabin down the coast
at Big Sur.''

"We are?''

''Yes, for the weekend.'' Blake led her to his Porsche,
which was parked just behind her car. He put the flowers in back, but she kept the roses, clutching them to her
breast. She looked up at him expectantly. His emerald
eyes were sparkling with emotion. She watched his wry,
stubborn mouth as he cupped her face in his hands, coveting her. Then he kissed her again. "Come on,'' he
whispered. ''We've waited long enough.''

CHAPTER TWENTY-TWO

As the Porsche sped along, Lindsay quietly watched the sea. The clouds billowed and broke in places, permitting the bluer hues of the afternoon sky to occasionally color the gray-green of the ocean.

When the vehicle rounded a curve at a promontory, she could see far down the coast to a point where the high bluffs of the land merged into blackened clouds, suggesting rain. Notwithstanding the threatening sky, the weather seemed unsettled and the possibility of seeing the sunset remained.

Blake drove the powerful car at high speed, but with a certain restraint and carefulness. He had total control, yet flirted with the limits of the situation. From time to time Lindsay would look at him instead of the sea, contemplating the implications of their freedom, feeling very much in his hands.

When they came to a long straight stretch where the highway ran for a mile or so without curving, Blake glanced over at her and took her hand. "You're looking wistful," he said softly.

"I've been thinking about our ordeal of the past few weeks. Just then I was thinking of Terry, as a matter of fact.

"What about Terry?"

"I spoke with her after our meeting this morning. She told me that what you'd said about Russell and her was true. Charlotte Phelps had said she'd lied, but I was curious if she'd admit that as well."

"Terry's not evil deep down, I suppose. Once she got her money there was no need to maintain the pretense of her story. I don't think she intended to hurt anyone, even me."

"You know, it's strange. I've felt bitter and resentful toward Terry the past few weeks, but after talking to her today, I felt pity for her. I realized she is just misguided."

"The whole situation was rather pathetic, actually. She admitted to me that the shooting incident was a hoax."

"Really?"

"Yes. She fired the shots herself then made up the business about them coming from a car like mine. Apparently she didn't tell the police she actually saw me in the car, but the possibility was enough to implicate me."

"What was her motive? To get revenge?"

"No, she told me she got the idea from something you or Millicent Woodward said about the fact that my hostility toward her would make me look bad in court. She saw it as a kind of pressure, I guess."

"Poor thing."

"Well, thank God she's got a reasonable attitude about Rusty. I don't know what I'd have done if she had tried to drag him into the suit."

"She does seem to love him but it's obvious she doesn't particularly aspire to being his mother. The impression I got this morning was that she'd be seeing him less in the future."

"Yes, I think that will be the case. She told me she's going to take the money and set herself up back east."

Lindsay thought of her anxious days after Max Bender had reported that Terry had returned to Blake's house. "What exactly was going on when Terry moved in at your place, Blake?"

"We were negotiating the settlement, and she was seeing Rusty. It had been quite a while since he'd seen her. Frankly, she was hanging tough on the hundred thousand. It took some doing to get her down to fifty."

"I think you were awfully generous at that, considering her case was a sham."

"I knew that and Terry knew that, but she's not stupid. The hang-up was over the release of Woodward & Bishop as part of the settlement. She knew she had me over a barrel."

Lindsay reached over and touched Blake's cheek. "You *must* love me to pay Terry fifty thousand dollars to save my hide."

"Would you think less of me if I made an admission?"

"What?"

"I didn't put up the money. Kenneth Woodward did."

Lindsay looked at Blake in surprise.

He shrugged. "Well, I told him it was only fair since *his* wife was the senior partner."

She laughed. "And he accepted that?"

"Not easily. He argued that he was in for weeks of misery. I countered that all he had to do was take Millicent to London or Paris for a long weekend."

Lindsay poked Blake in the ribs. "You fancy yourself an expert on feminine psychology, don't you?"

He winked at her. "I guess we'll see, won't we?" Blake pointed up the road. "My place is just up around the next bend."

A minute later they pulled off the highway at a point where a ravine cut through the mountain and ran down into the sea. The drive went through a thicket of trees along the side of the ravine, then curved out onto an open promontory several hundred feet above the surf. There, hidden from the highway was a rustic wooden cabin looking out over the ocean.

Lindsay helped Blake unload the car and while he opened up the cabin she stood on the porch looking out at the water, the bank of fog, and the multi-colored sky fading gradually into darkness. He came and stood next to her, his arm sliding comfortably around her waist.

"It's magnificent, Blake."

"Yes, it's my retreat. I love it here."

The salt air blew steadily against them, chilling Lindsay though she wore a bulky sweater.

"Would you like a quick walk on the beach to get a feel for the area? It'll clear the cobwebs of the long drive, too."

"Okay."

Blake closed the door to the cabin and led Lindsay by the hand down the path and wooden stairs to the bench below. It was high tide and the churning surf came tumbling halfway up to the foot of the steep cliff marking land's end. They walked along just beyond the reach of successive waves that slid toward them.

Lindsay shivered in the cold air and Blake put his arm around her, shielding her body against the force of the wind. They had gone half a mile or so up the long beach when the sky darkened and ominous black clouds came in from the sea.

"That looks like a rainsquall in the making," Blake said. "We'd better head back."

They were still a quarter of a mile from the stairs leading to the cabin and it was nearly dark. Only the white frothy turbulence of the surf was easily seen in the semi-light. Lindsay felt the fine salty mist blowing against her face from the crashing waves and felt a little trepidation at the power of the sea in the darkness.

Then, as they hurried along, great drops of rain started falling, at first in random splats, but a moment later in massive sheets. They sky seemed to open and loose a deluge upon them, so that within a minute they were both soaked through. Lindsay shrieked at the sudden havoc from the skies but soon realized there was no use in fighting it. Looking up at Blakes's wet face and feeling her own hair plastered around her head, she cleaved to him.

"Forgot my umbrella again," he said with an ironic laugh.

"I noticed," she called back over the fury of the squall. "It seems to be a habit of yours!"

They ran up the steps until Lindsay had to stop to catch her breath. She looked at Blake in the darkness, her chest heaving from the exertion. He waited patiently, holding her hand.

The rain had permeated her sweater so that it hung on her like a sponge, heavy, cold and wet. Her jeans were wet too, in fact, not a square inch of her was dry.

"You look a little damp," he said tweaking her nose. "Let's go before we get wet."

She tried to look scathing but the darkness protected him from her glare. Blake pulled her along, then, she taking two steps for each of his long strides, he pausing when she fell behind.

Finally they reached the porch of the cabin. He rummaged through his pockets as Lindsay shivered. "Did I give you the key?" he asked.

"Blake!"

He laughed and opened the door. "Guess it wasn't locked."

Her blow narrowly missed him, but she stepped quickly inside out of the cold wind. Blake closed the door behind them and flipped on a light.

"I'll get some towels. Get out of those wet clothes," he said.

When he returned a moment later Lindsay was standing on the rag rug in the middle of the living room. She had removed her sweater and was wringing out her hair with both hands. Blake wrapped one towel around her neck and began rubbing his own hair vigorously with the other. He had removed his sweater and was nude from the waist up.

Lindsay too rubbed her hair and face, then began unbuttoning her blouse.

"I'll build a fire," Blake said nodding toward the stone fireplace. "Why don't you go get in the shower?"

She stood in the small bathroom in front of the stall shower with its plastic curtain, peeling off her pants. The cabin was cold and she shivered, craving the warmth of the shower just as she had that night at his house in Saratoga.

Lindsay had been under the hot jet of water for about five minutes and her skin had finally begun tingling with warmth when Blake entered the bathroom.

She heard the curtain sliding back and turned in surprise to see his smiling face.

"It's a small water tank," he said with a grin. "Move over."

His body was cold and clammy for a moment but he soon warmed under the sensuous heat of the water flowing over them. When at last his body grew as hot as her own she melted into him, loving the strength of his arms about her. Then Blake took the bar of soap and began running it over her shoulders, back and buttocks as she clung to him.

"Blake, I've already done that."

He kissed her nose. "Yes, but I haven't."

HIS ARM LAY HEAVILY upon her naked breasts. The breathing of his half sleep fell against her cheek, coaxing her from the dreamy stupor of her fulfillment. Lindsay heard the pounding surf of the dark sea far below the cabin, and outside the little window of the bedroom she saw the moon breaking through the clouds.

After the storm had moved on, Blake had opened the window a crack for air, but as she watched the silvery face of the moon a gust of wind pushed it open wider, permitting the salty air to waft in over their naked bodies. The curtains billowed like the sails of a ship, and Lindsay pulled the down comforter up over them for protection against the cold air. As she did, Blake stirred.

He touched her cheek with his fingers and smiled, his white teeth barely visible in the moon-cast shadows of the cabin. He kissed her, sighing contentedly.

Blake remained silent, but she could feel an intensity building in him. He was looking at her face in the darkness. His index finger pressed softly against the fullness of her lower lip.

"Lindsay," he said tenderly. "How long will it take to get your parents out here from St. Louis?"

She felt her heart leap. "My parents? Why?"

"Don't you want them out here for the wedding?"

"Wedding?"

"Sure. After all you've put me through, the least you can do is make an honest man out of me."

Lindsay's eyes flooded. "Oh, Blake."

"Will you marry me, Lindsay?"

"Yes, Blake," she said as the tears began streaming.

He held her for a long time, letting her tears wet his own cheeks, kissing her hair and touching her face with his fingertips. Blake pulled the comforter close around them. "We're going to be so happy. And Rusty will too. He's very fond of you, Lindsay."

"He's a sweet child and I'm very fond of *him*." She touched Blake's lips. "He won't mind a brother or sister though, will he?"

"He's wanted a little brother for years. A sister will take some convincing."

Lindsay laughed. "I can see my two challenges already—the virtues of girls and facilities."

Blake rocked her in his arms. "Don't worry. You'll be great."

"I hope so," she purred. "I want to be."

"That's all that matters, Lindsay."

She ran her hand across his broad chest, snuggling against him. Blake gave a sigh of pleasure at her touch. For a long while their bodies cleaved in the cocoon of their recent lovemaking, their hearts beating together under their naked flesh. As Blake's lips lingered affectionately on her cheek, Lindsay felt an overwhelming sense of peace.

"I love you so," he murmured.

And she longed for the joy of that moment to be frozen forever in time.

Harlequin Intrigue

Because romance can be quite an adventure.

WORLDWIDE LIBRARY IS YOUR TICKET TO ROMANCE, ADVENTURE AND EXCITEMENT

Experience it all in these big, bold Bestsellers— Yours exclusively from WORLDWIDE LIBRARY WHILE QUANTITIES LAST

To receive these Bestsellers, complete the order form, detach and send together with your check or money order (include 75¢ postage and handling), payable to WORLDWIDE LIBRARY, to:

In the U.S.
WORLDWIDE LIBRARY
Box 52040
Phoenix, AZ
85072-2040

In Canada
WORLDWIDE LIBRARY
P.O. Box 2800, 5170 Yonge Street
Postal Station A, Willowdale, Ontario
M2N 6J3

Quant.	Title	Price
_____	**WILD CONCERTO**, Anne Mather	$2.95
_____	**A VIOLATION**, Charlotte Lamb	$3.50
_____	**SECRETS**, Sheila Holland	$3.50
_____	**SWEET MEMORIES**, LaVyrle Spencer	$3.50
_____	**FLORA**, Anne Weale	$3.50
_____	**SUMMER'S AWAKENING**, Anne Weale	$3.50
_____	**FINGER PRINTS**, Barbara Delinsky	$3.50
_____	**DREAMWEAVER**, Felicia Gallant/Rebecca Flanders	$3.50
_____	**EYE OF THE STORM**, Maura Seger	$3.50
_____	**HIDDEN IN THE FLAME**, Anne Mather	$3.50
_____	**ECHO OF THUNDER**, Maura Seger	$3.95
_____	**DREAM OF DARKNESS**, Jocelyn Haley	$3.95

YOUR ORDER TOTAL	$_____
New York and Arizona residents add appropriate sales tax	$_____
Postage and Handling	$___.7
I enclose	$_____

NAME _____

ADDRESS _____ APT.# _____

CITY _____

STATE/PROV. _____ ZIP/POSTAL CODE _____

WW3

EYE OF THE STORM

MAURA SEGER

A powerful portrayal of the events of World War II in the Pacific, *Eye of the Storm* is a riveting story of how love triumphs over hatred. In this, the first of a three-book chronicle, Army nurse Maggie Lawrence meets Marine Sgt. Anthony Gargano. Despite military regulations against fraternization, they resolve to face together whatever lies ahead.... Author Maura Seger, also known to her fans as Laurel Winslow, Sara Jennings, Anne MacNeil and Jenny Bates, was named 1984's Most Versatile Romance Author by *The Romantic Times*

What readers say about
HARLEQUIN SUPERROMANCE™

"Bravo! Your SUPERROMANCE [is]... super!"

R.V.,* Montgomery, Illinois

"I am impatiently awaiting
the next SUPERROMANCE."

J.D., Sandusky, Ohio

"Delightful... great."

C.B., Fort Wayne, Indiana

"Terrific love stories. Just
keep them coming!"

M.G., Toronto, Ontario